Lords of the Var:

THE

SAVAGE

KING

Michelle M. Pillow

Futuristic Romance

New Concepts

Georgia

Be sure to check out our website for the very best in fiction at fantastic prices!

When you visit our webpage, you can:
* Read excerpts of currently available books
* View cover art of upcoming books and current releases
* Find out more about the talented artists who capture the magic of the writer's imagination on the covers
* Order books from our backlist
* Find out the latest NCP and author news--including any upcoming book signings by your favorite NCP author
* Read author bios and reviews of our books
* Get NCP submission guidelines
* And so much more!

We offer a 20% discount on all new Trade Paperback releases ordered from our website!

Be sure to visit our webpage to find the best deals in e-books and paperbacks! To find out about our new releases as soon as they are available, please be sure to sign up for our newsletter (http://www.newconceptspublishing.com/newsletter.htm) or join our reader group (http://groups.yahoo.com/group/new_concepts_pub/join)!

The newsletter is available by double opt in only and our customer information is *never* shared!

Visit our webpage at:
www.newconceptspublishing.com

New Concepts Publishing, Inc.
5202 Humphreys Rd.
Lake Park, GA 31636

ISBN 1-58608-799-1
© 2005 Michelle M. Pillow
Cover art (c) copyright 2006 Eliza Black

NCP books are available at special quantity discounts for bulk purchases for sales promotions, premiums, fund raising, or educational use. For details, write, email, or phone New Concepts Publishing, Inc., 5202 Humphreys Rd., Lake Park, GA 31636; Ph. 229-257-0367, Fax 229-219-1097; orders@newconceptspublishing.com.

First NCP Trade Paperback Printing: July 2006

Author recommends reading books in order of release. Also check out the Dragon Lords series, which take place before the Lords of the Var.

Dedication:

To Amelia and My Readers. May you all find the one true Prince, who will give up everything in the galaxy just for you. (loincloth optional)

"To be ruled by a woman is to be ruled by weakness and kingdoms are only as strong as their rulers. A King must stand alone, beholden to none."--King Attor of the Var

Chapter One

Agent Ulyssa Payne grumbled and banged the communicator across her knee in a last ditch effort to make the very expensive piece of junk work. Her campsite was close, but it was cloaked so she couldn't see its exact location. She wouldn't chance revealing it until she made sure the perimeter was secure. If anything, experience in the field had taught her to be extra careful.

She knelt on the ground, looking up at the bright Qurilixen sky in frustration. The blue-green haze of the planet's atmosphere shone through the gigantic leaves of the forest. The planet was always cast in daylight due to its three suns, with the exception of one night a year when everything fell into perfect alignment. The evening she'd arrived with a shipment of Earth women on a Galaxy Brides ship, it had been such a night. She'd been forced to haul her backpack through rough, dark terrain while the Draig warriors partied with their mail-order brides.

"When I get back, I am so quitting the Agency," Ulyssa ranted under her breath, smacking the communicator harder in her frustration. She would never really quit. The Human Intelligence Agency was her life. It was her whole reason for being. "After this I am definitely taking a vacation. I'm going to have a bath, a bottle of hard liquor, and a rare steak as big as this forsaken hellhole, and a male prostitute--a mute male prostitute who only knows how to follow orders. First I'm going to get clean, then I will get drunk, and then I'm going to get laid."

It had been nearly five months since she had a man and he'd hardly been worth bragging about. The sex had been mediocre and afterwards he'd wanted to cuddle. She had more fun getting out of his bed than actually being in it. Ulyssa smiled, remembering how she'd scaled out his window and down fifteen stories while he went to the kitchen to get her a snack.

Part of the reason she'd been celibate since then was that she'd been in quarantine, uploading her mission, and in training. As soon as she was finished, the Agency had made her go undercover on a Galaxy Brides ship as one of the prospective brides. She'd spent a whole month surrounded by nothing but women, morphed into a hideous character she could barely stand, with a shipload of too-much-estrogen-producing females who talked of nothing but the men they were going to marry.

"Ugh," Ulyssa snarled in distaste. "Why anyone would ever want to get married is beyond me. Poor, poor, misguided fools. They really have no idea what they're in for."

The reddish trees of the alien forest were colossal, some of them spanning wider than an Earth home. Yellow ferns spread out about her, growing wild in the red earth of the planet's surface. She felt like a dwarf running around in the land of giants.

Only the inhabitants on the planet weren't technically giants, though they were quite large and fierce. They were all shifters--nothing but male shifters. It was a little fact the Agency had forgotten to tell her about. The northern half of the small planet was ruled by the Draig, a tribe of dragon shifters. The southern half was ruled by the Var, a tribe of man-cats. If not for seeing them quarrel from her perch in the trees, she would never have known.

From what she gathered from the Galaxy Bride uploads, radiation from their blue sun made female children rare. Over the generations, the radiation had altered the men's genetics to produce only strong, large male, warrior heirs. Maybe once in a thousand births was a Qurilixen female born. The fact that they had no women of their own was why the services of corporations like Galaxy Brides were so invaluable to them. In return, they would mine ore that was only found in their caves. The ore was a great power source for long-voyaging starships, all but useless to the Qurilixen, who were not known space explorers.

Good thing she was extra cautious and masked her scent before leaving camp. Shifters usually had a great sense of smell and the Draig warriors would have detected her presence in the forest for sure--and if not them the Var would have found her. If she had to choose, she was sure she'd rather be captured by the Draig. They appeared to be the more civilized of the two creatures.

The Qurilixen were classified as a warrior class, though they had been peaceful for nearly a century--aside from petty territorial skirmishes that broke out every fifteen or so years between a few of the rival houses. The best comparison anyone could make is that the men were like the warriors of Medieval Earth--the romanticized version anyway. The Qurilixen worshipped many Gods, favored natural comforts to modern technological conveniences, and actually preferred to raise, grow, and cook their own food--the true mark of a primordial society.

Although, it seemed times were about to change. The forest literally crawled with both races. She wasn't stupid. She could tell the planet was on the verge of an all out war. The last thing she needed was to get caught in the middle of it.

This was definitely a primitive planet, perhaps one of the most primitive she'd been assigned to in a long time. As far as she could tell, her campsite was on Var land. It didn't matter. It's not like she'd stopped to ask permission to set up camp. In fact, neither race knew she was there. She preferred to keep it that way. If Galaxy Brides went looking for her, their lost bride, all they'd find was a ghost trail to a woman who never existed.

Ulyssa growled under her breath, swearing every dark curse she knew. She needed to report to headquarters--if the damned communicator would ever turn itself on--and tell them her mission was over. Realizing she'd gone through the Galaxy Bride torture for nothing didn't make her happy. But, on the bright side, she'd gotten some permanent hair removal done and a few itchy battle scars removed, although such foolish luxuries hardly made her present situation worth it. Shaving had never been a primary concern and she would only collect more battle scars to replace the old ones.

Picking at the dried mud caked to her tanned skin, Ulyssa grimaced. She so needed a decontamination unit. Hell, she'd even try a primitive water bath, just so long as she could scrub clean.

Suddenly, the communicator lit up. She sighed, not liking the fact that she had to report to her superiors that her mission had been fruitless. She liked less the fact that she was trapped on a barbaric planet until one of the company ships could swing by and get her.

"Hello?" a sweet, elderly voice asked from the communicator.

"Agent 596," Ulyssa answered. The unit clicked.

"Report," a grim voice ordered from the small handheld unit, replacing the first computer generated operator.

"Ulyssa 596, codename Gena, Qurilixen," Ulyssa said into the unit.

"Go ahead," the voice answered.

"Target dead, killed by his own." Ulyssa pulled the unit back to add a bitter curse. She had just spent the dusky night in the forest, huddled by a tree while the Medical Mafia clones packed up camp. Her target, a leader in the Medical Mafia, Doc Aleksander, was killed by his daughter in self-defense. They assumed Doc had been on the planet to make a trade for some of the precious ore. "Daughter has disbanded family line, no information to be had."

"What?" another voice demanded, harder than the last. Ulyssa recognized the mission director, Franklin. She rolled her eyes. "What do you mean she disbanded the family?"

"Are we secure?" Ulyssa asked, careful to keep her voice soft as she glanced around the forest. The trilling call of a sofliar came from the dense underbrush, carrying over the hum of insects. All was peaceful.

"Yes, Agent, speak plainly," Franklin said.

"Doc is dead. Nadja has married one of the Princes from the Qurilixen House of Draig. She's disbanded the family and left everything to her mother. The Aleksander branch is ended. I'm transmitting a full report now." Ulyssa stopped talking and pressed a button. When the report was sent, she demanded, "Now, get me off this damned floating barbarian rock, Frank!"

"Got it," Franklin answered. "Good work."

Ulyssa snorted. She'd hardly call a fruitless mission good work. "What about my ride?"

"Well, Agent," Franklin cleared his throat, "to tell you the truth you don't have one. We didn't expect this to happen. The seers didn't predict Doc's death, only that he'd be on the planet. We were planning on having you there a lot longer than a few weeks."

"How long Frank?" Ulyssa asked, her voice hard.

"The closest ship is three months from there."

"Three months!" Ulyssa hissed. "I didn't spend a month on that damned Galaxy Brides ship, simpering like a morphed bimbo fool, grabbing my breasts and making inane comments, just to spend three hellish months on this nowhere planet for no darned good reason! You get me a ship faster!"

Franklin chuckled. "What? We'd thought you'd like pretending to be a girl for awhile 596."

Ulyssa frowned. *Great! Here come the 'you're worse than a man' jokes. Kick a little male behind, never call them back after you have your way with them, and you get branded a heartless bitch.*

"Ugh," she groaned. "I so need to get some action. This is getting bad."

"What was that, 596?" Franklin asked.

"Nothing, sir." Ulyssa fought the urge to laugh.

"How are your supplies?"

"I'll be fine."

"I know, Agent." Silence came over the intercom, but she knew he was still there. Very quietly, Frank said, "You take care of yourself, kid."

"Don't worry about me, Frank. I'm just like a cat, always landing on my feet."

"I know, Agent, I know. It's not the landing I'm worried about. It's those nine lives of yours. Don't use 'em up. You owe me a date when you get back."

"Dream on, sunshine." Ulyssa laughed, eyeing her rustic surroundings in displeasure. She kept the irritation from her voice. She knew if Franklin could get her off the floating rock sooner he would. "But I will let you buy me a drink. You owe me at least that."

"Done," Franklin agreed. "Contact only if there is trouble, otherwise call in eleven weeks."

"Know the drill, 596 out."

"Command out."

Ulyssa pressed the button to the communicator and watched it turn off before moving to latch it onto her belt.

"Three months," Ulyssa began with a dark frown. "Just gre--"

Suddenly, she froze, holding very still. The birds weren't singing and the forest had gone quiet--too quiet. Slowly, she reached for her leg, feeling blindly for her gun. Her thumb hooked around the leather strap, flicking in the dried mud caked over it.

A loud roar resounded from the trees, as she drew her weapon. She frantically pulled the gun, falling on her back as she turned toward the noise. She was too late. Two thick paws pressed into her shoulders. Fangs snarled at her from a hot mouth.

"Oh," she gasped, nervous. From her place on the ground it looked to be an overgrown mountain lion. "Nice kitty. Easy, big fella. Take it easy."

The cat snarled at her soft words and lifted a meaty paw to the side of her head striking her. As the paw made contact, it wasn't claws and fur that smacked her, but a very human feeling fist. Her visions swam. Pain shot through her face from her cheek. Blood trickled into her mouth, spilling over her pale skin in little rivers. When she looked back up, she gasped. It was no longer an animal that pinned her down but a naked man. His bright blue eyes glared into her with lethal intent.

"Look what I found wandering around in my kingdom," the man said with a dark laugh that left her cold. "A dirty little *gwobr*."

Without warning, he jumped to standing, hauling Ulyssa up by her wrist. Her feet flailed in the air before landing awkwardly on the ground. On reflex, she kicked. Her foot hit the man's very muscular waist. He dropped her wrist with a grunt, but did not double over. Ulyssa smiled, but her victory was small and short-lived.

Right as her foot landed back on the ground, a dozen half-dressed warriors poured out from the treetops as if falling from the sky. She squared off to defend herself, but she was outmanned by the gathering of blond Vars. They fought back with a liquid grace she'd rarely seen in a species, sleek and smooth of motion like ancient Earth ninjas. She tried to fight back, kicking and punching as she found her mark on hard steely flesh. But, within seconds, she was subdued.

Ulyssa screeched, showing the proper amount of feminine anger a barbaric people would expect. Her heart raced with adrenaline, but she never lost her cool. Heathenishly strong hands clasped ahold of her struggling body, lifting her high. She was bound and gagged with swift precision. She'd been caught unprepared, and in the end she was no match for their brute force. Panting through the gag, she fell limp.

One of the large warriors lifted her over his broad shoulder. In the Var tongue, the warrior said, "King Attor, what shall we do with her?"

Ulyssa was suddenly very grateful for her intergalactic translator chip. She'd been wary when the Agency implanted the little device into her ear. It couldn't translate every foreign word, but usually it was enough to understand what was going on. And, since it was a smart chip, it learned as she went and widened its vocabulary.

"Take her and have her cleaned so that I may examine her," the Var King, who'd first trapped her to the ground, said. She glared as he forcibly grabbed her chin to better study her dirty face. His strong body was completely naked and he moved as if unconcerned by it. The others were dressed in loose fitting tunic shirts and tighter pants. Ulyssa assumed they stripped as they shifted. "If she is anything like her sweet smell, I will enjoy her immensely at the victory celebration--just as soon as we send those Draig cowards into the ground where they belong."

The warriors cheered, their heated eyes lit with battle and bloodlust. Ulyssa tore her chin away from King Attor's grip. The King only laughed at her defiance.

"Oh, I'll take pleasure breaking you in, *briallen*. You'll make a nice little addition to my harem. If you're lucky, I might even breed you," the King laughed harder, prompting his men to do the same. The beefy shoulder beneath her stomach jolted with movement. Her hands tingled from the tightness of the binds.

One of the warriors handed the King a loincloth and he wrapped it around his waist, leaving his chest bare. With a look of severe consideration, the King didn't take his eyes from her, as he ordered his men, "If she gives you any problems, throw her in the dungeons until I return. I'll be more than willing to teach her the Var penalty for defying the King's order."

Ulyssa grunted against her gag, glaring and cussing at her captors until her face turned red. Attor leaned over and plucked a green plant with a yellow center from the ground. Squeezing it between his fingers, he rubbed the pollen beneath her nose. Instantly, her eyes darkened. She fell completely limp, fast asleep.

* * * *

One week later

"We can't make peace with the Draig! They're our enemies!"

At the sound of his brother's hard voice, Prince Kirill of the Var looked up from where he'd been studying his hands. The stresses of the last several days lined his eyes-- eyes that were so dark a brown they were often mistaken for black. He held still, not moving from the chair he rested in.

The old council hall was empty, except for Kirill and three of his brothers. Deep set, antique, cushioned chairs were set around a large, intricately carved fireplace. A fire burned brightly, giving the tomblike room light and warmth. Long pillows lined the red-carpeted floor. There were no windows in the old section of the castle, not even a little slit. As young boys, they had made the room their private fort. Now that they were older, they still convened there to relax and talk in private. The air was stuffy and unmoving, but the four Princes were too preoccupied to notice such things.

Falke, the Commander of the Guards, sat to Kirill's left. His stiff body was unmoving in its rigid discipline. Falke commanded the warriors at the castle and was in charge of the military. After a half century of command, he'd become hard and unforgiving.

Falke's counterpart and their younger brother, Reid, was Commander of the Outlands. Reid spent his days away from the palace, watching over the northern borders. Reid had a twin brother, Jarek, whom they hadn't heard from in some time. Jarek was off gallivanting around the galaxies. The twins were the only Princes with the same mother.

On the floor lounged Quinn, the youngest and sleekest of the Princes. His smaller stature had come in handy on many occasions. As boys, they'd fit him into tight spaces, making him the lookout or spy, depending on what mischief they were about.

"At least let us convene the old houses and vote!" Falke continued in his forbidding tone, breaking into Kirill's contemplation. Kirill took a deep breath. He couldn't blame Falke for his anger. The Commander had seen many battles with the Draig warriors and thus had seen the most Var deaths.

"And you, Quinn?" Kirill asked.

"I see the merit of both war and peace," Quinn answered in his quiet voice.

"Some ambassador you are," Reid laughed, throwing the cushion from behind his back to where Quinn lay on the floor. Quinn grinned and tucked the cushion behind his head to replace his folded arms.

Falke directed a frown to Kirill at the banter, his eyes begging for order. "I'll send more guards to the Outlands. We should make sure the borders are well guarded. If there is to be a battle, let it be away from our city."

Reid nodded. His smile faded slightly from his tanned features. "That would be wise. There has been no trouble in the shadowed marshes, not since father tried to kidnap Prince Yusef's bride."

At the mention to King Attor, the Princes grew silent. Their father had no love of the Draig and each knew he'd been the main cause of war in the past. Solemn eyes turned to the fire, as each Prince remembered watching their father's body burn at the burial rite.

Attor had not been a loving man, but he was still their father. They were royalty and royalty had no time for love or weaknesses. As the late King was fond of saying, *Kingdoms are only as strong as their rulers. The Draig are weak. The Var Empire will rise again.*

"Have you contacted Jarek and told him?" Kirill asked Reid.

"No, but I have sent messages through secure lines. It's hard to tell where he has gone off to. Last I heard he was on Tragon, but that was about six months ago." Reid shrugged. Then, to break the somber mood, he teased, "So brother, when you're crowned King, will you be keeping the lovely women in the harem for yourself?"

Kirill frowned, rolling his eyes. "Father collected women as Falke here collects weaponry. I have no idea what to do with them all. I have no wish for a lifemate, let alone several half-mates."

All Princes nodded in firm agreement. None of them looked to commit themselves to a woman--ever. Why bond to one when you could have many?

"According to law, they are your responsibility," Quinn said softly, chuckling.

Kirill shot him a defiant glare and growled. Quinn laughed harder, unconcerned. Sighing, Kirill gave up his feigned anger, lounged back in his chair, and threw a leg over the side. "I tried to give them freedom, but half of them didn't want to leave the palace. The other half has nowhere to go. And the crazy one, Taura, wanted me to bind her to father's corpse so that she may burn with him."

"It's the Roane way," Falke said, in defense of his birth mother. The other Princes just laughed. Taura was partly the reason Falke was so serious. Whereas all the others had the blood of Var and human in them, Falke was half Roane. The Roane were a naturally bold, hard people with strict discipline and rigid ideals. Taura had passed those traits to her son. As children, when the boys were playing and getting into mischief, Falke had been training to be a warrior.

"Ah, I suppose I'll have to at least meet with them all. How many could there be? Fifty?" Kirill asked.

"A hundred and sixty three, brother, by my last count," Quinn laughed. "Give or take a few dozen."

"It almost makes you respect our father, doesn't it?" Reid stood from his chair and stretched, prompting the others to do the same.

"The late King always had respect. It was the other emotions he had little use for," Kirill answered. With a thoughtful look upon his face, he strode from the old council hall, leaving his brothers to watch after him in wonder.

* * * *

Ulyssa grimaced, furiously shaking her head at the woman who tried to hand her a near transparent gown of black and silver. She looked warily over the line of young women already dressed in similar outfits. It had been nearly a week since her capture and the barbaric King had yet to keep his word and come back for her. It was really too bad, she had a few punches she'd like to give to him, right before she ripped off his precious manhood.

Ulyssa sighed. She knew it was actually better he'd not come for her. Killing a king would not look good on her resume, and it might hamper her escape. She highly doubted the barbaric Var would give her a fair trial. She grinned. She highly doubted she could win a fair trial in such a case. Murder was murder, after all, and no crime would be more premeditated than the death of King Attor by her hand--for that was all she thought about.

"I am not dressing up like a doll for any man," Ulyssa said to the woman, enunciating her words. She turned her back in dismissal. The woman finally gave up and left her alone.

When Attor said he had a harem, he hadn't been lying. She could only hope he'd forget about her long enough for her to break out of the lush prison. Scratching behind her ear, she again shook her head, widening her blue eyes at the persistent woman.

Ulyssa wore tight black pants and a black tank top. They were both hers, thankfully salvaged from when she arrived. They'd taken everything else, including her communicator and gun. At least they'd let her into a decontaminator. That was something, even if they had been checking her for diseases.

From the looks of the preening women, they expected company. Ulyssa didn't plan on sitting around and waiting for that company to arrive. Leisurely, she made her way around the room to a long buffet table. Picking at the food, she quickly ate. Then, grabbing up a goblet, she drank deeply of the wine. She'd have preferred hard liquor, but was happy that it was at least alcohol. No matter where she went in the galaxies, every race had some version of liquor.

"Getting drunk, the galactic pastime of champions," she mumbled under her breath with a small laugh of self-amusement.

The harem was just what she would have expected one to look like--silk and satin, pillows and furs, a water fountain in the center surrounded by fruit trees and yellow ferns. The floors were checkered gray and white tiles, constructed from a stone much like marble.

It took Ulyssa awhile to place where she'd seen the like before, but it finally hit her that the palace looked much like the old Moroccan architecture on Earth. She'd seen the ruins once as a young girl and had been fascinated by their intricate patterns. However, there was also a definite medieval castle influence at play within the basic structure.

There was an aviary in the center of the room where a loud sofliar sang some sad song--nonstop, over and over again, until Ulyssa wanted to wring its feathery little neck. She'd read historical documents about such places as harems on Earth, long ago. She'd never thought she'd live to see the set up firsthand.

Ulyssa eyed the women in disgust as she took another bite. She was again trapped with simpering females who did nothing all day but primp and preen, as they waited for one man to come and choose them for sex. She couldn't say they were worse than the women on the Galaxy Brides ship, but they were just as pathetic.

Ugh, no thank you!

The harem just proved once more how barbaric a planet Qurilixen really was. She was a little amazed to know they had the capability for space travel. Yet, they chose not to employ the finer technological advances in life and instead opted for a simplistic existence.

She'd been all over the galaxies and had seen many things. The Var people were still too primitive a race for her liking, but their talent for art and design had to be admired. Never one to slow down and look at the finer things in life, Ulyssa was amazed to find herself staring at the intricate carvings over the arched doorways leading from the harem, or the particularly beautiful, symmetrical patterns of brilliantly displayed colors--blue, red, orange, gold, green--inlaid into the walls. A particular circular design was quite dizzying when stared at too closely. She blinked, reaching out to touch the bumpy surface in fascination.

The imprisonment would have been bearable to Ulyssa if she still had a mission. She functioned much better when she had a purpose to occupy her thoughts and keep her busy. Now her only goal was to escape her prison and wait three months for a ship to come pick her up. Good thing she had a back up communicator at her camp or the ship would never be able to locate her. She was deep cover and that meant no body transmitters. They were too easy to find in a full body scan.

Thinking about her situation, she frowned. With her camp under cloak, it might take three months just to find the site. She'd been unconscious when carted to the Var palace, and she had no idea in which direction to start walking. The dire prospect of her situation didn't faze her. In fact, it did quite the opposite. It excited her beyond measure.

Seeing the opening she'd been waiting for, she watched as the harem guard helped a servant carry in a large tray of what looked like a roasted pig. As they grunted and strained under the heavy weight, Ulyssa slipped behind their backs and out the door without notice.

If luck stayed with her, all the halls would be empty and she wouldn't be forced to fight any of the man-cats. Not that she was too scared to try. They might be able to subdue her in a group, but if it was one on one, then she was sure she could take them down.

The long hallway walls of the Var palace were smooth, inlaid with intricate tile mosaics. The hallway itself was empty. She grinned, feeling her blood stir at the hint of danger. Adrenaline pumped into her veins, electrifying her as nothing else could. Without pausing to look around, she sprinted down the hall and took the first corner.

Chapter Two

Ulyssa continued down the hallways, rounding several more turns. She blindly tried to navigate her way to something that would give her a hint of escape. The halls were like a maze and she soon realized she was lost within them.

Hearing a noise behind her and fearing it might be the Var harem guard, she slipped around a corner to hide. Almost instantly, she crashed into a warm, firm chest. Ulyssa jerked back in surprise, just as two strong hands clamped about her arms like a vice.

"Relax," a voice said. The dark, rich sound sent chills down her spine, erupting beneath her flesh in spurts of sensitive longing. Every inch of her tingled. She fought for breath. The man chuckled, a seductively low sound, and asked, "Where do you think you're going?"

Ulyssa jerked, turning around with a defiant scowl. Her mouth opened, ready to do battle with whatever manner of creature dared to touch her. As her gaze met two dark, very curious eyes, she froze. Her heart nearly stopped beating in her chest. She couldn't breath, could barely think. Desire, hot and liquid, shot over her at the sight of the handsome man who held her. Never had her body reacted with such fierce awareness, as to be struck both deaf and dumb.

Dark stubble shadowed the man's chiseled jaw, matching the long black hair that spilled down over his broad shoulders. He was perfectly built, not too broad and not too thin. Even motionless, she could tell he'd move with the liquid grace of his kind. There was something slow and seductive in the way the Var carried themselves--like hunters crouched ready to attack, stalking their prey. She'd seen the athletic quality in all the warriors, but never did the prospect of being their prey excite her until that very moment.

Black leather bands with silver studs gripped tight to his biceps and wrists, secured taut on both of his arms. His shirt appeared to be one piece of material with two narrow straps over the shoulders. It was held together by black cross lacing beneath his arms, leaving his sides and waist exposed.

Ulyssa nearly swooned as torrid images swirled in her head. He didn't wear the tunic of the guards, so she wasn't worried about him arresting her and dragging her back to Attor. In fact, she wasn't worried about anything at all for the moment. Unbidden, her eyes continued down, over his frame. He didn't move to stop her, didn't shake her arm to get her attention. Unconscious of the action, she licked her lips, suddenly famished for male attention.

His pants were of the same material as the shirt, soft, yet molding to his firm, delicious body. A belt matched the armband, clinging around his narrow waist. More cross lacing reached from the knee, over the outside length of his thighs, leaving no indention of firm muscle to the imagination, as it revealed tanned flesh all the way up his hip. She flexed her fingers, itching to reach forward, to dip beneath the material to feel him.

A low rumbling sound broke into Ulyssa's thoughts. She blinked in surprise, having nearly forgotten where she was, what she'd been doing. Before she could think to protest, her captor pulled her forward into his muscled chest and pressed her back into the wall.

The stone along her spine was cold, making a strange contrast to the hard heat of him along her thin frame. She gasped, feeling trapped by his body. His thick arousal grew between them, unmistakable in its desire. The pressure sparked a very liquid reaction inside her loins. Her nipples puckered hard against her shirt, tingling as her hastened breath caused them to rub along his chest. Ulyssa shivered, her head screaming to fight and run. She couldn't move. A euphoric trance held her in its web, drowning out reason.

"When a woman looks at a man with that much invitation, who is he to deny her?" the Var man said in his low, rumbling tone. Passion made his words sound hoarse. Warm breath fanned over her cheek, causing her to shiver in anticipation.

The man boldly moved against her and Ulyssa felt the all too real press of his desire rocking gently into her hip. She felt his heat to her breasts, further budding her nipples into hard, beckoning points. As she looked up into his deep-set eyes, eyes that swirled with amber flecks within the darkened sea of brown-black, she knew she was in trouble.

Prince Kirill tried to take a deep breath, trying in vain to make his body pull back from the soft woman he trapped against the wall. He couldn't make his limbs obey. Every nerve screamed at him to continue. His body was stiff with the stress of many days. It had been a long while since he'd had a woman, even longer since he'd had a woman so lovely as this creature before him.

She had yet to speak with words. But what she didn't say with her voice, she more than screamed with her wide, blue eyes--eyes that were dark, eyes that sparkled with the stars of deep space. He could see how a man could easily get lost in her gaze. She was the most beautiful vision he'd ever seen. His whole length trembled, ready to answer the primitive call of her body to his.

Her hair was a peculiar shade of blonde and red, pulled back from her face into a bun that rested neatly above the long nape of her neck. He itched to pull the locks free, but he held back. Glancing down over her toned body, he growled in pleasure.

A thought flickered in his head as he wondered who she was, what she was doing alone, walking unescorted in his section of the palace. As her lips parted, the thought fled and he didn't care. He needed to release the tension from his body, the hard throbbing ache in his loins. His heart pumped hard in his chest, swirling lust into every limb. He was ready to claim her. It would be easy to pin her to the wall and have his way with her right there in the empty hallway. He would too, if she'd but allow him.

Suddenly, thought returned to him. "Are you one of Attor's?"

Ulyssa blinked, looking momentarily stunned. She slowly shook her head in denial. In a low, throaty tone, she whispered, "No."

Kirill groaned, feeling the moist heat of her desire radiating from her thighs. Her eyes dipped to his mouth just as her tongue edged along her bottom lip in invitation. He pushed his body more firmly against her. Letting her feel the full length of his arousal, he rocked his hips, grinding along her clothing. A slow, seductive smile curled on his mouth as he invited her to his kiss with the simple lifting of his jaw. To his great pleasure, she leaned in, accepting his offered mouth without hesitation. Her lips were warm, soft, and when she tilted them in offering, she moaned ever so lightly.

Ulyssa saw him move, his confident mouth curling up in masculine invitation. His strong, male scent drew her in, tempting her senses, teasing her desires. Without thought, she leaned forward to kiss him, drawn to discover if he tasted as good as he looked. Her lips parted. Her fingers ran up the side of his stubbly cheeks to pull him closer. His long hair was like silk as it brushed the back of her hands.

Not once did she stop to think that he was a stranger to her, that he wasn't even all human. At the moment, she didn't care. He was solid and real and so very hot. It had been so long since she knew a fraction of the longing she now felt in the madness of his arms. And, if she was perfectly honest with herself, she wanted to see just how wild the Var cats were in the bedroom. With their grace and natural prowess, she just bet they made for worthy lovers.

She heard a soft, feminine sigh and realized it came from her lips. Startled, she pulled back just as his velvet tongue was about to delve inside her mouth. The brief touch sent a shockwave through her so intense that she leaned forward to accept it.

Kirill pulled back, a question in his gaze as he tasted her on his mouth. His pleasant expression faded into a slight frown. Holding her at arms length, he asked, very seriously, "You drank nef, did you not? Quite a bit of it if your glazed eyes are any indication."

"Nef?" Ulyssa repeated, trying to squirm past his hold, wanting to be back against his hard body. She pressed her ear to her shoulders, wondering if the translator was broken.

A slight frown of disgust came to Kirill, as he easily slipped into her language, "Try to concentrate, human. You did belong to the King. You were one of his."

Ulyssa blinked, trying to understand his low words. His change of language didn't help her confusion. Why was he holding her away from him? What happened? Her heart pounded in her head, fueling her desire tenfold. She shivered uncontrollably. Her body was wet, ready, pulsing with fierce abandon. "No, I don't belong to anyone--only myself."

Again she tried to lean forward and again he held her back, gripping her shoulders firmly in his strong hands. Ulyssa moaned throatily. She glanced over his body to his lean hips. His arousal pressed strong against the confines of his pants. In a trance, she reached to touch it.

Kirill chuckled, artfully avoiding contact with her searching palm. As if to himself, he mused, "If I didn't smell the unmistakable scent of human on you, I'd have sworn you were a rare Var female. You're bold and assertive."

Ulyssa blinked, wondering at the comment and the approval she detected in it.

"Come on," Kirill urged. "Let's get you out of here. It's obvious you don't know what you've done. I would lecture you about drinking that which you don't know, but I don't think you'd be able to understand me right now anyway."

Ulyssa again blinked in confusion. Why was he talking? She looked down her body. Did she smell bad or something? Was he married? What happened to make him stop? She frowned. Was it just her or were her breast swollen and tingling? She looked down at them and was sure they looked larger than normal. Humming softly, she cupped her breasts in her palms, feeling the instantly gratification of the caress. A small sound of wonder escaped her and she suddenly felt dizzy, as she tweaked her nipples.

Kirill groaned, leaning over to pull her hands down. "Ah, you do drive a man to distraction, don't you, human?"

Ulyssa turned to glare at him. He chuckled to see her look.

"What is your name, human?" he asked.

"Ulyssa," she slurred without thought, turning back to contemplate her achy breasts. A finger dipped beneath her chin, drawing her attention back up to the dark eyes. She sighed prettily, simpering like a fool and not caring.

"Lyssa, I'm Kirill. I'm going to take you to a different part of the castle to sleep off the affects of the drink you took. Do you understand?"

Ulyssa frowned at his condescending tone. Her eyes narrowed in disgust, before getting distracted by his mouth.

Kirill laughed softly. "I am sorry, little one, but you will just have to miss the pairing tonight. You're in no condition to choose a mate."

Ulyssa snorted, not paying attention to him.

Kirill frowned and glanced around the empty hall, as if struggling with a decision. Finally, taking her by her arm, he walked her down the hallway, away from the harem. He didn't look at her again as he led her through the long halls, winding around turns until she was completely lost. Ulyssa didn't care. She couldn't stop staring at his face, as she simpered like a witless maid.

* * * *

"What a nightmare," Ulyssa grumbled, stretching her arms over her head. Satin sheets cocooned her body, gliding over her naked flesh in a tickling caress. For a moment, she smiled and arched her back at the feel of luxurious comfort. An unfamiliar wave of contentment washed over her.

Suddenly, she froze in mid-stretch. The relaxation in her body was replaced by a slow building of stress in her limbs. Her eyes popped open and moved around in her head. She was naked, in a strange bed, in a strange stone room. This wasn't good sign.

Ulyssa shot up, sitting on the bed. The large bedroom had a smooth stone floor with woven rugs. She could tell that, like everything else in the Var palace, great attention had been paid to the detail of their making. Staying true to style, the large marble fireplace was carved to perfection and sported a comfortable fire. The bed, covered in dark blue satin sheets and a matching blue and silver coverlet, dominated the floor. Seeing the two arched doorways leading from the room, one with a door and one without, she frowned.

"Where the hell am I?"

Ulyssa threw the covers from her body and edged to the side of the bed. Her bare feet dropped down on the floor. Walking to the entrance without a door, she peeked in. It was a long closet, filled with nothing but clothes cut to fit a man. A flash of a sinfully dark gaze came to her. She closed her eyes and took a deep breath.

"Think, Ulyssa, reason it out."

Lyssa.

The name was an echo in her head. She shivered, recalling a deep, rich, Var accented voice. She knew it wasn't Attor. Had she slept with the bearer of that voice? Surely if she had, she would have done so with a plan of escape. She could remember no plan, but she could recall every detail of a firm body next to hers in the hallway, grinding and pressing her into the wall. Hell, she'd been ready to screw his brains out right there. Why hadn't she? It wasn't like she was shy.

Ulyssa frowned, wrinkling her brow in deep thought. The night unfolded slowly in her mind, foggy yet real. She'd escaped the harem. A man found her. She'd come on to him with no thought of escape.

Ulyssa grimaced, but was not embarrassed by her actions. She'd wanted him and had gone for him, no big deal. Then, he'd rejected her. She scowled, stuck on the memory. He'd rejected her? Now, how was that possible? That *never* happened.

"Nothing happened," she whispered, not sure if she felt relief or irritation. Her pride stung at the memory, but she tried her best to ignore it. Lightly, she scratched her naked backside as she went in to explore his enormous closet. It was bigger than her entire quarters at the Agency. Rubbing the back of her neck, she continued to frown. "He brought me back here. I took off my own clothes and made a pass at him. He then left me here--alone, unfulfilled. Huh. What the hell is that all about?"

A long, rectangular window commanded the far wall of the closet, letting in the soft light from outside. She could see a balcony beyond the window with stone and iron railings along the edge. The dusky green-blue sky spread out before her and she realized the bedroom was high off the ground. A majestic display of forest and mountains stretched before her. She could even see a clear lake tapering off into the distance. Its glassy surface reflected the three suns.

Ulyssa was stunned into momentary silence at the awe-inspiring sight. There was something quite magical about the Var palace, something that stirred a suppressed part of her being. She thought it best not to explore that part of her soul. Some things were better left hidden.

A quick scan of the rooms proved he'd taken her clothes with him when he left. She searched the closet for something decent to wear and found a cross-laced shirt, like the one the man had worn the night before. The shirt was too big for her smaller frame, but she didn't care.

Not caring that she was stealing, Ulyssa slipped the garment over her head and adjusted it to fit her smaller size, pulling the laces tight. She did the same with a pair of pants, lacing them up along her thighs. Using the extra length of cross-laces, she made a makeshift belt around her waist. Then, finding a floor length jacket with long sleeves, she pulled it on. There was no way she'd get into his boots so she didn't even try, opting to remain barefoot for the moment.

"Not bad," she murmured, admiring herself in a mirror as she unbound her hair only to pull it back again. She found it easier to work if it was out of her way.

Walking through the bedroom, she slowly opened the second door and peeked out. The light was dim after the brightness of the bedroom fireplace. Slowly, she closed the door and edged forward. From what she could tell, it looked like a living room, complete with a couch and chairs, more arched entryways leading to various parts of the house.

"Here kitty, kitty, kitty," she whispered, a little too spitefully. Whoever the man was, his rejection stung and she reacted to it. "Are you in here, you little furball?"

She waited and got no answer. Squinting to see now that the bedroom light didn't shine behind her, she crept through the living room. As she passed one of the decorative arches, she saw a long kitchen and dining area. She ignored it, going instead to the arch with a door. Thinking it led outside, she pushed it open. Instead she found a large bathroom. A rectangular mosaic tub took up the far wall with many waterspouts coming from the sides. Next to it was perhaps the biggest water shower she'd ever seen. Well, she'd never actually seen one, but the Agency did have pictures. Through the textured glass, she detected a bench seat.

"Hum," Ulyssa mused with an irritated glance around the room. "Maybe I'm looking too high. I'm sure there has to be a little cat door around here somewhere."

* * * *

Kirill watched the door to his bedroom open. He'd been sitting in the dark, trying to relieve the stress headache that built behind his eyes for the last week. The pain started at the base of his skull and radiated up to his temples until he could hardly see straight.

A heavy responsibility had been thrust on his shoulders, a responsibility he really hadn't prepared himself for--the welfare of the Var people. King Attor had not left him in a good position. He'd rallied the people to the brink of war, convinced them that the Draig were their enemy, and even went so far as to attack the Draig royal family.

Kirill would see peace in the land. However, he knew the facts didn't bode well for it. The Draig had a long list of grievances against King Attor and the Var kingdom.

Before his death, Attor had ordered an attack on the four Draig Princes, all of which ended horribly for the Var. The worst was when Prince Yusef was stabbed in the back, a most cowardly embarrassment for the Var guard who did it. If he hadn't been executed in the Draig prisons, he would've been ostracized from the Var community. Luckily, Prince Yusef survived or else they'd already be at battle.

Attor had also arranged for the kidnapping of Yusef's new bride. Princess Olena had been rescued or else that too would've led to war. The old King had tried to poison Princess Morrigan, the future Queen, on two separate occasions. She too lived. And those were only the offenses that Kirill knew about in the few weeks before Attor's death. He could just imagine what he didn't know.

Kirill sighed, feeling very tired. He'd known since birth that the day would come when he'd be expected to step up and lead the Var as their new King. He just hadn't expected it to be for another hundred or so years. His father had been a hard man, who he'd foolishly come to look at as invincible.

"Here kitty, kitty, kitty." His lovely houseguest's whisper drew his complete attention from his heavy thoughts.

Ulyssa bent over like she expected him to answer to the insulting call. He dropped his fingers from his temple into his lap and a quizzical smile came to his lips. As he watched her, he wasn't sure if he was angered or amused by her words.

"Are you in here, you little furball?" she said, a little louder.

She wore his clothes. Never had the outfit looked sexier. His jaw tightened in masculine interest, as he unabashedly looked her over. All too well did he remember the softness of her body against his and the gentle, offering pleasure of her sweet lips. She'd made soft whimpering noises when he touched her--yielding, purring sounds in the back of her throat. Even with the aid of nef, he was surprised by how easily and confidently she melted into him. The Var were wild, passionate people and were drawn to the same qualities in others. He suspected she'd be an untamed lover.

Too bad she'd belonged to his father first. In his mind, that made her completely untouchable--though none would dare question his claim if he were to bring her to his bed. Technically, by Var law, she belonged to him until he chose to release her. For an insane moment, he thought about keeping her as a lover. He knew he wouldn't, but the thought was entertaining.

Kirill's grin deepened. Ulyssa strode across his home to the bathroom door with an irritated scowl. It was obvious she didn't see him in the darkened corner, watching her. He detected her engaging smell from across the room--the smell of a woman's desire. It stirred his blood, making his limbs heavy with desire. And, for the first time since his father's death, his headache relieved itself.

"Hum, maybe I'm looking too high. I'm sure there has to be a little cat door here somewhere."

His slight smile fell at her words. It was easy to detect the mocking in her.

"Where's your little kitty door, huh?" Ulyssa whispered to herself, her blue gaze searching around in the dark.

Kirill grimaced in further displeasure. He watched her open the door to his weapons cabinet. Her eyes rounded. She nodded in appreciation before closing the door and continuing her search for an exit.

She stopped at a narrow window by his kitchen doorway. Her neck craned to the side, as she tried to see out over the distance. Kirill knew she looked at the forest. From under her breath, he heard her vehement whisper, "Where exactly did you little fur balls bring me? Ugh, I need to get out of this flea trap, even if I have to fight every one of you cowardly felines to do it. I've fought species twice as big and three times as frightening. A couple little kitty cats don't scare me."

If this insolent woman wanted to play tough, oh, he'd play. Curling gracefully forward, Kirill shifted before his hands even touched the ground. He let one thick paw land silently on the floor, followed by a second. Short black fur rippled over his tanned flesh, blending him into the shadows. His clothes fell from his body and he lowered his head as he crept forward. A low sound of warning started in the back of his throat. He was livid.

Ulyssa froze, hearing the growl behind her. She really hadn't expected anyone to be in the room or else she never would've ranted like she had. Biting her lip, her eyes automatically scanned for a weapon as she turned.

Seeing the oversized panther stalking her, its body low against the ground as if she were its prey, she gasped. "Oh, whoa, easy there big fella. Are you one of them or are you just a pet?"

Ulyssa had fought all kinds of alien species and yet somehow her training hadn't prepared her to face a wild animal like this one. She could see the tempered speed in the panther's streamlined body. Steeling her nerves, she looked him in the eyes and reached out the back of her hand. "Are you in there, Var ... warrior ... man? Can you hear me?"

The animal roared, loud and long, brandishing his deadly fangs. She jolted back in surprise. His jaw snapped shut, as if he would bite her. His beastly yellow-green eyes narrowed in warning.

Ulyssa lost all bravado as she backed into a wall. Her heart let loose, hammering in her chest. Adrenaline rushed through her veins, making her shake. Her breath came out in ragged pants. She was terrified, too frightened to scream.

The animal crept closer. To her shame, she felt tears threaten to fill her eyes. Some agent she turned out to be! Her programming for this planet didn't include animal combat. Weren't you supposed to cower before wild animals and let them have dominance? Or was it the other way around? For the life of her, she couldn't remember. It's not like they had many wild animals left running around Earth these days. Those they did have were in locked conservatories, kept away from human interference, and left to their own devices.

The panther roared, bringing her attention back to the trouble at hand. Ulyssa recoiled, lifting her arms to protect her chest and face as she pressed into the stone wall. A dark blue banner waved near her nose as she turned her head away. The image of a styled panther fluttered before her. She whimpered, closing her eyes. Her body tensed, bracing for the initial attack. Silence followed and she couldn't move.

"Shhh," a gentle whisper soothed. "I didn't think you'd be so scared of me."

Ulyssa gasped, recognizing the burr of Kirill's voice from the night before. She felt the gentle brush of warm fingers on her cheek. On instinct, her hand balled into a fist and before she'd even opened her eyes, she swung for him. She didn't like being scared and the fact he'd been able to frighten her pissed her off. Her fist met with his jaw, knocking his head back on his shoulders. But, to her amazement, he didn't stumble away. His head lowered, a controlled movement, and his dark eyes pierced into her. Slowly, he flexed his jaw.

"You bastard!" She glared at him. "How dare you try and scare me? I should tear you apart!"

"Mmm," he smirked. Ulyssa's heart nearly fluttered out of her chest at the sultry look he gave her. He wasn't worried by her threats. Her mouth went dry. His fingers glanced over her neck, past her racing pulse. "Like you tried to tear me apart last night?"

"I-I," she stuttered, at a sudden loss. Had she attacked him last night? Fighting the haze of memory, she tried to recall. His eyes drifted to her mouth. She could feel his heat pouring over her, soaking into her skin.

"You tried to offer yourself to me and, when I refused, you threatened my life."

Licking her lips, Ulyssa's gaze followed his lead and moved down over his body. To her surprise, she discovered his chest was bare. Hard muscles moved beneath his skin, rippling over the surface in male perfection. The heady scent of man came over her, like an intoxicating perfume that left her panting. Her gaze moved over his strong arms, wondering how they would feel holding her. Not an ounce of fat marred the look of him.

Then, very slowly, his words sunk in. He'd refused her! It was like a slap in the face. Her eyes rounded in horror.

"You're fortunate, briallen," he murmured. "If it had been tonight, you'd have died for the offense."

Kirill stepped back from her and turned. Ulyssa watched him walk away. Her eyes rounded in surprise to see that he was completely naked. A wave of fiery longing swept through her at the sight. She couldn't help it. In a twisted way, his rejection only made her want him more. She loved a challenge--and this man was defiantly the most handsome challenge she'd seen in a long time.

Luxurious waves of black hair flowed over his back and shoulders, drawing her eye down the hard muscles surrounding his spine to his narrow hips. His taut buttocks moved with power and grace. She wanted to touch it, grab it, control it--control him. Too bad she really didn't like him. But, then again, when did you have to like the person to sleep with them? It's not like she wanted to stand around making small talk first. It's not like she wanted to get to know him at all. Handsome men never had anything interesting to say.

Ulyssa licked her lips in anticipation. She smiled, not even hesitating before following him to the bedroom. He was cute. Her shots were up to date. If he tried to talk, she'd just have to gag him to shut him up, or at least put his mouth to a better use. Giving a little practice wiggle of her hips, she thought, *I'm not drunk now. Let's just see him try and refuse me again!*

Chapter Three

Kirill had locked her out. Ulyssa paused and tried the handle a second time. Yeah, he'd definitely locked her out of his bedroom. Her cheeks flamed. Placing her hands on her hips, she tapped her foot in anger. Well, if he was going to be a prude there wasn't a damned thing she could do about it. Stupid fool was missing out on the best sex he'd ever be offered.

Pounding on the door, she yelled, "Hey, pussy cat! Mind telling me how to get out of here?"

To her surprise, the door opened. He was fully dressed, as he had been the night before, in seductively tight black. She pulled away from the door to let him pass.

"Don't tempt me to shift, woman. I won't be so kind as to turn back next time." Kirill's voice was hard. He brushed past her to the living room, leaning over to pick up his clothes from the floor. Under his breath she heard him mumble something about ripping out her bothersome throat to shut her up. She thought it better not to ask him to clarify the entire statement.

"Sorry," she answered, rolling her eyes at his back and making a face. Going beside the bathroom he pushed a tile. When an opening appeared in the wall, he tossed the clothes inside and walked to the kitchen. The hole closed behind him.

When he ignored her half-hearted apology, she followed him to the kitchen and demanded softly, "So, how do you get out of here?"

"Do you ever quit talking?" he asked, seeming amused. "The morning is a time of silence and reflection of the day."

The kitchen was constructed of industrial metal against stone. Despite the fact that they were in a castle, it was very modern. Ulyssa watched him open a cabinet and take out a bowl. She did her best not to smirk. Next, he grabbed a jar of milk from the fridge. She bit her lip to keep from laughing. Oh, it was just too easy--kitty cat with his bowl of cream. Unable to resist, she asked, "Having breakfast?"

He shot her a puzzled frown. Ulyssa snorted as she tried not to laugh.

"What's wrong with you now?" Kirill demanded. His brow furrowed.

"Um, nothing," she managed, still struggling for control.

"You are a strange one, aren't you? I don't suppose you escaped from the medical ward?"

Ulyssa's expression fell.

"Guess not," he answered for himself. Taking a metal container, he poured a powdery substance into it and then added the milk. He handed her the bowl. She stared at the gruel with a look of disgust. He put the milk away, grabbed a spoon, and thrust it into the bowl. "Here, eat. Then I will bring you back to the harem."

Ulyssa's stomach growled, as if to answer for her. She was famished. Slowly lifting the spoon, she tested the mixture with the tip of her tongue. It tasted bland, like milky paste, so she braved a small bite.

"It's only been one night of pairing," Kirill said, moving through the kitchen to the dim living room. He paused to stretch his arms over his head. "If you're lucky, some of the willing bachelors will still be without a mate."

"Excuse me?" she choked, dropping the spoon into the bowl she carried with her. "What exactly is this pairing thing you want me to do?"

"The Var bachelors come to woo the half-mates, at least those who haven't bore children to King Attor. Those who wish it will be married." Kirill stopped stretching and turned to study her.

"Oh, no," Ulyssa said, shaking her head. "Not a chance in hell! King Attor is not pawning me off on some....."

His brow rose in warning, as if he could sense her coming insult. She choked it back with some effort. She wasn't use to curbing her tongue.

"...some man," she finished weakly.

"You're right," Kirill said. "King Attor isn't. I am."

"You? Who are you to decide my fate?" Ulyssa took a threatening step forward and scowled. "You're just some ... I don't know what you are. Some guard? What do you care if I marry?"

Kirill's arms crossed over his sturdy chest in a very domineering manner. His head tilted arrogantly to the side. He said nothing.

"Oh, I see. You're a guard and you've picked me to...woo." Ulyssa sighed. "Listen, I'm really flattered, but I'm--"

"I have no wish to mate," Kirill stated.

"Oh, then I'm sure we can come to some sort of an arrangement." Ulyssa shot him her sweetest smile, letting her lashes flutter over her eyes. It was a look she saved for special occasions such as these. It was a look that men could not resist.

Kirill's didn't move, except to blink, as he showed no masculine interest.

"Fine," she grumbled. Snarling, her eyes rolled heavenward. "Listen. Let me be perfectly honest. I don't belong here. I don't want to get married and sweep up fur balls for the rest of my days. As you can see, I'd surely make any Var's life a living hell. I'm just not made to be a--"

"What is this place, hell?" Kirill interrupted. "How do you live a place?"

"It's both a place and a concept. Human sinners go there when they die and--*Argh!* It doesn't matter!" Ulyssa waved a hand toward him in distraction. "It's bad--very bad! It's like being burned alive and tortured at the same time, every day, all day, for all eternity. That's what being married to me would be like."

Kirill frowned, eyeing her as if she was insane.

Ulyssa forged on, "So, if you would kindly tell King Attor that you didn't see me and point me in the direction of the nearest exit, I'll gladly get out of here. You'll never have to lay eyes on me again."

As if an idea suddenly hit him, he sighed. "You haven't been told?

"Told what?" Her frustrated grumble was audible.

"How can this be?" Kirill asked. His face softened, as did his voice. "Were you not in the harem? I'd have thought they'd make an announcement. Taura is usually one to make sure the harem runs smoothly."

"I ... I didn't exactly talk to the other women there," Ulyssa answered, remembering how they avoided her like she was a plague carrier. "Why do you ask?"

"I'm truly sorry to have to tell you this, but King Attor is dead. He died a week ago in battle. I was under the impression his half-mates were informed of this."

Ulyssa kept her face blank. The King was dead?

"If it makes you feel better, he died bravely," Kirill offered.

"What do I care?" Ulyssa shrugged. Her mind raced with questions and schemes. With the King dead, the castle could be in a state of turmoil. It might just work to her advantage. Or, everything might be on lockdown, and it could work against her. "Attor was a barbaric jerk. I say good riddance."

After she said the words, she wanted to take them back. What was it about this man that disarmed her and made her think more about sex and less about survival? Kirill's eyes fell but she didn't notice. When he again looked at her, his face was hard.

"So, who's a girl have to bargain with to get a little freedom around here?" she asked, flippantly.

"Me," he answered.

Ulyssa focused on him once more, shooting him a playful smile. Her brow rose on her face, as she asked, "Oh, yeah? Why you, sweetheart?"

"Because I'm Attor's oldest son and the future King of the Var." Kirill's words were light, but deadly.

Ulyssa paled, instantly sorry for her offhand remarks about his father. She'd never had said them if she'd known. She stood, speechless, her mouth slightly agape. His eyes glittered with golden threat and, for a brief moment, she thought he would shift and tear her apart. To her surprise, Kirill turned from her and stalked away into the darkness.

In the shadowy corner, she watched as a door opened to offer in light. She wanted to kick herself for not seeing it before--the front door in plain sight and unlocked. Kirill's handsome body filled the frame before the door closed once more.

Ulyssa was spurred into instant action, afraid he'd lock her in. When she got to the door, she threw it open and looked out into the long hallway. Kirill was gone and she was free to go.

* * * *

Kirill stormed down the castle halls, eager to get away from the aggravating woman in his home. He didn't have time to deal with her. He didn't want to deal with her--not today, not ever. Let her go. What did he care if she escaped? It would be one less of Attor's women to worry about.

On most days, Attor's women were free to go about the castle, though they chose not to. However, until a new King was officially crowned, the castle was kept under tight lock and key. After his coronation, it would be up to him to decide the women's fate. Already, most of them expressed an interest in marrying the Var soldiers. It was a wise, logical decision, as they'd be given their own home and be taken care of. Most Var chose to mate for life, others half-mated and were still very happy and content. The women would be provided for, cared for, some even loved.

Kirill suddenly stopped. Unbidden, his eyes turned behind him, looking back toward his home. He swallowed. No matter how he tried to deny it, he wanted the frustrating wench. Ulyssa. *Sacred Cats!* She was beautiful, fiery, bold. Her very smell stirred his blood, making him want to pounce and ravage. Only once did she show her fear of him, though he'd detected it at other times--a faint smell, one that was suppressed and well hidden.

He couldn't blame her for fearing his panther form. He'd done everything he could to frighten her. But, when he saw her brave façade crumble and her body tremble in the most feminine way, he couldn't continue. He wanted, no needed, to give her comfort. The realization made him pause. Her nearness quickened him and stirred his blood. If he was honest with himself, his body needed her, desired her more than he had any other in a very long time.

Needed? He needed no one. He couldn't. He was the future King. Had not his father said that all Kings must stand alone, beholden to none?

"To be ruled by a woman is to be ruled by weakness." He could hear his father's gruff voice clearly, as Attor's words renewed themselves in his head.

"I don't need her. I need release," he growled low under his breath, moving to stalk the hallways once more. "She's but a stranger. She's not special. Any woman will do, so long as her thighs spread and her body is soft. I don't need anybody."

Kirill turned, glancing once more over his shoulder.

"I don't need anyone."

* * * *

Ulyssa was again lost in the maze-like hallways of the palace. It was strange, but out of an hour of wandering, she'd only come across one guard and he'd been easy to avoid. She shook her head. Security in the palace did seem to be lacking, that was for sure. If she were in charge ... wait. What was she thinking? She wanted nothing to do with this heathenish place.

She frowned, looking down the endless halls with a sense of boredom, trying to remember if she'd seen a particular pattern before in the wall. The mosaic tiles started to look alike and she developed a migraine from concentrating on them, as she tried to memorize their unique designs. It did no good. She was most definitely lost--not that she'd been found in the beginning.

Ulyssa's thoughts turned to the future King of the Var. She should have known he was royalty. His very barbaric, powerful nature radiated off his graceful form. He was regal and strong. There was a keen intelligence to his gaze, a sturdy caution, a quiet thoughtfulness. Ulyssa was trained in how to read people. Shifters were no different than humans, once you studied their habits. Everything needed to know about her enemies was in their actions and expressions.

The fact that he'd not shown anger at her words against his father spoke volumes. This was a man who would bide his time, patiently waiting for the perfect moment to strike. A hot-blooded man would've had her killed for such slander, or at least would've beaten her within a centimeter of her life. Not Prince Kirill. He was cool, calm. He was a force to be wary of and he was definitely the perfect man to lead the primitive Var nation. She was glad she wasn't going to be around long enough to see his rule.

Ulyssa stopped paying attention to where she was going, as a small smile came to her face. Prince Kirill was definitely one of the most handsome creatures she'd seen in a long time, and she had seen many. Her body heated and melted just thinking about the way he moved. Her arms ached to touch him. She'd just bet he was graceful in bed. Such a pity she wasn't going to find out.

Almost as badly as she wanted to test his skill as a lover, she wanted to test his skill as a fighter. With those animal reflexes, she just bet he'd be a worthy combatant, even without shifting. Oh, and his weapons! She'd nearly swooned in excitement to see them. Her fingers still itched, wanting to draw down the many swords from the weapons cabinet. She knew a few defensive moves with a blade, but she really wanted to learn more. There never seemed to be time at the Agency for archaic weapon training. Almost all species she dealt with used a type of gun. The ones that didn't weren't handled by her unit.

"Halt!"

Ulyssa blinked at the command, surprised but not afraid. She turned to see a large Var warrior standing before her. The man was half-shifted, his features not all cat and not quite human. He wore the Medieval-like tunic of a guard. A light tiger striped fur covered his face and neck with orange and black, mimicked by the fur on his hands. His voice was a gravelly pitch, as if garbled by the beginnings of a roar.

Ulyssa grinned, looking forward to a little sport. A brow rose artfully on her features. There was only one of them and she so wanted to test her abilities against Var in a fair fight. "Yes?"

"You're not to be walking the halls," the tiger man said.

Ulyssa tried to hide her smirk. "Oh? And why's that?"

"Because it is forbidden the night of the coronation," another voice answered.

The second Var was behind her. Ulyssa froze. She hadn't heard his approach. There was no growl to his tone, only a flat dominance. The blackness in the voice gave her chills. Slowly, she turned. Before her was a large warrior, perhaps the largest Var she'd seen yet. She grimaced. He would not be so easy to beat. Even without his impressive build, she detected a quality to him that screamed militant warrior.

"I--I have permission," Ulyssa answered weakly. She hated herself for stuttering.

"Permission?" the large warrior repeated, giving nothing away from his overly serious face. Then, turning to the tiger man, he ordered, "On your way, Navid."

"Yes, Commander Falke," the tiger, Navid, answered.

Ulyssa didn't bother to watch the guard obey. He'd become the lesser of her worries.

Falke turned back to her and again prompted, "Permission?"

"Yes," Ulyssa lied, lifting her jaw. "From Prince Kirill."

Falke's brow rose, urging her silently to continue.

"He has chosen me for his woman," she said, watching the man's face carefully. "I spent last night in his room. So I demand that you let me be on my way before you incur the future King's wrath."

"Navid, come back here." Falke leaned forward to sniff her. His eyes dipped over her attire. At great length, he nodded. "My brother has chosen her as his woman. Take her and have her prepared for him, then deliver her to Prince Kirill's chambers."

He was Kirill's brother? Oh, hell, I've really done it now! Great going, Ulyssa! Ulyssa thought with a brief wave of panic.

"That won't be necessary," Ulyssa began weakly, swallowing down her nerves. She glanced over her shoulder at Navid. His thick arms were crossed over his chest, as he waited for her to comply with the Prince Falke's order. Turning back to the Commander, she shook her head. "I...."

Ulyssa did the only thing she could think of, she took off running. Passing the smaller Navid, she hooked him across his throat with her outstretched arm. The man fell back. With lightening speed, Falke was on her, pouncing from behind and tackling her to the ground. Her face slammed into the hard stone floor, jarring her near senseless at the impact. A light moan escaped her lips.

"If my brother wants you, he will have you. You wear his clothing and you have his smell," Falke said, unaffected by her escape attempt. She tried to struggle at his words, but his one hand held her pinned to the floor. An unforgiving knee pressed into her lower back, stifling her breath. She gasped just to stay conscious. "On your way, Navid. I'll handle her. She better speak the truth for, if she lies, she'll bear the King's wrath."

Navid bowed and left, glaring at her as he did so. Ulyssa knew he didn't take kindly to being out-maneuvered by a woman in front of his boss. She didn't care. It was his fault for thinking she'd be a complying female who'd follow orders.

Falke hauled her up from the ground with a swift leap into the air. Ulyssa stumbled while he landed effortlessly on his feet. Without another word, the muscular Prince tossed her over his shoulder and sprinted down the hall. It was all she could do to hold on.

* * * *

Kirill's coronation was short, just like all of the Var ceremonies. They found no reason to draw out the legalities of an event and turned right to the celebration. As the Preost spoke, his eyes had scanned over the crowd. Most persons within the royal palace were present and made to swear allegiance to the new King. The banquet hall was packed full, but Ulyssa wasn't there. He wondered why he felt disappointment in her absence. He wondered why he thought of her at all.

The banquet hall was a splendid affair with a high domed ceiling of glass that let in the diffused light of the three suns. Music poured from stringed instruments, playing the traditional songs of his people. Flowers swept over the walls in long garlands, their fragrance sweetening the hall.

Dancers from Attor's harem weaved about the tables, entertaining the men with their seductive movement. Silk and gauze clung to their bodies, flowing like ocean waves from their tight flesh. Kirill watched their movements in distraction.

He was now responsible for every soul in the hall before him, and many more souls beyond the palace walls in the Var city, and more still beyond that. It was a heavy burden. From that moment on, every Var life was dependent on him. Every mouth that needed to be fed would be his to feed. Every wrongful death would be his to avenge. Every quarrel, no matter how small, would be his to decide. It was a difficult responsibility, but one he must bear alone.

Kirill's stomach knotted to think about it. There would be no one to shoulder the burden of his centuries of reign. His brothers would help, but they could never understand. He only wished he'd been more prepared for his father's death, but none had expected the indestructible Attor to fall.

Looking around the hall, Kirill was glad that most of his father's women had chosen mates. Once a decision was made, the Var found no reason to wait. They'd be leaving the palace that night after a quick mass marriage ceremony.

Kirill's attention was caught by one of the guards, who came to bow before him. Behind the man was a line of attractive women. Kirill hid his slight smile. A woman to warm his bed and temper the fire in his loins was just what he needed to relax and momentarily forget his burden. Regally, he nodded at the guard, who then motioned the women forward. One by one, the lovely creatures bowed before him. First, a red head with bright green eyes caught his notice, followed by a mystical temptress with hair as dark as deep space. Her gaze sparkled with mischief.

Kirill debated between the two, eyeing their displayed breasts and the curve of their hips. When choosing a lover, he knew he didn't have to look beyond those few simple things. For a moment, he considered taking both. With the stress he'd been under lately, he wasn't sure he could properly pleasure both of them at once. In the end, he chose the dark temptress.

With a lift of his hand, he motioned her forward. The woman smiled, coming closer to him. Without hesitation, Kirill asked, "You haven't been with the late King?"

"No, my lord," the woman answered meekly.

Kirill nodded, pleased with her sultry voice. She would do well to fulfill his body's needs. "You wish to be with me in my bed?"

"Yes, my King." There was no hesitation in her answer. Her lips stayed parted and she shot him a look of pure invitation.

"Very well. The rest may go," Kirill said.

The women bowed, their disappointment evident. It was a great honor to be chosen as the King's lover and if a woman could please him enough to be made a mistress, well that position was almost as grand as being a wife. However, all knew that the Var Kings did not usually share their power with a Queen.

"Your name?" Kirill asked of the woman.

"Linzi, my lord," she murmured. Her eyes dipped boldly over his form.

Kirill saw her attraction to him, an attraction she didn't try to hide. Instantly, another set of eyes flashed in his mind--eyes of entrancing dark blue. He scanned the hall, looking for red-blonde hair, hair that would stand out in a crowd. His body lurched, wanting Ulyssa. Her scent was still in his head. Remembering the sound of her voice drummed fire into his veins. Her allure to him was potent, more potent than any other had been.

"My lord?" Linzi asked, looking over her shoulder at the crowd to see what he stared at.

Kirill's attention focused once more at the sound of her voice. He sighed, hiding his disappointment in not seeing Ulyssa. She was probably long gone by now. It was just as well. He didn't need the kind of distraction a woman could become, especially right now as he fitted himself in the role of a King.

Slowly, he stood from the throne chair that commanded the hall. The milling crowd parted to let him through, eyes turned to him in respect. The exotic dancers spun out of his way and bowed low as he moved passed. Linzi followed meekly behind him without having to be commanded.

Once they were out of the hall, Kirill turned and gave the woman a smile. He held out his arm for her to take. She did without hesitation. There was no shyness in her as she looked at him. She knew well what he wanted from her. There was no modesty in sexual things for the Var. Sex was as natural as breathing. Although Linzi was not Var by blood, she, like so many others, had adopted the Var ways as her own.

Gently, the King said, "Come, Linzi. Let us go to bed."

* * * *

Ulyssa's nostrils flared in anger as she struggled against her bonds. That oaf Falke had tied her to Kirill's bed like some sort of coronation present. Her wrists were bound over her head and her legs were loosely tied to the bottom posts, conveniently keeping them open. She'd actually been surprised when he didn't tie a big, red bow over her breasts. The nerves of these men, thinking they could just do as they please with a woman wherever and however they wanted!

Ulyssa wasn't sure what made her angrier--the fact that she was tied to the bed, or the fact that Falke made her put on a dress. She grimaced looking down at the skimpy ensemble. Barely two pieces of transparent material, the black and silver dress had a short front piece and a longer back piece, held together by side cross straps that ran over her naked hip and sides, finally to loop over one shoulder. With a pull of either strap, the dress would come completely off. Ulyssa knew it was probably the exact function the Var had in mind when they designed the awful thing.

Hearing a noise, Ulyssa froze. A door closed and a small sound came from the other side of the bedroom door. Tensing, she glared toward the sound, pulling hard at her restraints in a renewed effort to be free. There was a crash followed by a very feminine giggle. Suddenly, the bedroom door flew open. It was thrown open with a hard push, banging loudly as it hit the wall. The woman giggled again, a truly nauseating sound to Ulyssa.

Kirill's back was to her. A metal crown was on his dark head. Animalistic groans of pleasure came from him as he kissed the dark woman in his arms. Ulyssa watched in stunned, frustrated silence, as Kirill's hands run over his lover's body. His palms cupped her breasts, the thumb rubbing in slow circles over her nipple. The woman kept giggling, until it was all Ulyssa could hear in her numb brain and the sound annoyed the hell out of her.

A low sound grew in the back of Kirill's throat to answer the irritating laugh, bringing Ulyssa from her trance. The rumbling sent shivers over her spine. A heated, unreasonable jealousy lit like fire in her blood as she watched them together--especially since she'd nearly burned for him since their first meeting. Without thinking, she growled, "If you want to use the bed, then you best help me get off it first."

Where did that come from? Ulyssa was shocked by her outburst. She watched as Kirill stopped in mid-kiss. His firm lips drew back from the woman's and his hand fell from her breast to his side. He turned confused eyes to look at her. Ulyssa wiggled her fingers at him in greeting, drawing attention to her wrists above her head. She pressed her lips together, giving him a mockingly wry smile.

"You?" the stunned woman by his side began. Her wide eyes roamed over Ulyssa. Suddenly, she bowed low, "Forgive me, my lady. I did not seek an introduction. I am Linzi. I didn't know the King already had a first. I didn't know to seek your permission."

Kirill frowned and opened his mouth to speak. Linzi's words stopped him.

"I'm sorry for tempting you, my lord. I'll spend the required thirty days in exile from you. If you wish to have me then, you know where to find me." Linzi bowed and rushed from the room.

Kirill didn't even try to stop her from going. A rueful expression crossed his features and his heated gaze turned to the bed. Seeing her, a frown grew between his brown-black eyes. Ulyssa met his stare dead on. The challenge between them was once more renewed.

Chapter Four

"Cute little girlfriend you have there," Ulyssa said dryly, "nice and submissive. I'm curious, does she have to ask permission to get on her knees and give you a blow--"

"What are you doing here, Lyssa?" Kirill asked, crossing his arms. He had no qualms about checking out her bound form on his bed. Interest lit inside him, as he unabashedly studied her tantalizing position.

"Uh, in case you're blind, I really don't have a choice but to be here at the moment. Your barbarian of a brother, Falke, tied me here." Ulyssa again wiggled her fingers for dramatic effect, but his eyes weren't on her hands. She tried to draw her legs together, but it did no good. If he were to lean over just a little further, he'd see right up her skirt. Moisture pooled between her thighs, making her more than ready.

"And why would he have done that?" Kirill asked, coming to stand beside the bed. A slow, delicious smile curled his lips. A soft light shone from the closet, giving a pleasing dimness to his bedroom, casting their skin in a romantic softness that seemed out of place in their battle of the wills.

"I don't know," she lied. Her voice dipped and she couldn't stop herself from looking at him.

"Hum." Kirill studied her a moment longer before shrugging. "Suit yourself. I know my brother wouldn't have tied you there without cause. Until you're ready to speak the truth, I'll be forced to leave you where you're at."

Kirill made a move to leave. Ulyssa tensed.

"Fine!" she yelled after him as his hand touched the door. "I was trying to escape this damned palace--which I'm sure you're well aware is one giant maze. Some guard stopped me, then your brother showed up out of nowhere and..." Ulyssa sighed, rolling her eyes in her head. "And I might have told him you chose me to be your woman. Now untie me."

"You said what?" Kirill paled slightly. His eyes darted around to hers.

"Gawd! You don't have to look at me like that. Okay, so I'm not your type. You don't have to rub it in. I'm not a freaking leper!" Ulyssa glared at him. What in the hell was wrong with her for a lover? She was ever bit as attractive as that harlot she'd just chased out of the room with her presence. "Besides, you'd be lucky to sleep with a woman like me--if you could even handle it!"

"I didn't choose you," Kirill said softly. A strange expression came to him. "Why would you say that?"

"Hello? Are you even hearing me? I said I was trying to escape. I thought it would get me a free hall pass." Ulyssa shrugged. "Now, I told you what happened. Untie me."

Kirill's lip curled slightly, but he ignored her otherwise. Slowly, he walked to the fireplace and stuck his steel crown on the mantel. Very thoughtfully, he ran a light finger over the metal edge before moving to smooth back the long length of his black hair.

"Don't you understand what it is you have done?" Kirill asked.

"No." Ulyssa watched him closely. He turned to her, his gaze dark and poignant. Whispering, she asked, "What?"

"You've declared yourself my mate," Kirill said. "My first half-mate to be exact. It gives you power in my home. All it would take is my declaration and you'd be my lifemate, my wife."

"What?!" Ulyssa nearly screamed as she began bucking anew. "I'll be no man's wife! Now you untie me this instant, you heathenish, savage ... jerk. What's your race's obsession with getting married anyway? Why don't you join the modern age, you primitive ... cat man! Don't you even dare think to--"

"*Luckily*," Kirill stressed by way of interruption, "for both of our sakes, I'll never make such a declaration. I've no use for a wife. And I certainly don't wish for one that would try to burn me alive every day."

"What? *Oooh!* I said it was like being burned alive, *like* ... oh, never mind!" Ulyssa glared hotly at him.

"Either way, I've no use for a wife," Kirill said, hiding his smirk.

"Great, so it's agreed. Untie me and point me to the nearest exit." Ulyssa relaxed against the bed. Her arms ached from her constant pulling. Her finger throbbed from lack of blood and her wrists were beginning to sting from being rubbed raw.

"I'm afraid that's no longer possible." Kirill turned to her and made his way across the room to stand above her.

"What in the hell are you talking about, not possible?" Ulyssa's eyes narrowed, as she stared up at him. Man, but he was handsome. If he weren't so damned frustrating, she'd try to get him to lie on top of her. Tingles erupted all over her skin. Suddenly, her binds didn't seem like such a bad thing. Her nerves reached out to him, wanting him.

"You've declared yourself my first half-mate." Kirill's eyes softened as he looked down at her.

"Yeah, so?" she demanded, growing rigid as she fought to control her lust for the barbaric King. Her lips pressed tightly together. "I take it back. I'm not your woman. There, taken care of. Now ... let ... me ... go!"

"My kind cannot take back such declarations, especially on the same day they're made. To do so would dishonor us both. It would be assumed either you lied or I misused you and later denied it. Either way, it's not a good way to start my reign as King--with scandal."

"Tell everyone I lied. You'll not be looked down upon. In fact, you can say you banished me from the palace as punishment. It'd solve both our problems." Unbidden, her eyes began a journey over his hard body. He was gorgeous to be sure. Her gaze took in his broad shoulders, his slender waist, his perfectly proportioned hips. Seeing the hard bulge pressing against his pants, her mouth went dry. She wished her hands were free so that she could pull open the laces at his hips to better see. But, being as her hands were occupied, she'd gladly use her teeth--if he'd just step closer.

"You'll be dishonored."

Ulyssa's eyes flew up to meet his. His features were lined with vast amusement.

"I don't care what your people think of me. So what I'm dishonored." She widened her eyes and declared mockingly, "I'm sure I'll get over it."

"To be dishonored in my culture is to face either imprisonment or death." Kirill's eyes roamed over her body, devouring her form as she had his. His gaze stopped to leisurely stare at her breasts. He purposefully licked his lips. "If I let you go, you'll be hunted."

"Well, oh dire one, tell me. How do we get out of this mess?"

"There's only two ways I know of," he answered.

"The first?"

"Death."

"I don't suppose you'd be willing to die for me, would ya stud?" Ulyssa asked with a raise of her brow.

"No." Kirill grinned mischievously at her--a truly wicked smile. Tremors again coursed through her at the look. He was really too attractive, just looking at him made her mind wander to naughtier things.

"And the second?" Her voice came out a whisper. His smile widened. Ulyssa grew nervous. "What's the second way?"

"You have to stay here, in my home, and be my mistress."

It took awhile for the shock of his bold statement to set in. Ulyssa stared at him, waiting for the laughter that was sure to follow such a declaration. The laughter never came. Even as her body leapt with fire at the idea of being his lover, her mind rebelled. She would belong to no man. She could be no man's mistress.

Lightly, he continued, "You'll stay, and your body will release mine."

Kirill eyed the beautiful woman tied to his bed, waiting for her reaction to his words. Her face was blank, but it didn't matter. He could see the disbelief in every subtle movement of her form. Her breath caught and held. Her fingers curled into light fists. He'd known the statement would irritate her.

"In return, mine will give you pleasure," he whispered with confidence. He watched her body shiver at the words.

Sacred Cats! She was ravishing to behold. From the view he was afforded of her silky hip all the way up her side to the roundness of her breast, he knew she was naked beneath the traditional gown. Her darker nipple pressed against the transparent material, outlined to perfection.

The darker region between her thighs drew his attention. Already, he knew she desired him. He could smell the scent of her as it filled his head. His mouth watered, eager to taste her. His lips parted slightly, wanting to taste the cream of her skin, the flavor of her essence. He wanted to ignite the passions he felt simmering beneath her fiery surface and at the same time slake his own burning needs.

He'd been shocked to find her strapped down as an offering to a King. He didn't doubt how she said she got there. Trust Falke, his ever-dutiful brother, to follow the old traditions to the letter. If this woman declared herself the future King's woman and then, as he suspected she had, tried to escape Falke as he made her ready, his Commander brother could've very well tied her down without a second thought. A King's wish in such matters was always followed.

She was strong, so frustratingly stubborn. Those traits were clear. But, beneath the stubborn exterior, he detected a vulnerability that made every fiber in his masculine being want to protect her and keep her safe. It'd been there in her eyes when he'd scared her in his shifted form. She'd never be more to him than a half-mate, a lover. But, to possess her, would be an honor worthy of a King.

"No."

"No?" Kirill's brows rose in surprise. What did she mean no?

"That's right. No. I'll not be your mistress," Ulyssa said. "I don't want to be."

"It's a position of great honor," he countered.

"Uh, still, no thanks. I'll pass." Ulyssa grinned smugly at him.

"You are in no position to negotiate." Kirill would never take an unwilling woman, but she had started the game between them and frankly he was amazed that she said no to him. He tilted his head and made a great show of taking a deep breath. Her longing filled him like a sweet, intoxicating perfume. "Besides, your body says you'd like very much to be my lover."

Ulyssa's mouth fell open, before she grumbled wryly, "Nice try, barbarian. If you were going to ravish me, you'd have done it last night. Now, let me go before I get really mad."

"Perhaps I should ask nicely before you make your decision." His voice practically growled as he grinned like a boy about to test a new sword. Slowly he made his way down to the foot of the bed, keeping his dark eyes on hers.

Gradually, Kirill's gaze slid down her frame, over her breasts, her waist, past her hips, until finally it stopped at the apex of her thighs hidden beneath the dark gown. His body curled forward as he moved onto the bed. Crawling on all fours, he came above her. His knees fitted between her loosely bound legs and he placed his palms down on the bed, outside of her thighs.

Slowly, he looked up at her, taking his time as he studied her body beneath his. Dark hair spilled over his shoulders and down his back. A light of promise filtered into his piercing gaze.

Ulyssa's heart nearly stopped at the meaning in his expression. Her breath came out in raspy pants. For the life of her, she couldn't think of a single thing to say. Kirill licked his lips as his finger drew forward to her knee. Lightly, he touched her and she trembled. Her eyes widened. A torrent of moisture pooled between her thighs and made ready for him.

Watching his finger as if it was the most important task in the world, Kirill drew it in light circles up her inner thigh. The back of his hand edged up her skirt by agonizingly small degrees. Her leg twitched, falling slightly open in invitation. The movement caused his hand to still in its progress over her skin. Kirill moaned softly, leaning over to brush his lips against her raised knee. He didn't kiss her, just allowed his lips to discover the texture of her skin in a brief caress.

Ulyssa's body jerked violently, giving away the depths of her need. Her center was wet, hot, nearly burning in anticipation. Her hands worked against the ties, fighting to be free. His lips brushed along her knee another time and she again jerked. Ripples of pleasure shot through her at the simple caress. Her back arched, offering itself up in invitation. She wanted more from him, so much more.

Kirill groaned in approval of her passion. She was so purely wild in her untamed responses. Even though he knew a part of her fought what stirred between them, she wanted him. Suddenly, he stopped and pulled his hand back into a fist. Sitting between her legs, he studied her intently.

"What?" she began, confused. Her lids fluttered as she searched for him in the dimness. "Why'd you stop?"

"You belonged to my father, Lyssa," he stated simply.

Ulyssa tensed. "I belong to no man, especially not your father."

To her surprise, a smile flashed over his features at her words. "I truly pity any man who'd love you with his heart, for it'd be a weary battle to win yours."

Ulyssa felt the instant sting of tears at the words, but blinked them back. She didn't care to wonder why the truth would feel like such a hard kick in the gut. Hadn't she always said the exact same thing? But, to hear it from him seemed ... painful.

Kirill's hand reached once more for her thigh, pushing the skirt up higher. His voice a low rumble, he asked, "Do you want this?"

"It's just sex, Kirill," she answered, still hurt by his words and covering it with her straightforward way of talking. "I've had my intergalactic travel shots and I can't get pregnant. We have nothing to worry about."

He stopped, considering her words.

"What? I can't call you Kirill? Do you really want me to shout out Your Royal Highness?" Ulyssa smirked.

Kirill came forward and brushed his lips against hers. It was a kiss they both felt all the way down to their toes. Whispering along the corner of her mouth, he said, "No, in bed you may call me whatever you wish. In public it is my lord, my King, or King Kirill."

"You do realize that I'm not staying here." Ulyssa bumped his nose playfully with hers.

"You realize I can't permit you to leave quite yet," he answered, rubbing back.

"I wasn't asking for your permission." She reached her tongue to trace the seam of his lips, trying to tempt him to madness. He tasted like wine--warm, delicious. "You have no power over me."

"I can't allow you to leave." Reaching out with his tongue, he did the same to her. His dark eyes bore down into her blue ones. "And I have power over everything in my land."

"It would seem we can't reach an agreement," she whispered. Her long lashes fluttered over her eyes, as the tips of their tongues touched and tangled in slow circles.

Kirill sucked her tongue's tip into his mouth and closed his lips around it as he slowly pulled back. "Mm, so it would seem."

Ulyssa moaned, unable to take the drawn out seduction. Her body hummed with fire. She needed him to fulfill the ache his nearness stirred. Parting her lips, she pushed up, ready to claim his mouth with hers in a searing kiss. He pulled back, as if he'd been anticipating her advance. He let a slow smile form on his mouth as he paused, letting her know that he was in control.

Then, just as eagerly, he closed the distance and gave her what she craved. His tongue delved between her lips, sweeping past the barrier of her teeth to possess and explore as his mouth sawed heavily against hers. She met him fully, no hesitation. Her teeth bit lightly into his bottom lip, as she sucked it into her mouth. Their loud moans intermingled in the bedroom, echoing off the walls.

"Mmm, you taste sweet," he said into their kiss. "Like berries."

He roamed his hands over her sides, touching her skin through the laces. Reaching the side of her breast, his thumb slipped beneath the material to settle under a soft globe.

"You skin is like silk." Kirill's kisses moved from her lips, trailing over her jaw to her throat. Small animalistic noises escaped him as he softly devoured her. Everywhere he touched a fire ignited in her flesh. She'd been with men, but none had provoked such a response as to make her lightheaded and giddy. "And it tastes like cream."

Ulyssa shivered in feminine pleasure. Never had she felt more like a woman than she did when he spoke to her. She suddenly didn't mind being helpless to his whim.

"Mmm, berries and cream." Kirill's hands slid down to her hips. He licked her earlobe and then he sat back to watch as he pulled her skirt over her waist. His lids fell heavy over his eyes as the small thatch of hair was revealed to him. "I want to eat you all up."

Pleasure exploded as his mouth lowered onto her wet mound. Instantly, his long tongue met with her feminine lips, parting them so that he may take a deep taste. Ulyssa cried out. His hands held her steady as he lapped up the cream of her body. Her hips jerked and she almost climaxed against him. His low chuckle of pleasure reverberated between her thighs, vibrating against her.

Teeth grazed the center nub of her desire. He licked her opening, only to suck gently. Ulyssa screamed. Kirill sucked harder, milking an orgasm from her body.

Bright lights exploded beneath her closed lids. Her teeth bit hard into her lip, nearly drawing blood as the tremors overtook her. Her body became rigid as she bucked up from the bed, straining the bonds. She came hard against his mouth and still he wouldn't stop, wouldn't let the torment end. Only when she was weak and panting, begging him for mercy, did he pull back.

A satisfied expression came to his dark features. He sat back, reaching to pull off his belt. Ulyssa fought for control, for reason. Her eyes devoured him, trying to focus as the tremors subsided. Soon, his shirt was unlaced and pulled over his head, revealing the bronzed perfection of his smooth chest.

Ulyssa was almost too weak to move, but as she watched the slow seduction of his stripping, she found herself ready for more. Only, this time, she wanted him buried inside her. Her eyes moved down to the bulge of his arousal. Instead of revealing it to her curious eyes, he reached to untie her legs. Once freed, he gently massaged the blood back to her ankles. Her feet worked restlessly on the bed as he took his time touching her. Her legs stayed open, waiting for him.

Seeing her gaze still trained on his erection, Kirill asked in a dark tone, "Would you like to see it?"

Ulyssa nodded. Breathless, she panted, "Yes."

He smiled and stood beside the bed before tugging the laces along his thighs. The material slid off him to the floor. He stood proud, naked before her, letting her look her fill. His body was all sinew and muscle. Not a measure of fat marred his perfect, smooth frame.

Ulyssa's eyes darted to his arousal and she gasped in pleasant surprise. If anything, the smooth shaft was larger than it should have been on his slender body. She wasn't sure if the enormous size excited or terrified her. It didn't take long before her excitement won out. No wonder he had no qualms about undressing for her. With a weapon like that, it was a wonder he didn't roam about naked all the time.

"Mm, come here," she purred.

Reaching over with her foot, she ran her toes along his inner thigh. His movements were refined, stalking, graceful, as he crawled over her once more. She loved to see the dominating grace of his muscles as they rippled beneath his skin. His fingers found her laces and slowly parted her from her clothes, kissing her flesh as he leisurely undressed her. She writhed wildly against him, rubbing her calves restlessly over his back, his hips, along his sides, wherever she could reach.

As his lips latched onto a ripened nipple to suck it gently, she growled, "Ah, untie me. I must be doing something wrong, because I'm on fire and you're calm. Let me loose and I promise to make you lose control."

"Don't make promises you can't keep," he said into her breast, moving to flick her other nipple with his tongue.

"What the hell is that suppose to mean?" she demanded, stiffening. She rounded her eyes in horror as if he'd hit her. Moving her leg along his side, she tried to buck him from her body. Her eyes became moist and she blinked to keep from crying out in dismay and embarrassment. She struck him repeated along his waist with her thigh. He grunted, but did not stop his mouth's onslaught.

Kirill rose up coming to her lips. His leg trapped hers down, burning into her with his thick arousal. An arm wound its way to her thigh to hold it still so she couldn't strike again. She suddenly became aware of just how strong the man-cats really were.

Kissing her thoroughly breathless, he pulled back. Contemplative, he brushed back her golden hair and asked softly, "What happened to the confident woman who would dare defy a King?"

Her throat worked nervously, she couldn't move. His eyes stared at her, confident and sure and so in control. It looked to her as if he didn't feel the passion at all. Yet, there was tenderness in him too, and that made her nervous. She ignored his softer side, concentrating on being angry and hurt.

"Get off," she growled. "We're done here."

"That's not what you wish," he stated, self-assured.

Ulyssa frowned. Damn him if he wasn't right.

"The nef you drank, which made you feel such great uncontrolled passion, gives me the restraint I need to see to your pleasure first. In doing so, I will increase mine." Kirill stopped to kiss her again before moving to rim her ear with his tongue. Nibbling a tender lobe, he continued, "That's why I can't lose control. It has nothing to do with your many charms. The nef controls the beast within my kind. That's why we drink it, to temper ourselves back."

Ulyssa frowned, not liking his unfair advantage. She wanted him as frantic and needy as she. Though, his explanation did mend her wounded pride.

"If my drinking of it displeases you, Lyssa, I won't before coming to you in the future," Kirill said.

Ulyssa tensed. Very carefully, so there was no mistake, she said, "This night is it, Kirill. There will be no *in the future*."

Kirill moved his hips to settle between hers in a graceful slide. She shivered as his hard heat neared her delicate opening. She was ready for him, so ready. Her body released a torrent of cream at his nearness.

"Is that a challenge?" he asked, a bold smile on his firm lips.

"No," she shot, glad that her voice came out hard and sure. "It's a fa ... ahhhct."

Kirill thrust forward as she spoke, cutting off her words as he imbedded his shaft deep inside her. Her eyes widened in amazement as his lips found the pulse at her neck. He nipped her skin, holding still as he let her tight body adjust to him.

Ulyssa was no untried virgin and yet tears of pleasure-pain stung her eyes. She gasped in surprise. All logical arguments left her until all she could think was that he was larger than she'd first thought.

"Do you hurt?" he asked, his voice impassioned, when she held still. His tone was concerned, but his lips didn't stop their achingly torturous movement against her flesh.

She shot forward, forgetting everything as she turned her mouth to capture his. She kissed him hard and long, moaning in pleasure. He growled into her mouth and she breathed in the sound of it. Her hips moved, urging him to thrust.

To her surprise, he slid deeper still until his hips were seated flush against hers. Every fiber inside her being reached for him. She arched, pressing her stomach and breast to rub against his heat. He moved, slowly at first, as he worked his body in a tantalizingly precise rhythm against her. He took it easy, driving his hard shaft in shallow thrusts until she got used to his size.

Fire and tension pooled in her hips, stoked to a fevered pitch. Her cries of pleasure joined his softer grunts, as she squirmed for more. She tried to hook a leg around his back. With a growl, he grabbed it and slung her knee over his shoulder, opening her wider to him. The tempo of his hips built, faster, harder, digging into her, rocking in and out of her warmth in long strokes, until they pushed against each other in searching need.

Kirill lifted up. She watched his muscles, swimming wonderfully erotic beneath his skin. He was perhaps the most beautiful man she'd ever seen--rugged yet refined. His dark hair tickled her breasts. Her arms strained. She wanted desperately to touch him, but her bonds were too tight.

"Oh, my! *Kirill!*" Ulyssa screamed into the bedroom as she neared her rocky climax. Suddenly, an earthquake let loose inside her skin her she shook with the force of it. Her whole body tensed, helpless against the tides of passion.

Kirill's yell joined her, just as loud and violent as he too stiffened. He froze like a glorious statue above her, his body tight, his mouth opened wide, the cords of his neck strained. Her passage clenched him, spurring on his release, milking the seed from his body.

As the tremors subsided, Kirill fell forward. His elbows braced his weight so he didn't crush her. Playfully, he licked her cheek before rolling off her. Within seconds, he had her hands untied and was massaging the feeling back into them.

Ulyssa watched him, weak and in awe of his gentle strength. He said nothing as he dropped her hands and pulled her into his chest. He held her to him, curled intimately around her naked body.

She felt the hard length of him pressed protectively to her skin. Her head nestled onto the crook of his arm and her back stretched along his strong frame. His knees bent forward into the backs of hers. A strong arm draped over her waist and his fingers wrapped possessively around her soft breast, over her heart. She'd never been protected before, not even as a child. It was a strange sensation, one she didn't want to dwell on.

Ulyssa felt Kirill's breath deepen in sleep. She shivered, staring out over the dimly lit bedroom to the closet door. She knew that the balcony was there, beyond the window. She wondered if she could use it to escape. Never had she just slept beside a man once she'd gotten what she wanted out of him.

Her heart beat fiercely against his warm palm, pounding so hard it kept her awake. But, great sex or no, she would never be a King's whore. A strange ache built in the pit of her stomach. He was by far the best lover she'd have had.

* * * *

The next morning, Ulyssa stole some clothes from Kirill's closet and slipped from his house well before dawn. The palace halls were quiet as she made her way. She was still lost, but the idea of being trapped forever within the palace as a mistress stiffened her resolve to escape. She would belong to no man, even if that man was a King.

Chapter Five

Kirill stretched his arms over his head, arching his back against the mattress. With a half smile forming on his lips, he sighed in contentment and reached over to pull the warm female body back into his embrace. He'd slept better than he had in a long time and the nightmares that plagued him since his father's death were gone. He felt great!

His hand met with the empty expanse of sheets causing the smile to fade from his features. Frowning, one dark eye opened to follow his hand. He rolled on his side to search the bedroom for Ulyssa. She was gone.

"Lyssa," he murmured lightly, sitting up. His voice was hoarse from sleep and he cleared his throat, only to call louder, "Lyssa?"

Kirill's body was ready for her, as was evident by the heavy protrusion beneath the sheet. A growl grew steadily in his throat as he leapt out of bed. He frantically checked his closet and balcony, then his home. She had truly left him.

Scratching his naked stomach, he looked down at his erection in disappointment. The knot of stress again came to his shoulders, settling all the way down his spine. His eyes darkened as he strode into the closet. The last thing he needed was his mistress, a woman marked by his very potent scent, roaming alone about the palace declaring that she is unattached. For Kirill had no doubt Ulyssa would insist on trying to leave him. Such scandal wouldn't bode well for his reign. The Var prided themselves in many things, not the least of which was being able to please a woman in bed. If a King--a man of supposed great power and even greater wisdom--couldn't keep a woman happy longer than one night... Well, it would be disastrous.

Kirill didn't want to think about it. He hurriedly dressed in a light tunic and pants. He then slid leather boots over his feet. They reached up his calves. Pulling the shirt laces tight, he walked out of his home.

Once in the hallway, he looked in both directions only to find them empty. "Siren, find Lyssa ... uh, make that Ulyssa."

He only had to wait for a brief moment, before the castle's mainframe answered in a sultry female voice that dripped of seduction, "No record of an Ulyssa, my lord."

Kirill grimaced. He wasn't sure there would be, but it'd been worth a try. Her DNA had yet to be programmed into the castle's central computer, so it was impossible to track her exact location electronically.

He started to walk away, only to stop. Going back to his home, he rushed to his bedroom and scanned the sheets. He found a strand of red blonde on the pillow and took it. Going back to the hall, he pressed a series of tiles on the circular pattern in the wall. The tiles didn't move as he touched them. But, as he finished and pulled his hand away, the whole center circle pulled into the wall to reveal a screen.

Pressing a button, he lightly set Ulyssa's hair into the tray that slid out. Smiling, he said, "Siren, meet Lyssa."

"Lyssa recorded, my lord," the computer answered in a tone that dripped honey and almost sounded like a pout. "Security clearance?"

Kirill thought of that and finally said, "Ten."

"Prisoner class, my lord? Would you like me to notify the guards that she is not in her cell?"

"Ah, no, Siren, better make that a ... uh ... eight clearance." Kirill grimaced slightly. She'd have freedom to roam the palace but wouldn't be able to make it outside the building without him being notified.

"Very good, my lord, Lyssa stored."

"Now, Siren, find Lyssa for me," Kirill stated again, pressing a button to retract the computer and replace the wall to normal.

"Lyssa is outside the royal office, my lord, and does not appear to be moving on. Door sensors are picking up a vibration. The lock is being picked. The palace guards have been notified and are en route."

Kirill took off running in the direction of the royal office before Siren finished. Her voice followed him as he moved down the hall. He frowned. Why would Ulyssa try to go there? Was it possible the woman was a Draig spy? After what King Attor had done to the Draig royal family, he wouldn't blame them for taking the defensive. But, even if he understood, he couldn't allow it. He had a duty to protect his people, even if that meant fighting in a war he didn't personally believe in. If Ulyssa was a spy, the Draig had definitely chosen her well.

Kirill didn't know why it irritated him to think that she'd only slept with him out of deceit, but it did. He didn't wish to delve too deeply into the feeling. She was rare, that was all--a mystery, a diversion, a good bed partner.

Well, if he was honest with himself, she was more than just good in bed. She'd been phenomenal. Just thinking of it made him run faster to find her.

"You stupid hairball, get off me!"

Kirill quickly suppressed his grin as he rounded the corner. Falke held Ulyssa tightly in his grasp from behind, as she continued to spout profanities at the great Commander. A dozen soldiers surrounded the pair, appearing confused.

"What? Scared little kitty cat needs all these warriors to help him out? Can't take out a single girl on his own?" she taunted.

Falke's eyes looked over Ulyssa's shoulder to his brother. She jerked up, kicking out at one of the staring guards. He took a step back rather than touch her. The men looked to the King for guidance. Kirill knew they didn't wish to lay a hand on his mistress without permission.

Falke gave what Kirill knew to be the closest thing he had to a smile and nodded in approval. Kirill grimaced. Trust Falke to approve of a woman acting like a harpy.

Ulyssa's wide blue eyes landed on him and he felt a spark of electricity shoot through his core. She again wore his clothes. He didn't like that she took them without permission, but damned if she didn't look sexy all the same. She shook with a renewed force. Falke tightened his grip. She yelped in pain and instantly stopped struggling.

"Kir--" she began, only to correct herself. "My lord, would you mind telling this oaf of yours to get off me!"

The guards gasped at her hard tone. Falke's breath caught behind her back. Kirill's brows furrowed together, as he looked at her in displeasure.

Ulyssa's eyes darted around at the men. She visibly swallowed only to add, "Ah, please, your royal ... highness ... sir."

Kirill sighed and affected a bored, unconcerned pose. His arms crossed over his chest and he looked down his nose at her. "You must forgive her. My little mistress likes to play games."

The men looked at him expectantly. Ulyssa's mouth fell open and he rushed on to keep her from talking.

"She so wanted to be hunted as my prey. I couldn't help but to indulge her whim." Kirill stepped forward to leisurely run the back of his knuckles over her cheek and down her throat. Her eyes narrowed in warning just as he was about to dip to a breast. He somehow knew she wouldn't take kindly to being groped in public. A part of him willed his hand to continue, but he was too wise to press his luck. She was being quiet. He wouldn't give her cause to start screaming.

Kirill felt the jealous eyes of the guards on them. Ulyssa was a beautiful woman and bold enough to fire any Var's blood. But, the fact that she liked to tease the hunter said much about her wildness between the sheets and this excited them, too. The ancient hunter in them, long suppressed by their societal codes, always drifted beneath the surface waiting for an excuse to play. It was part of the reason they drank *nef*, to calm the inner beast.

"I should've warned her to stay within my section of the palace," he continued, not holding her gaze for long. He motioned his hand to the guards. "You may go. I'll reprimand her in private."

Ulyssa's heart raced in her chest, more from seeing Kirill than being captured by his brother. She felt his nearness and wanted him again. His hair was handsomely disheveled about his shoulders, making him look wild and incredibly sexy. Her breasts were only too eager to remind her how the silken locks felt brushing against them. To her shame, her nipples puckered against her stolen top. She glanced down briefly and, when she looked back up, Kirill stared at the treacherous little buds.

She quietly watched the guards bow and leave her alone with Falke and Kirill. The mighty King still stared at her chest when she turned back to him and she cleared her throat to get his attention. His dark eyes flashed to hers, glittering with a golden promise. Her stomach fluttered and she couldn't move. His look said he wanted her. His lips parted as if he could already taste her. There was possession in his eyes, possessiveness over her. She felt him in her head, heard his low voice--a quiet murmur she couldn't make out. Shivering, she struggled anew.

"Tell your oaf of a brother to let me go!"

Kirill nodded at Falke that it was all right. Falke loosened his hands. Her elbow instantly wrenched back to slam into her captor's tight midsection. She yelped in pain, catching the elbow to her chest and cradling it. The Commander's breath caught, but he didn't double over like she planned.

Tearing away from them, Ulyssa glared accusingly as she rubbed her injured arm. "You're lucky--"

"Siren, unlock the royal office please," Kirill interrupted softly.

The door instantly unlatched and swung open. Kirill walked into the royal office, ignoring Ulyssa's outburst. She growled and stormed in after him. Falke shut the door behind her and left them alone. She wondered if he kept guards.

The royal office was much like the rest of the palace, with the same beautiful tile work on the walls and the same medieval castle feel to the structure. A large barren fireplace was dwarfed by the even larger sidewall. Long banners hung on either side of it. A long, woven rug of red and blue lay on the floor. Its intricate pattern was perhaps the loveliest she'd ever seen. Next to the rug were large chairs, so deep they'd nearly swallow her in comfort if she were to use them. On the opposite wall there was a long, empty stone desk and more chairs, a couch, more rugs and tile patterned designs.

Ulyssa ignored the beauty of the stately room. When she looked at the desk, Kirill was leaning against it, his arms crossed over his chest. A leisurely smile arched on his features and he made no qualms about looking her over with his heated eyes.

"How dare you treat me like that in front of your men!" Ulyssa's words came out in a hiss and her eyes narrowed to shoot daggers. "I don't belong to you and I'm most certainly not your mistress! And did you actually say I like being your prey?"

"You are my mistress." Kirill stayed calm, unmoving, seemingly unaffected.

"I am not," she hissed. "I belong to no man, especially not some chest-thumping savage King! I'm warning you Kirill, either you let me go or I'll--"

"Regardless of what you call yourself, you must stay here as my woman." Kirill sighed. "I marked you last night. All the men smell me on you. Your position in my home is being announced as we speak. Falke will see to that, being as   castle   security   is   his   duty."

"Listen," she broke in, raising her finger at him to emphasize her point, "just because we had some great sex, doesn't mean you own me or that I'm going to fall over panting at your heels."

"You really have no choice, Lyssa. My mark binds you to me. I will be able to find you if you run." Kirill lowered his jaw and gave her a meaningful look. "There is no escape."

"You dare to ... to mark me without my permission! My God, what sort of people are you? Though, it's no wonder you're a tyrant. Like father, like son, eh?"

"I asked for your permission. I asked if you wanted me to be your lover, you said yes. You allowed me to make love to you, mark you as mine."

"I allowed you to fuck me!" Ulyssa screamed at the top of her lungs, her eyes wild. She felt trapped. His eyes narrowed in warning at her tone and she pressed her lips tightly together. She hadn't meant to say it that loud, though she refused to apologize. The silence drew out between them, each staring at the other, contemplating the other's position.

"You speak too much," Kirill said at last, pushing away from the desk to go to her. His lips curled up at the side. "Let me put your mouth to better use."

Ulyssa's eyes automatically dipped down to the bulge between his thighs. She didn't understand him. He was angry, she'd bet her life that he was, and yet he wanted to sleep with her. She swallowed nervously, knowing how easy it would be to bend to his will and let him have his way. Blinking, she stiffened her back and resolve. She forced a look of disinterest to her face and settled her fist along her hips.

"No thanks." Ulyssa stiffened. "I'm kind of in a hurry and need to get going."

"Where is it you need to go?" he asked. When she didn't show invitation, he passed by and settled down into one of the comfortable chairs. She rolled her eyes heavenward and made a face before turning to follow him.

"That's none of your concern." Ulyssa sat across from him, nearly getting swallowed in the chair's folds. She struggled slightly before giving up and relaxing into the comfort of it. Leaning her head to the side, she could see his face clearly. He was studying the barren fireplace.

"Everything in my kingdom is of my concern." Kirill looked her over. His features fell and she could see a look of distaste come over him, as he admitted, "Besides, you were here with my father. Why do you suddenly need to leave now?"

"Argh!" she fumed. Sitting forward in the chair to glare at him, she growled, "Let's get this straight. I wasn't here with your father. I've never slept with your father. I don't like your father."

"Ah, but you were in the harem," Kirill said. "I checked. The women remember you well. They said you were ... *moody.*"

Ulyssa paled as if he'd slapped her. "I don't care what they think of me, the simpering fools."

"Ah, yes, I do wonder where they got that impression," he mumbled sarcastically under his breath. She didn't think he was funny.

"I only met King Attor once." Ulyssa did her best to stay reasonable and calm, but his nearness distracted her. It was almost as if she could smell him on her skin. Her nerves reached out to be with him. Her body begged her to give into his, to let it feel the touch of his incredible hold one more time before she left. How much of a hurry was she in anyway? "And that was when he kidnapped me in the forest with a bunch of blond warrior idiots."

"If what you say is true, I'm sure my father had his reasons," Kirill said. Her mouth opened, but before she could comment, he added, "What brings you to Qurilixen? Why were you in our forest?"

Ulyssa didn't readily answer.

"For all I know, you're a spy to be dealt with." Kirill sat forward to mimic her hard, blank look.

"I'm not." A tension built between them, snapping through the air with electric fire. "I was brought to the harem about a week ago. I was in the forest camping, minding my own business, trying to get rescued from this accursed place, when he *kidnapped* me. Now, all I want is to get back to my campsite. Besides, I could really care less what you and your fellow felines are up to. Your planet is of no concern to me. I mean, in case you haven't noticed, there's a much larger, much more interesting galaxy of planets out there."

"That doesn't explain what you're doing here," he murmured, refusing to be bated to anger. His lids lowered over his eyes and she got the impression he barely listened to her words. His gaze started roaming to her chest. The edge of his tongue flicked over the corner of his mouth.

Ulyssa's eyes stayed steady and she gave nothing away. Using all her training, she lied, "I was shipwrecked. I was waiting to be rescued when your father took me. He also took my communicator and I'd like it back."

"Rescue?" he prompted. His lips stayed parted and she could remember the feel of them on her body. She trembled. She tried to fight him, but couldn't.

"This is madness!" she thought, trying her best to concentrate. She tore her eyes from him to look around the room. She began to sweat and her limbs shook as she tried to calm her racing pulse. Images assaulted her, fantasies that were best left unknown. She had to look at anything but him. She wanted to jump across to his lap and kiss the irritating confidence from his lips. She wanted to make love to him right there on the chair until he was under her complete control.

"In three months…" she whispered, barely paying attention to her words. She could feel his look tunneling into her, piercing her, undressing her. She wiggled uncomfortably in the chair, suddenly wanting to give him something to look at. Her stomach tingled and she became hot. Moisture gathered between her thighs. "…my ride will come get me and I'll be off this planet forever."

"Mmmm," he answered, as if tasting a fine wine. "Where's the wreckage?"

"I parachuted." Her eyes could no longer keep from moving over him. She was drawn to be next to him. It was beyond her control. Before she knew what was happening, she stood. Kirill smiled at her. His arms settled back, wide and inviting. She couldn't resist as she crossed to stand in front of him. "I believe it crashed past a big red mountain to the north. You'll find the wreckage there."

"That'd be Draig land," he said, thoughtful.

Ulyssa shrugged. She already knew that. With them on the brink of war, there would be no way for him to confirm her story--at least not in time to do anything about it.

"You say help is coming?" Kirill's hands turned out, the palms facing up.

Ulyssa didn't stop to think. She crawled onto his lap, straddling his hips with her knees. Her fingers hesitated before lifting to smooth back the material covering his hard chest. Her breath came out in a soft pant at the contact. Her words were carried on a slight moan. "Yes in three months. I'm going to camp until then."

"Why not stay here in the palace? It's more comfortable than the forest."

"But--" Ulyssa drew her hands away and tried to pull back. He grabbed her hips and held her to him.

"I'll make you a deal, Lyssa. You stay here and be my mistress until your ride arrives." Kirill's fingers tightened and he pulled her hips closer. "I can feel that you desire me. We have already been together and you have admitted the sex between us is great."

"I don't want to be your mistress," she tried to protest.

"Accept the title of it, Lyssa. Act happy with me, be seen with me, live in my house, be submissive in public and, in three months time, I'll let you go." Kirill gripped her, rocking her hips lightly along his tight body. She felt him tense beneath her thighs as he waited for a response.

"Do you promise that, no matter what, you'll release me?" Ulyssa couldn't believe she was even considering his offer. This man was definitely more complication than she needed. She'd be better off in the forest.

"Yes."

"What assurance do I have that you will honor what you say? Royalty is infamous for breaking their word all the time." She didn't think it was possible, but he stiffened more. His eyes narrowed and his face turned a subtle shade of red.

"You dare to question my word of honor?" he demanded through gritted teeth. He gripped her almost painfully and her hips stopped moving.

Ulyssa considered him for a moment. What'd she really have to lose? Either spend three month being eaten by alien bugs or spend the time with a handsome lover in lush surroundings being taken care of like a Princess? Whether he kept his word or not, she'd be leaving.

"Then it's a deal," Ulyssa said. "On the condition you give me back my communicator. It was a gift and I can't afford to replace it."

"Done," Kirill agreed. "In three months, considering you have told me the truth and you are indeed going to be rescued from a shipwreck, I give you my word of honor to let you leave. As to your communicator, I'll ask around. If I find it, you'll have it."

"Done," Ulyssa said with a smile. "Agreed."

A smirk came to his handsome feature, lighting them with a playful light. "What is it humans say? Shall we kiss on it?"

"Close enough." She gave a small moan and leaned over to meet his mouth with hers. Just as her lips brushed against his, the door to the royal office opened. She sat up straight and leaned over the edge of the chair. She grimaced at Falke, as if to say: *What are you doing here? Go away.*

Falke bowed, giving her a mocking smile. "My lady."

"Commander," Ulyssa said, not moving from Kirill's lap. She smiled. Well, if Kirill wanted her to declare herself his mistress, he was going to get a mistress. "Do you mind? I'm trying to service the King's manhood here and your presence is really a distraction to my concentration."

She felt Kirill stiffen beneath her legs, right before he shook with contained laughter. Falke looked at her, showing no emotion--not even shock. She was secretly impressed, but wouldn't let her new arch-nemesis see it. Suddenly, spending three months figuring out ways to irritate Falke had some appeal.

"My King," Falke said, keeping his steady eyes forward. Ulyssa saw well he detected her new game and welcomed her to the challenge of besting him. "Prince Olek and Prince Zoran have arrived with a small Draig guard. They request an audience."

"Take them to the hall and give them refreshments. Find Reid and Quinn." Kirill didn't bother to look at his brother. Instead, his hand played with Ulyssa's cross-laces, untying them just enough for his finger to dip beneath the under curve of her breast. "I'll be right there."

It was all she could do not to moan aloud as Kirill's finger swept up over the soft globe to her nipple. He rubbed it in small circles. She absently reached for his hand to stop him.

"Very well, my lord," Falke said. He bowed, though Kirill couldn't see it, and left the room.

Ulyssa pulled back to look at Kirill. His features fell in disappointment as he glanced at her hand atop his, stopping his fingers from exploring her breast.

"Prince Olek and Zoran?" Ulyssa asked, dying with curiosity. She knew they were Draig, but wanted to know what they were doing at the Var palace. "Enemies of yours?"

Kirill let out a small, derisive laugh. "I wish I knew."

She felt a tension building up in him as he took his hand from her shirt. With great ease, he picked up her hips and lifted her off his body, planting her firmly on the floor. Wearily, he stood. For a moment, he studied her, giving away nothing. His hand lifted and he cupped her face.

"You should go back to my home," he said at last. He moved to turn.

"Ah, I can't," Ulyssa answered. "Besides, shouldn't I come with you? You know, make a submissive public appearance or something."

"Not to this. This kingdom's concerns are not your own." Kirill turned to move toward the door. "If you wish it, I'll introduce you to my brothers later at dinner. For now, go to my home."

Ulyssa frowned, not liking how he ordered her about. "I can't go to your home, oh mighty ruler."

Kirill sighed, turning to look at her.

Before he could speak, she rushed, "I don't know the way. It took me two hours to wander this far."

"Siren," Kirill announced. "Send Navid."

"Oh, um." Ulyssa lifted her hand and shook her head.

"What is it now?"

"I kind of ... well, I knocked him down when trying to escape Falke yesterday. I don't think he'd be too happy to help me." Ulyssa gave a sheepish grin and shrugged. "He was in my way."

"Siren, cancel Navid. Send me Talure." Kirill sighed, shaking his head. "I don't know what I've gotten myself into with you, but try to behave while I'm gone. Just promise me you'll try."

"You'd take the word of a lowly captive?" she teased.

His face fell. He didn't get the joke. Preoccupied with thoughts of direr things she couldn't begin to guess at, he merely answered, "Think of our arrangement as you wish, Lyssa. Only, remember it was you who claimed to be my woman, not the other way around. I'm trying to make the best of our situation. I expect you to remember our bargain. I'll hold you to your word."

Ulyssa watched him leave. She moved to follow him, but as she pulled the door open a tall, slender guard stood in her way. Even though the dark blond warrior was smaller than the other Vars she'd seen, he was still rugged and handsome. Didn't this race have any ugly men? She nodded her head at the man. "Talure?"

"My lady," he answered with a respectful bow.

Ulyssa saw him sniff the air as he leaned toward her. She suddenly wondered if she smelled bad. All the Var kept trying to sniff her--Falke, the guards. Did Kirill's marking leave her a little pungent? When Talure turned his back to lead the way down the long hallway, she lifted her armpit and inhaled. She couldn't smell anything too offensive. "Hum."

"My lady?" Talure asked, turning to glance over his shoulder just as she was lowering her arm. His brows furrowed together in the beginning of a grimace.

Ulyssa turned a subtle shade of pink. She lifted her hand like she was stretching in a pitiful attempt to hide what she'd been doing. "Ah, I didn't say anything."

Chapter Six

Kirill sat at the head of a long table in the main hall, listening patiently to Prince Olek as he spoke. The Draig Prince's light brown hair hung to his shoulders and was braided from the temples down. He had straightforward green eyes that appeared to see everything around him and yet they gave nothing away. Smile lines edged his mouth as if he laughed often, but he wasn't smiling now. Olek was the Draig Ambassador and, from what Kirill could tell, he was an honest man who really did want peace between their two kingdoms.

The Prince's temperamental brother Zoran, on the other hand, reminded Kirill of Falke. Zoran stared at them with a thinly concealed rage. Falke returned the dark look. Neither man had made a move of aggression, but both looked ready to strike at the slightest provocation. They had the same thick, sturdy build to them--a build that came from decades of war and training.

Zoran was the Draig Captain of the Guard and his presence demanded respect. He was the hardest off all the Draig brothers and Kirill knew he would not be satisfied by the outcome of their meeting today. Zoran, like Falke, would not cower if they were to go to war. When Kirill looked at the two Commanders, he knew neither would bend. War would be a bloody option for both houses.

"You know I can't admit to something of which I have no knowledge," Kirill said at last, doing his best to be diplomatic. The Draig wanted answers. He couldn't blame them. But, what they wanted, he couldn't and wouldn't give. "If King Attor ordered the attacks on your family, I don't know about it. We have no records of these events."

Zoran tensed. Olek merely nodded. Kirill was fairly sure his father had done the things they accused him of, but refused to voice his suspicions to the Draig Princes. To do so would be to add fuel to the already raging fire between their people.

"I can assure you," Kirill continued, "that I don't share my father's views of our kingdoms. As I have said before, it's my hope that the House of Draig and the House of Var may find peace."

Falke tensed next to him. Quinn caught his eye and nodded in silent agreement. Reid, who stood behind them, didn't move.

Slowly, Olek stood and extended his hand. "I'll pass your words onto my father. It, too, is my hope we can reach an understanding."

It was Zoran's turn to tense. His jaw flexed as he too stood up. His voice a hard growl, he stated, "There is much to consider, however."

"Yes, much," Falke answered in harsh agreement.

Kirill took Olek's hand and clasped it briefly. They both sighed, knowing the Commanders had faced each other often in battle over the many decades. No matter how hard they wished it, peace would not be gained overnight.

"And pass along my congratulations to your family on the Princesses' pregnancies. You're truly blessed to have all four with children at once," Kirill said. His words were more of an acknowledgment that he knew what happened on Draig land than a congratulations to the royal family. It served to remind Zoran they were not ignorant of Draig affairs. "May your line stay strong."

"As may yours," Olek said.

Kirill thought of Ulyssa. Why did she pop into his head at such a moment? He could sense that she wasn't telling him the whole truth, but he didn't believe she was a spy for the Draig. Whatever it was she was hiding, he could think of worse ways of pumping her for information than doing it in his bed.

Olek bowed before turning to Zoran. Zoran motioned to a group of Draig soldiers sitting nearby. The dragon shifter guards stood and followed the Princes from the hall. Falke followed behind them to escort them out without having to be asked.

"What do you think?" Reid asked when they were alone. He sat where Olek had been, grabbed the pitcher of Qurilixen ale from the table, and poured himself a goblet.

"I think they are like us," Quinn said. "They want peace, but they don't know how to trust us. How can we blame them?"

"How indeed," Kirill said.

There was a long moment of silence. Suddenly, Reid grinned. "Are the rumors true, my King?"

"What rumors?" Kirill blinked, confused. Reid laughed, prompting Quinn to do the same. Grumbling, he added, "And stop calling me my King. It sounds mocking coming from you."

"The rumors, *my lord*, that you have chosen a first half-mate so quickly after your coronation," Quinn said. His thoughtful blue eyes sparkled with much amusement.

"Yes, *my lord*, and that you favor chasing her naked about the halls," Reid added, laughing harder.

"Ah, stop calling me my lord, you insolent wretches," Kirill muttered, feigning irritation. He'd known he'd be in for some good-natured teasing from them. "It's a good thing I favor you both or I'd have you thrown in the dungeons."

"And that she likes to run away from you wearing your royal garb so that you may track her," Quinn added.

"Oh, and what about the one--" Reid began, only to be interrupted when Kirill slapped the table.

"Enough," Kirill growled. He frowned to think of his arrangement with Ulyssa. "Yes, I've taken a mistress. Her name is Lyssa. You'll meet her tonight at dinner."

"It's true? I thought that surely the rumors were false." Reid gasped in amazement. Unexpectedly, he nodded in masculine approval. "Lyssa, you say? But didn't you leave here with Linzi after the coronation?"

Kirill rolled his eyes. Reid had a predilection for bedding many women and didn't care who knew it.

"You'll bring her here, to the hall?" Quinn asked, a little surprised that the King would bestow such an honor to a woman so soon. King Attor never allowed his women to dine with him in the hall, no matter how long they carried his favor. "Are you thinking of mating to her?"

"Sacred Cats, Kirill!" Reid exclaimed, horrified. "Why would you do something like that? Have you gone mad?"

"I assure you I'm quite sane. I've no intention of taking a mate." Kirill's voice was stern. "I merely thought it wise to have a woman in my home to tend me."

"But, why not take the harem? That way, afterwards, you can send her away. And why take one when there are so many willing?" Reid shook his head, stunned. "Surely you don't wish to sleep with only one woman. What'll be said of you, Kirill? You are King. You'll be expected to fulfill many. You should be taking a dozen women to your bed at a time, if only to prove your manhood! Do you wish for our people to see you as weak? Can you not handle more than one woman, brother?"

Kirill scowled at Reid's insult to him. He glared, slamming his fist down hard on the table. The goblets fell over at the force of his blow. "Well, Reid, you appear to have too much time on your hands. Instead of questioning my prowess, why don't you find something of use to do? Oh, I know. Why don't you cook for us tonight? I wouldn't want to ruin my reputation by bringing Lyssa to the hall."

Reid grimaced. Kirill knew his brother considered cooking to be woman's work. To call upon him to do it was a suitable punishment. Quinn, seeing Reid's look, laughed.

"We'll be at your house at seven. Quinn, inform Falke of our plans. I expect you both there." Kirill grinned.

"Why'd you have to bring me into this? What did I do?" Quinn pouted, though he was hard-pressed to hide his grin.

Kirill moved to leave, only to turn. Smiling, he said, "Oh, and Reid?"

"What?" the brother grumbled.

"Do not disappoint your King." Kirill smirked. "You'd better hurry. I've quite a royal appetite."

"We'll be lucky if he doesn't poison us." Quinn whined in his most mournful tone. The smirk on his face belied his words.

Reid growled. He picked up a goblet and threw it at Quinn. The youngest brother ducked, backing away. The goblet hit the stone floor, making an awful racket as it bounced.

"See you tonight, brother," Quinn taunted, sprinting from the hall before Reid could clobber him.

* * * *

Ulyssa stretched her arms over her head and yawned. The large bath was filled with hot, steaming water. Though her training had included the concept of a water bath, she'd never actually soaked in one. Boy, had she been missing out! She had half a mind to stay in the tub the entire three months.

Finding bottles many of soaps, it took her awhile to decide which to use. In a decontaminator, all one had to do was push a single button and go. Finally, choosing the best smelling of the liquids, she dumped a large amount of purple soap on her head and smacked it with the flat of her palms until it was squished into her hair. A trail of suds gushed over her face and she screeched in dismay as it ran into her eyes. Bending over, she held her breath and dunked her face straight down into the water. Furiously, she rubbed her eyes until the stinging stopped.

She sat up, sputtering and gasping for breath. Part of her hair was plastered to her cheeks and she grabbed a towel off the wall to swipe the wet locks back. Never one to quit, she grabbed the bottle with purple soap and squirted more into her hand. It pooled between her fingers. Ulyssa froze, staring at her goo-covered palm. All of a sudden, she screamed at the top of her lungs and jumped up in terror. Horrified, she hopped out of the tub, tripping and hollering her way from the bathroom.

* * * *

Kirill slowly walked down the long hallway, lost in deep thought. Reid's words still stung. He knew his brother was only saying what he, himself, had not wanted to admit--that having Ulyssa in his home could be perceived as a weakness to his kingdom. The Var people were used to King Attor and his ways. And, whereas there was no law stating Kirill couldn't claim a woman for his own, the fact that he had brought Ulyssa so quickly to his home might affect the public's opinion of him.

Already, some were weary of his decisions. Many of the old houses, led by Lord Myrddin, believed they should attack the Draig and avenge Attor's death. The fact that Kirill had not done so did not sit well with the Attor's loyal supporters. Kirill could not discount their opinions, as they were well respected, powerful men within the Var community.

"What a mess," he muttered under his breath.

He thought of sending Ulyssa to live in the harem. But, the fact that the people believed her to be his chosen first half-mate, and his mistress, also meant that they'd see her banishment from his bed as a sign of indecision. The Var prided themselves on being decisive and confident. Ulyssa had said she was his, and so he must keep her--at least for three months. Three months was little time in his world, but he could only hope to find a way out of their situation by then. Three years would have suited his purpose better.

Still troubled, he made his way home. Weary from his meeting with the Draig, he shut the front door behind him. A shrill scream echoed from the bathroom. He jolted in alarm and turned to the sound of terror. Kirill froze, his eyes wide as he watched the bathroom door.

Ulyssa slid across the marble floor on her naked back, leaving a trail of soapy water in her wake. Her arms and legs flailed in the air as she tried to stop. He would have thought it comical, if not for the sound of her panic.

Believing she was under attack, Kirill sprung into action. He leapt over the couch, flying through the air to land next to her sprawled body. As a reflex, sharp claws grew from his fingertips and fangs from his gums. Ready to defend her, he sniffed the bathroom. He could detect no danger. In fact, he could detect nothing at all.

"What is it?" he asked in a near growl. He slowly retracted his claws and fangs. His eyes glimmered with a golden-green interest as he looked down at the floor. His body was tense, his blood stirred, ready for a fight--for action of any kind. The heightened state of his senses easily turned to the naked woman beneath him, covered in soapsuds. He licked his lips, watching the little bubble trails make their way over her flesh from her hair.

Ulyssa whimpered and tried to stand. "I ... need ... a medic."

"What?" Kirill asked, leaning over to hear her. He inhaled, trying to detect blood and smelled nothing but the fragrance of soap mixed with the distinctness of her womanly scent. The aggression moved down his body to gradually fill his loins.

"I need a medic!" she yelled in frustration, shaking. "I ... there's something wrong with me. I'm ... *melting*!"

Kirill's eyebrows furrowed together in confusion. He looked her over. She looked fine to him--more than fine. He hid his grin.

"This human word, *melting*. Does it mean burnt?" he asked, wondering if he didn't understand her. Her flesh was a darker shade of red from hot water, as if she soaked for a long time or was scalded. He leaned over to help her stand when what he really wanted to do was crawl forward onto her, trapping her wet form beneath him. With much effort, he refrained.

Gripping her arm in his firm hold, he hauled her up. Her feet slipped as she struggled to find footing. He held her before him. Instantly, his eyes went over her naked body, first taking in her wet soapy breasts. His mouth went dry.

Red blonde trails of wet hair stuck to her shoulders, ringing down around the side curves of her breasts. Her dusky nipples were puckered and hard, standing proud from the creamy globes. His gaze followed the soap trails down her flat stomach to where they were held captive by the narrow strip of nether hair between her beautiful thighs. His mind went blank, unable to perceive anything but the idea that the soap would make him glide so sweetly into her tight body.

Every primal instinct inside him roared to life. His body responded in the only way it could. His shaft grew with a sudden force of desire, pressing and throbbing against his tight pants. If not for the nef, he would've tossed her over the back of his couch and had his wicked way with her-- whether she was ready for him or not.

"No, not burnt. I'm withering," Ulyssa said in a panic, not seeing his sudden discomfort or the fact that he eyed her like a beast after a meal.

Kirill's darkening eyes darted up to her trembling lips before looking at her pale face. Her eyes were a little red where she'd rubbed them and her hair stuck up at places from her scalp. It took him a moment to comprehend her words. She looked comical. He couldn't help himself, as he started to chuckle.

"Here," a panicked Ulyssa demanded. She held out her hands for Kirill's inspection. "It's not funny. Look! I think I used acid or something. I'm withering away."

Kirill looked down at her fingers as she shoved them up into his face. He grabbed her hands to pull them back so he could see. Her body shook violently. He could smell her terror and it stirred an odd protectiveness within him. Looking at her hands, he laughed anew. Her fingers and palms were red from the heat and wrinkled from too much time spent in the bathwater.

Ulyssa jerked from him and tried to step back. Her feet slipped on the soapy stone and she ended up falling forward into his arms. Kirill caught her with a grunt.

"I'm glad you think my dying is so funny, you ... you savage!" She struggled against him, but her feet slipped and she only ended up jerking around in his arms.

Getting a closer view of her soap-smothered hair, Kirill couldn't stop laughing. The troubles of the Var and Draig melted from his mind. "Just how much soap did you put onto your head? Half the bottle?"

"Oh, it was the soap wasn't it! Was I not supposed to use the purple? Does it do something to humans?" Her wide blue eyes looked at him, pleading with him for help. "Is it for morphing? What's it turning me into?"

Kirill let his arms wrap around her waist and he pulled her intimately close to keep her still. Ulyssa gasped and stopped breathing as the fire of his arousal hit her stomach. She made a weak sound in the back of her throat and he could smell the instant downpour of her desire for him.

"You're not dying," he said calmly, softly. His dark gaze dipped possessively to her mouth. "You stayed in the water too long. And the soap you used is for the skin, not the hair. Have you never taken a bath before?"

"Decontaminators," she sighed by way of an explanation. She shivered from the cold against her naked back now that the scare was over.

Kirill let a sexy smile line his features. "Hum, well, as long as you're undressed and wet, I might as well teach you how to properly use the bath."

"I don't want to go back in there," she said in all earnest.

Kirill leaned forward to nuzzle he cheek with light kisses. "Mmmm. How about the shower? I'd very much like to have you wash me and you do need to rinse off."

"Hey, I'm not your maid," she growled, trying to push him away. His gentle laughter over her predicament stung.

A blush of embarrassment tried to sting her cheeks, she swallowed it back.

"Ah, but you are my mistress, Lyssa, for three months at least. And I have needs a mistress must tend to," he said, a low crackling in his throat as he rubbed his hard erection into her wet stomach. Soap and water soaked into his clothes, sticking the material to their flesh.

"I agreed to be ... *subservient*...." Ulyssa cringed, barely able to say the word aloud, "....in public, but in private you have no power over what I do."

Kirill pulled back and frowned. His hand moved to her arms to hold her away from his body. Very serious, he stated, "I am King."

"Didn't take long for the title to go to your head, did it?" she mocked.

Ulyssa took a deep breath, trying to slow her racing heart. She'd been truly terrified. Now, it just seemed silly and she couldn't help but be humiliated. She didn't do well embarrassed, so instead she did the most natural thing--she started an argument.

Besides, if this man thought she'd play housekeeper and bedwarmer slave for three months, he was sorely mistaken. Letting her voice dip into a sultry murmur, she proposed, "Tell ya what, your highness. How about I behave and act submissive in public and you be submissive to me in private. I think it only fair."

Kirill's features hardened. Very sternly, he stated, "A man can't bow to a woman, Lyssa, and still call himself a man."

She trembled at the low timbre of his words. The distance between them was agony. She was hot for him. Her stomach stung with the discomfort of her desire.

"What kind of nonsense is that?" she shot. Placing her hands on her hips, she faced him without thought of her nakedness.

"It's logic," he stated. "A man ruled by a woman is ruled by weakness."

"So women are weak?" She would never admit it, but she'd thought about him all morning, until she was nearly mindless with desire. Suddenly, playing washerwoman didn't sound so horrific. In fact, if it gave her a chance to feel his hard body for herself, it could be downright pleasurable.

"Yes," he answered without flinching. His hand rose to caress her cheek. She didn't move. Softly, he continued, "They're the softer sex. They're to be ruled, protected. It's why their bodies are softer, slighter than a man's. A man who dares to love a woman will have weakness in that love for he'll consider her opinion over his. And, if the enemy wishes to strike him, they will strike his heart to get to him. I'm a man who must lead a kingdom. Do you think I can do so if my people think me weak? I can't afford weakness. I'm the highest Var power on Qurilixen, just below our Gods. So, you see, a King can never be subservient. I can't bow to you--not even in private."

Ulyssa considered his barbarian logic and continued to stare at him. She detected a sadness in him, a loneliness. She saw the strain of his position in his eyes and was sorry for it.

"Kingdoms are only as strong as their rulers," Kirill said. Then, seeming to struggle, he added, "I don't want you making too much of our time together. Nothing can come of it. I'll never be able to commit to you fully."

Ulyssa almost laughed. "Think pretty highly of your skills as a lover, don't you?"

His shoulder lifted in a manly shrug, as if he had only been stating a fact.

"It's good to know the Var King doesn't have self-esteem issues." This time she did giggle. "Don't worry, your most royal highness. I think I'll be able to pry myself from you when the time comes."

"Lyssa," he began in warning to her insolent tone.

"Easy, highness." Ulyssa licked her lips. She kind of liked his Me-Man-Hear-Me-Roar attitude. She'd never put up with it for a lifetime, but it was damned sexy in a lover. Forcing a playful pout to her lips, she asked, "So you can't even play? How sad."

"Play?" Kirill asked, confused.

"Leave work at the door--that sort of thing. You don't see me stressing over my job."

"Ah, but your job isn't ruling half a planet." Kirill gaze moved over her face, taking her in. He looked as if he wanted to say more, but he held back. His eyes shifted with gold, turning from their dark depths as he looked intensely at her.

Ulyssa felt her body stir with more than just desire. She didn't like it. He had said it himself. Nothing could come of this. She didn't want anything to come of this, did she?

Ulyssa swallowed. No, definitely not. She had a job, a ... mission. Well, she'd have a mission once the Agency picked her up of the barbaric rock of a planet she was trapped on--new mission, new adventure. Her eyes dipped to his mouth and back to his eyes.

She sighed. That must be what her problem was. She was bored! That's why she spent too many hours contemplating Kirill! She wasn't preoccupied with him. She was preoccupied with boredom. Just because the unattainable was before her didn't mean she had to fight to obtain it. What did she want with a King anyway?

Relaxing now that she had it all figured out, Ulyssa let her lids fall languidly over her eyes. She gave a small, sexy moan. This was just sex. The barbaric King was just another adventure to be had. Leaning into him, she pursed her lips. "You're very serious, you do know that, right? You should loosen up a little--relax."

"And you're very naked," he answered, letting his gaze fall over her. His fingers glided down over her shivering skin to ring circles around an erect nipple.

"Mm, and very cold." Ulyssa inhaled a shaky breath. With each pass of his finger, shock waves erupted beneath her skin, traveling down her stomach to make her body even more ready.

"Fire," he stated loudly and the fireplace blazed. His lips parted as he leaned over to flick his tongue over a ripe nipple. "Come with me to the shower and warm up."

Ulyssa gasped.

Kirill's lips captured hers before she could answer. His words were a command and she found she didn't really care. His mouth sawed passionately against her, instantly weakening her knees. She fell forward into his chest, moaning in delight of his touch.

She wasn't sure how he did it, but he was absolutely, hands-down the best kisser she'd ever experienced. There was something to the confidence of his movement, reflecting the grace of his body. It was in the way he tasted, the way he teased and gave. His tongue probed and conquered her mouth until she was left panting and weak.

Her arms wrapped around his neck and pulled his body tight to hers. She soaked in his heat as his arms lifted her from the floor. Walking with her slender body dangling along his tightly wrought one, he carried her to the bathroom.

Parting from the kiss, he stated hoarsely, "Shower on."

The shower sprayed warm water. Ulyssa's fingers moved to work the laces on his shirt. Kirill pulled back, dropping his arms to the side at her insistence to let her undress him. His eyes burned into her as he watched her naked body. Deftly, she pulled the shirt off his shoulders, stopping to kiss and touch the length of his chest. He hadn't let her explore the night before and now she itched to feel every hot inch of his smooth flesh, to discover if he tasted as good as he looked.

Ulyssa loved the graceful way his muscles folded beneath his tanned skin when he moved. His dark eyes pierced, watching her, fighting to command her. Ulyssa might play, but she wasn't his to control. A smile twitched on her lips as she realized she wanted what he said was impossible. She wanted to make him her bed slave. She wanted him to bow to her, even if it was only in private.

Turning his own look on him, she stalked around him as if he were her prey. Kirill's dark eyes narrowed and his nostrils flared, as if he could sense her intentions. Ulyssa touched his back, rubbing at his neck, up into the silky locks of his hair. She pressed her chest into his back as her fingers trailed down over his strong arms. His firm backside hit her stomach, taut and sculpted beneath the pants. Exploring him thoroughly, she finally made her way to untie the laces at his hips.

Kirill was panting heavily by the time she worked the first lace loose. His chest moved as he fought for breath. Her hands dipped along the cross-laces to the perfect indentions of his buttocks. Her touch curved around his flat stomach, edging the waistband from his skin, tickling the divot of his navel. She let him feel the cooled tips of her breasts at his warm back, rubbing lightly along his skin.

Then, with a catlike smile curling her features, she pulled back and moved to the shower. When she turned, his sharp gaze was on her. She stood, holding the door open as he stared. The hot water hit her skin, warming her even more, washing the remnants of soap from her flesh.

Kirill's pants were still hooked on his erection where she left them. She waited to see what he'd do. Slowly, he kicked off a boot and then the other, refusing to take his eyes off hers. Ulyssa let the shower door stay open as she moved her head into the stream of water. She let the shower rinse her hair, aroused by the fact that he watched with such interest.

"You're very beautiful," he stated. The tone wasn't warm, just matter-of-fact. He nodded his head in approval. "And bold."

"And you are still dressed," she pointed out with a tilt of her brow. She placed her hands on her hips and gave him an insolent grin.

His hands moved to his waist. With a flick of his fingers, he pushed the waistband off his hips, letting it glide to the floor. "Better?"

Ulyssa felt her smile freeze on her face. She tried to be calm, but the mere size of his towering erection seemed so much more daunting in the light. She felt a momentary wave of panic, but quickly squelched it with a throaty chuckle.

"You fear me?" he asked, stopping in mid-step as he came to her. A look of confusion passed over him. He took a deep breath.

"No," she lied, scrunching her face.

Kirill's eyes narrowed, but he said nothing. He took another step and stopped. "You wish this?"

Ulyssa frowned. Of course she wanted it! She'd made that obvious, hadn't she? Her body trembled and she realized she was a little nervous. The insight took her by surprise. How could she be nervous? She'd been with men before. She'd been with him before. And how in the world was he detecting it?

"Mmmm. If you keep talking, your highness, I'll have to start without you." To prove her point, she took her hand to her stomach and edged it down toward her hips, letting her fingers slide in the water on her skin. She cocked her head to the side and naughtily licked at her mouth.

Kirill didn't hold off any longer. A growl sounded in the back of his throat. He darted forward to pull her into his arms, not even pausing as he pulled the stall door shut behind him. His naked form pressed against hers, forcing her back against the shower wall.

Ulyssa felt him all along her body. The water slid between them, making his muscles glide over her softer form. His thick arousal settled between her hip, hotter than the water. She moaned, stirring and rubbing along his entire frame as he held her trapped. His hands explored her, commanding her flesh as he boldly touched wherever he desired--her breasts, her hips, around to cup her firm backside and pull her forward. He rocked his hips to hers, growling in pleasure as he kissed her.

"Ah," she panted, breaking free to breathe.

Kirill didn't stop. His lips slid over her wet jaw to her throat, devouring her with his mouth. He nipped her skin only to soothe the irritation with his long tongue.

Remembering that she wanted to be in control, Ulyssa pushed him hard. He didn't budge. A strong sound of refusal grumbled out of his lips as he continued to kiss her.

"I want ... I want to..." Ulyssa tried to speak, but his lips were wreaking havoc on her flesh. His palms cupped her breast, lifting it to meet his mouth. He sucked her nipple hard until it was surrounded by heat and velvet. Animalistic sounds of possession came from him, vibrating against her. "Ahhh, Kirill, please. I want to touch you."

Ulyssa realized she begged, but she couldn't help it. His mouth kissed too perfectly. His body felt too good. She trembled in anticipation.

His lips tore from her and he stood to meet her eyes. "And I want to bury myself inside you."

Before she could protest, he slid his hands around to her backside and lifted her off the ground, gliding her back along the stall wall. Kirill was going to get his way first, not that she minded one bit. Ulyssa grabbed at his neck, holding on. Without even flinching, he delved forward, slipping his erect shaft between the lips her moist opening. He let the tip dance just inside the entrance, teasing and testing her.

Her body was wet, more than ready. She wanted him. Her hips bucked in offering and he grinned.

With so much control that it drove her mad, he pushed into her slick passage, filling her body by small, agonizing degrees. He watched her face closely, taking in every one of her reactions. Her eyes rolled in her head. Her lips parted, as she gasped for air. The shower hit their bodies, caressing them like millions of fingers, heightening the pleasure.

Ulyssa nearly swooned as he finally pressed fully into her body. Seating himself to the hilt, he paused. She kicked him with her thigh in protest. Kirill chuckled and shot her a confident grin.

"Is this what you want?" he asked, low and hoarse. His fingers gripped into the cheeks of her backside, spreading them ever so slightly. Holding her up with ease, he began to move. He licked and teased her throat as his hips pulled back only to thrust in shallow strokes.

"Yes!" Ulyssa cried, beyond caring that he had all the control. He felt too good, too right. "Yes! Oh, my, yes! Please, yes, more! Give me more, Kirill."

At her words, he gave her more. He stroked up into her tight passage, hitting harder against her core. Ulyssa screamed in mindless pleasure. Her back hit the shower wall, but she didn't care. She twined her fingers into his long black hair, liking how the wet length blanketed her skin. His grunts joined hers as he thrust, hard and fast and deep inside her.

Ulyssa wrapped her legs around him, urging him on. She could feel the strong muscles of his backside beneath her calves. He rocked himself into her with a violent force, conquering her depths. The tension built inside her hips. She was close, so close.

Slipping her hand between their bodies, she tweaked her center nub with a finger, rubbing it in small circles. Instantly, her body twitched. Ulyssa screamed. Kirill growled in approval. He moved faster, harder, deeper, seating himself until he had no more to give.

Her body convulsed around his hard shaft as the strong force of her orgasm hit her. Tears came to her eyes from the pure intensity of the moment. As her passage clenched down on him, Kirill let loose. He yelled, the sound that of a true savage. He delved one last time and released his seed deep inside her.

They stood frozen in time, her back helpless against the wall. His body stayed buried deep inside her. Slowly, he let her slide down, pulling out at the same time.

Confidently, he said to her, "See, it's not so bad to be controlled by a man."

He moved to kiss her and she jerked back. "What did you say?"

"I said you didn't mind my dominance over you," he stated more clearly. He moved to kiss her lips again, and again she jerked back.

"You don't control me!" Ulyssa pushed him hard. He was caught off guard and his foot slid. She stormed past him, out of the shower. Grabbing a towel, she wrapped it angrily over her body.

His eyes were dark with challenge. "Do you need me to prove to you who controls whom again? I saw your plan, Lyssa, but it can never work. You won't command me."

"You bastard!" she hissed, gripping her towel tighter to her chest. He'd screwed her to teach her a lesson? The very nerve! She looked at his features. He thought he was bending her to his will? He thought she was a simpleminded little female ready to fall over at his feet? Well, she'd show him just how serious she was. Holding up her hand, she said, "I no longer wish it."

Kirill froze in mid-stride, feeling as if she'd kicked him. He looked at the woman before him. He knew she'd reached fulfillment and yet she did not look pleased. In fact, she looked livid. Wisely, he kept his distance.

"You don't mean that," he stated. He looked down his body, forcing her to do the same. His shaft was beginning to lift anew, readying for her. "I can smell that you want me again."

"I don't care what you smell." Her chin lifted and she pried her eyes away from his erection. "I no longer wish this."

"Is this ... how you play?" he asked, thinking it might be a game.

"No, I'm deadly serious, your highness." The title was spat from her lips.

"We had an agreement," Kirill said. He tried to keep his tone level, but it was hard. "You must remain as my mistress for three months."

"Oh, I know what I agreed to," she answered, scornfully. "And I'll behave in public. But in private, you aren't getting another thing until you beg me for it. It's about time you learned a little humility you savage jerk!"

"A King doesn't beg," he roared, losing his cool. He knew he was only repeating his father's words. But that didn't make them any less true. His eyes swirled with dark passions. His tense body shook. "A King cannot beg!"

"Then this mistress no longer pleases," she growled.

Kirill swiped his hand at her and she flinched, recoiling back as if he meant to strike her. His eyes rounded and he was hurt that she would assume such a thing. Giving a single, curt nod, he whispered softly, "It will be as you wish, Lyssa. I won't touch you."

Ulyssa watched him leave her alone in the bathroom. When he was gone, she ran to the door and slammed it shut. Instantly, she fell to the floor--weak. She didn't know what happened, but she felt branded by him and she didn't like it. Somehow, when they came together, the very savage Var King had managed to touch her soul. And the very idea of it terrified her.

Chapter Seven

Ulyssa stayed huddled in the bathroom like a coward for all of five minutes. Then, taking a steady breath, she assured herself she was in control of her emotions. The force of her orgasm had taken her by surprise--that was all. That's why she got all emotional on Kirill. But, the force of his words still stung. No man would ever control her.

Her heart leapt at the challenge he put forth. If he'd have just left well enough alone, they'd have spent the entire three months doing incredibly sinful things all over his home--probably even all over the palace. She was a woman confident in her sexual appetites. But his royal highness wanted to play dominance. Well, no man had ever dominated her before and she'd be damned if he'd be the first. She'd just have to make his life torture until he couldn't stand it any longer.

Walking tall into the living room, gripping her towel regally around her body, she was surprised to find the fireplace had heated the room to a pleasant temperature. She looked at the bedroom and swallowed. Kirill came from within, holding a black dress over his arm. He stopped, his eyes still dark as he looked at her, but they were guarded now.

He was dressed in his usually dark attire. The studded armbands around his biceps gleamed in the firelight. Her eyes roamed unbidden over his body, more familiar now with it since she'd had a chance to explore it for herself. Her body heated even as her mind rebelled.

"We go to Reid's home tonight to dine so that you may meet my brothers." Kirill lifted the dress toward her. "You can wear this."

"No thanks, I prefer pants."

"Lyssa," he began, exasperated. Then, sighing, he shook his head. "You must wear this tonight. You are a woman and this is tradition."

"Your tradition sucks," she grumbled, stomping across the marble floor to snatch the dress from him. She pushed past him into his room and slammed the door behind her.

Kirill sighed and didn't move. The tension was back in his body. His head throbbed with renewed force. He didn't know what he'd done to make her so mad. He'd explained his position to her. He could not, would not beg her to sleep with him. Kings just could not beg. It was simple.

Then, with a shrug, he assumed she would come around. If she didn't, he'd just have to make her life torture until she couldn't stand it any longer. A devious smile came to his face. He was sure he could make her so hot for him that she'd soon forget her words and submit again--and again, and again, and....

* * * *

Little, unevenly winding trails worked through the thick fold of colossal trees. Strange yellow ferns grew over the red Qurilixen soil. Ulyssa trampled them with her feet as she walked.

Prince Reid's home was deep within the forest, north of the palace, near what Ulyssa assumed would be Draig territory. She was surprised to find that Kirill walked alone with her. There were no royal guards behind him, no entourage of soldiers--just them and the wide open forest. She wondered if she could make a run for it.

The air was fresh and the sky, from what she could see peeking in through the shelter of branches above, was of a clear greenish-blue. The green leaves of the surrounding foliage were overlarge due to the excessive heat and moisture they received. Ulyssa had seen the three suns peeking from the clouded sky--two yellow, one blue--when they passed through the back way of the palace from the Var city.

The city surrounding the palace looked to be a large one that rolled down the countryside from the front gate. The homes were constructed of gray bricks, contrasting to the red earth, with the same beautiful workmanship seen within the palace--though more simplistic and rectangular in design. From what she could tell, the city thrived.

Kirill briefly explained that the royal family only used the front entrance for ceremony--usually when leading the troops to war. Otherwise, it was much faster just to take the side stairs out of the palace directly into the forest. When Ulyssa asked about palace security, he merely roared and two very large mountain lions were summonsed to their side. Even in shifted cat form, they bowed their heads before sprinting back to disappear into the trees.

Ulyssa looked around, wondering how many Var warriors watched them. Maybe they weren't as alone as she had thought.

"We're not being followed," Kirill said at her side, without even glancing at her. Her head whipped forward and they continued on in silence.

The air was surprisingly warm for the evening hour. Birds sang beautifully in the distance. Little noises of insects came from all around. Various woodland critters shuffled away in fright, strange creatures she had gotten closer looks at when she camped.

Suddenly, remembering the rustic campsite, she wasn't in such a hurry to run from the palace. Besides, she was going to thoroughly enjoy bringing Kirill to his knees. She looked over at him and smiled. He tensed, his eyes narrowing in suspicion as they turned to her direct attention. She couldn't blame him. She'd been rather cold to him since the shower.

"Mmm, so beautiful out," she murmured in her sultriest tone. She let her lashes sweep over her blue eyes. "Does your planet always look like this?"

"This season is the longest," he answered, seeming to relax. "But there's also a short winter. The Draig get hit worse, as they have the larger mountain range."

"Why are you fighting the Draig? Because they are different than you?" Ulyssa was truly curious. Both seemed like proud, strong races. After discovering the first species of aliens, humans had put aside their petty interracial issues and they'd became simply human. That had been centuries ago. Could it be the Var and Draig simply had primitive race issues? It seemed a silly thing to fight over, but it happened often enough.

Kirill opened his mouth to answer and then hesitated. He stopped walking to turn to her.

"What?" Ulyssa asked.

"I'm not sure you're to be trusted," he answered truthfully.

"Why? Because I refuse to sleep with you again?" she demanded.

"Ah, so you haven't changed your mind. I thought maybe since you were again speaking to me..." His dark eye searched hers, before he shrugged.

"There's no reason not to be civil. So, what's going on with you and the Draig? What do you have against them?"

"In truth, I have nothing against them. The battle I fight now was my father's war." Kirill hesitated. He didn't know what made him confess such a thing, but he did feel better having said it aloud. He looked at Ulyssa. Her wide blue eyes stared back at him--not judging, not assuming. It was rare that anyone looked at him anymore in such a way. He realized she was the only person he could say such a thing to, for she was the only one around him who had no vested interest in peace or war.

"Listen, I've been meaning to tell you something." Ulyssa's hands wound nervously together before she let them fall again to her sides. "I didn't mean to insult your father."

Kirill merely nodded and she said no more about it. They walked in silence. He reached out to touch her shoulder and pull her to a stop next to him.

"Are you sure you wouldn't change your mind?" he asked. "We aren't due at Reid's for awhile longer."

Ulyssa turned to him, not needing to be told what he meant. The same thing had been on her mind since she declared she wouldn't submit to him again. She stayed strong. Artfully manipulating her cleavage as she again walked, she asked, "Are you ready to beg for it, your highness?"

"You know I won't." As he spoke, his gaze was predictably on her chest.

"Then, I'm afraid I'm famished and wish to get to your brother's early." She shot him a brilliant smile, blinking as innocently as she could muster.

Ulyssa just smiled. The Var King was hot-blooded, though he hid it well. It would take no time at all before he caved to her. Her smile turned into a full grin. Her plan was working a lot faster than she thought it would.

Kirill's expression darkened. He watched her from the corner of his eye. Sacred Cats! She was beautiful. The black gown hugged her slender frame, pulling tight and low across her breasts. Cross lacing worked up the side of the gown, exposing hints of flesh. The skirt flared around her hips to her knees. On her feet, she wore thigh high boots that disappeared beneath the hem of the skirt. Kirill wanted nothing more than to follow the boots up with his hands. He wasn't fooled by her play of innocence and they both knew it. He walked faster. Under his breath, he muttered, "By all that is Sacred, you are a stubborn briallen!"

* * * *

Reid's home was built aboveground, in the colossal trees of the forest. At first, Ulyssa didn't see it from the forest floor. Kirill led the way in moody silence, only to stop beneath a thick overhang of leaves near a large stone bolder. Pushing the branches aside, he revealed a narrow staircase carved into the stone side of the rock. The rock was pressed flat to tree trunk, which was much wider than the old redwoods back on Earth.

"After you," he said, quietly.

Ulyssa hesitated, looking up around the trunk.

"I assure you, it's perfectly safe."

Ulyssa shivered. He stood very close to her back. She could feel his heat, the tickle of his breath on her neck. A momentary wave of lightheadedness passed over her, causing her to sway on her feet.

"Something wrong?" he asked in a tone that had dipped to a low timbre. She felt a hand whisper over her hip, skimming down along the top of her thigh, dangerously near the bottom curve of her backside. The touch was light, but it was enough to remind her how good his hands felt against her flesh. Every nerve lurched to attention.

"No," she whispered, trying hard to control herself. She stumbled forward, climbing around the steps.

Kirill walked behind her, enjoying the soft sway of her hips as she moved. He was almost positive she did it to tantalize him. He could smell her desire for him, teasing his senses almost as badly as her nearness did. It was a wicked game they played, but he found he much enjoyed their battle of the wills. He wouldn't give in first, couldn't give in, but it'd be a grand thing to watch her try to make him.

They climbed the steps around the base of the thick tree, making it half way around until they came to a door carved into the trunk. A small window was fitted into the wood, but Ulyssa couldn't see through the dark drape that hung over it on the inside. She looked curiously at Kirill.

"Your brother lives *in* a tree?" She tried to hide her amusement.

Kirill reached from behind her and knocked on the intricately carved entryway.

"The King knocks?" Ulyssa mused, whispering over her shoulder.

Kirill's face had come close to hers. He didn't pull away as her mouth turned to his. Leaning slightly closer, so that when he spoke his lips whispered against hers, he commanded, "Behave yourself, Lyssa."

A roar sounded from the inside followed by laughter. Kirill gave the door a light nudge and it soundlessly swung open. Ulyssa gasped. Inside, the tree had been hollowed out, forming polished wood floors with gorgeous natural swirling designs, and walls carved to look like rustic planks. The ceiling, also of wood, spiraled high revealing the home had at least two levels carved into it.

Kirill took her arm and led her up two stairs from the small opening of a front foyer to the main living area. The main level was circular, except along two flat sides were walls were left and rooms carved out behind them. An intricate door was carved into one of the flat walls, leading to a bathroom on one side. The other wall had an opening in it with a bar and barstools, revealing a large kitchen behind it.

Light filtered in from outside from little holes in the ceiling, reflecting off a small glass and mirror dome. In the center of the first floor was a comfortable living area adorned with thick, red couches and matching chairs, throw rugs woven in the same designs popular in the palace.

Ulyssa instantly recognized Falke as he stood up from a chair only to bow at his brother. From the corner of her eye, she saw Kirill wave him down. Falke sat.

"You've met Falke, our Var Commander of the Guards," Kirill said, taking her arm and leading her in. Falke again stood and curtly nodded. Ulyssa shot him an impish grin. She had not forgotten her stoic nemesis so easily. "And there on the floor is Quinn."

Quinn waved lazily and shot her a handsome smile from his place lounging on the floor. He lay on his back, his knee drawn up with a foot leisurely laid across it. A shock of lighter colored hair fell over his bright blue eyes.

"Believe it or not, he's our Ambassador." Kirill turned to the two men. "Quinn meet Lyssa."

"Quinn?" Ulyssa whispered to Kirill, a little daunted by the idea of being in a room full of Var Princes. "I thought you said we were visiting Reid? How many brothers do you have?"

"Only four," Kirill said, almost apologetically.

"Our father was a busy man," Falke added, rising to his father's defense. "He didn't have time for breeding."

Quinn chuckled and sat up. "Ah, don't mind these barbarian brothers of mine, my lady. They tend to forget that Earth culture is different than our own. Here it's considered a low number to have only five sons. Most families have anywhere from twelve to fifteen."

"There could be more," Falke defended. "King Attor went many places."

Quinn grinned, but nodded in agreement of the possibility.

"Fifteen?" Ulyssa squeaked. "I think five is more than enough. As it is, I suddenly feel very sorry for your mother."

Falke and Kirill looked at her, confused.

"You know, having five children. Being pregnant that many times," she explained.

"We do not have the same mother." Falke frowned.

"None of you do?" she asked.

"Well, Jarek and Reid were born together in one birth," Kirill said.

"Twins," Quinn clarified with an easy smile.

"Oh, right, the harem," Ulyssa said. She let her eyes fall down. She'd never be part of such a thing. A husband with hundreds of wives? Wait. What was she thinking? She wouldn't be one wife to one husband.

"By All That Is Sacred!" A shout sounded from the kitchen area followed by a roar of anger and a wave of black smoke. "So help me, if you weren't King...!"

The rest of the insult was muffled. Quinn and Kirill laughed. Even the stoic Falke's lip gave a little twitch, though he stayed rigid in his chair.

"Reid!" Kirill hollered. Ulyssa jumped in surprise at the sound and turned to look at him. His serious tone didn't match his playful features. He winked at her. "That better not be my dinner."

"I'll tell ... what you ... dinner ... you ... royal pain...." was Reid's muttered response. There was a loud crash, followed by a series of bangs. Reid stormed from the kitchen holding two drinks.

Prince Reid was dark featured and moved with the steady grace of his brothers. Muscles formed his body and he carried them proudly, as if he expected women to swoon at his feet. Stopping in front of his brother, he blinked in surprise as he openly checked Ulyssa out.

Slowly, he handed the two goblets to Kirill. Then, a devilish grin curling his features, he said, "Welcome, my lady."

"Back off Reid," Falke demanded, his voice full of warning. "I can smell your pheromones from here. She's the King's woman."

Reid's brow rose and Ulyssa had the distinct impression the look of masculine invitation was meant to aggravate Kirill more than entice her. She felt Kirill stiffen next to her. A hand came possessively to her elbow and she just couldn't help herself, as she murmured huskily, "My pleasure, Prince Reid."

Ulyssa offered her hand to him, her eyes narrowing, daring him to keep it up. Reid pulled back in surprise and hesitated, obviously not expecting her to respond so carelessly to him. He glanced at Kirill and slowly took her hand in his. He held it briefly before letting go. Reid backed away. Though his smile faded, his eyes lit with curious mischief.

Ulyssa turned to give Kirill an innocent smile. His eyes searched her face and she let nothing show. Her heart sped as she detected a hint of jealousy in his gaze.

"So, I believe there's one more?" she questioned.

"Jarek is out exploring the galaxies," Quinn answered behind her back. "We don't expect him back any time soon."

Ulyssa broke eye contact to turn to him. Teasingly, she said, "Well, it would appear he's the lucky one."

"My lady?" Quinn asked.

"Well, by the smell of it, we'll be starving tonight."

Three of the brothers started to laugh, even Falke. Reid rolled his eyes. "Yeah, yeah, very amusing, my lady, very amusing."

* * * *

The meal Reid prepared was bad. No, it was worse than bad. It was completely inedible. The roast, or what had once been a roast, was charred to resemble a large, black rock. Only too happily did the brothers catapult it off the long balcony carved into the second level of the home. The roast launched, hit a tree and, inflicting more damage to the bark than to itself, plummeted to the forest floor with a resounding thud. Rich, masculine laughter rang over the forest as birds squawked and flew away in protest.

Luckily, Quinn had smuggled a basket from the palace when he came. It was filled with cold meat and a creamy cheese-like dip. Dipping chucks of meat into the cheese, they ate in the living room, lounging in relaxation as they talked. No one treated Ulyssa like an outsider, as they told stories of their childhood growing up in the palace.

Ulyssa found the Princes to be very charming, even Falke though he hardly smiled. As she watched him, she saw a more subtle movement to his features--mainly in his steady gaze. He had more emotion than his brothers seemed to give him credit for. Over the course of the evening, she felt guilty for giving him a hard time. From what she could tell, he got enough harassment from his brothers that he didn't need it from her, too.

"...so Falke was covered in mud from head to toe," Reid said, laughing hard as he told another of his endless list of boyhood stories. It was obvious he'd been the proud instigator in many of the incidences. "We must have been what--?"

"Fifteen to twenty years," Quinn supplied.

Hearing Kirill laugh next to her, she peeked from under her lashes at him. His laugh was deep and rich. The mere sound of it gave her chills. It was a Kirill she hadn't seen at the palace. Here, with his family, he was almost serene.

"Anyway, here's Falke covered in mud and the Lithorian Ambassadors are on their way. Mind you, he's set to be the official greeter when they arrive. The King was very rigid on the point that they must be pleased in every way. Well, why we were dousing Falke in mud, Quinn sneaks into his bedroom and steals all his clothes." Reid laughed harder. Gasping for breath, he said, "The only thing left him was a dress Quinn stole from the harem."

"They believed it was ceremonial garb," Falke grumbled, trying to keep a stern face. "I had to wear it every year they came for ten years."

Ulyssa burst with laughter, imagining the stoic Falke in a dress.

"It's a good thing too, or else they might have stopped trading with us," Kirill said. "The King would've put Falke in the dungeon if that happened."

"And what do they trade?" Ulyssa asked.

Reid laughed harder. "Chocolate."

"Chocolate?" Ulyssa repeated in disbelief.

"King Attor had a sweet tooth," Kirill explained, as if it made perfect sense.

Ulyssa hid her frown. A father who would lock up his son for ruining a trade agreement over chocolate? She liked the dead King less and less. How hard it must've been for them, growing up with such an emotionally vacant man as a father. She imagined it would have been worse than her childhood--with no father at all.

Setting her plate on the floor, Ulyssa didn't think as she leaned back on the couch next to Kirill. She slipped her body naturally by his. She felt his breath catch before his arm moved to drape possessively over her shoulder. His firm body cradled hers naturally to his side and his fingers glanced over her arm, the tips moving in a light, absentminded caress. He smelled so good. God help her, she wanted him.

"Ah, to be so young again," Reid laughed.

"This couldn't have been very long ago," Ulyssa said, studying the brothers. "You all look hardly thirty."

They all laughed harder.

"Ah, to be thirty again." Reid sighed with much dramatics.

Ulyssa frowned, pulling back to look at Kirill. "If he's over thirty and you're the oldest ... just how old are you?"

"Ninety-eight."

Ulyssa's eyes widened and she waited for him to say he was joking. "You're kidding right."

"Ah, yes, he's a young King, to be sure," Falke said. He raised his mug, prompting Reid and Quinn to do the same. "But, he'll be a great one."

"Agreed," Quinn said, toasting.

"Agreed." Reid raised his glass and nodded.

"The hour grows late. I should get you home," Kirill said, pushing up from the couch. The statement was said with an intimacy that made Ulyssa nervous. Home. She'd never really had a home before, never really longed for one like the other kids in the orphanage. Going back. That meant a night of trying to keep herself from giving into her desire for him. Seeing the softer side of Kirill's life wasn't helping her resolve, nor was the insight into his father's ways. It explained much about why he was the way he was.

Ulyssa affected a yawn and stood. Slowly, she nodded. She didn't like the tenderness that crept into her chest as she took Kirill's offered arm. With quiet good-byes they took their leave.

Quinn sighed, as the door shut behind the couple. The three Princes sat in silence for a long moment, their face drawn in thought. Thoughtfully, the youngest Var murmured, "She does something to him. She relaxes him, balances him. It's almost strange to behold."

"I noticed it as well," Reid said, not exactly smiling at the insight, but not frowning either. "It's almost as if he carries her scent as well. But, how can that be? How can a human woman mark our kind?"

Falke remained quiet. Quinn shrugged, not knowing the answer.

"Did you see the possessiveness in him?" Reid asked. All three turned their serious gazes to the door, as if they could still see the couple.

"What do you think it means?" Quinn sighed.

Falke sat forward, bracing his elbows to his knees. His low tone crackled over the tree home. "I think it means, brothers, that our King just might have met his woman. If he's not careful, he'll find himself lifemated to a Queen."

* * * *

The forest was dim and cast with shadows in the late hour, yet the suns still provided enough hazy light to see by. Ulyssa kicked idly at the trail with her feet as they walked. She'd dropped Kirill's arm to walk down the front steps and hadn't touched him since, though she desperately wanted to.

"What is it?" Kirill asked, catching her soft eyes on him. His hands were threaded behind his back and he walked easily by her side.

Ulyssa refused to say what she was thinking, because she was too unsure where her thoughts were leading her. So, instead, she asked, "You're not afraid to walk alone without guards?"

Kirill chuckled. "Should I be?"

"Well, I mean... What if someone sent an assassin after you? Or wanted to kidnap you? Such things happen to royalty all the time. What about the Draig? Are they not a threat to you?" Ulyssa swallowed nervously, refusing to look at him, though she felt his eyes studying her intently.

"Are you concerned about my wellbeing?" The words were soft, probing.

She swore he drew closer to where she walked, but she didn't look up to confirm it. Taking a deep breath, she lied, "Not really. I was just curious as to why you would risk it. You could be ambushed."

"I can defend myself," he answered, a bit hard. "There's no reason for me to hide in the palace. The Kings before me did not hide and neither shall I."

"I'm not saying to hide. I'm just wondering why you don't have a guard walk with you when you're about or, if not a guard, your brother, Falke. I'm sure he'd come back with us if you asked him to."

"You do not think I can defend you?" he demanded, his jaw tightening. He turned to her and his hand snapped onto her jaw, squeezing her as he forced her to look at him. His dark eyes glittered with green-gold anger and she could see the threat of a shift in him. A peculiar sensation slithered over her flesh and she was sure claws grew over her neck, near her pulse. His voice tempered with a roar, he growled, "What have I done to deserve such talk of dishonor from you?"

"What? Dishonor? I--"

"Rest assured," he hissed at her. "I don't need Falke to protect what is mine."

"What is yours?" she repeated, stunned. Her heart nearly stopped beating in her chest. Was he claiming her as his? A curious feeling washed over her at the thought.

"Yes, my property," he clarified, though the statement came a little too late.

Oh, Ulyssa thought ruefully in growing outrage, *his property. I see. His property. That pigheaded barbarian jerk! I'll show him property!*

"What in the hell do you mean--?" Ulyssa began, raising her hand to push his chest.

"Shhh," Kirill ordered, turning his head away from her. His eyes scanned the forest. "Quiet."

"Don't you--*owph*!"

One of Kirill's hands darted forward to cover her mouth. The other pulled the back of her head until she pressed into the hard fold of his chest.

"Someone's coming," Kirill said under his breath, directly into her ear. She struggled against his hold. He ignored her weak protests as he sniffed the air. "Walk behind me and behave yourself."

Just as quickly, he let her go. Kirill walked, not watching to see if she followed. Ulyssa stood still, gasping for breath, and refused to move. She'd be damned before she'd walk behind him in submission. She crossed her arms over her chest, cocked her head to the side, and stared after him.

Kirill noticed she didn't follow him and suddenly stopped. His fingers lifted and, without turning around, he motioned for her to come to him. She didn't move.

As he turned to look at her, Ulyssa nearly laughed to see the tension in his body. His eyes glared out in anger, but she was too irritated by his words to care.

"King Kirill."

Ulyssa's smirk fell to hear the voice. She blinked, lifting her jaw proudly. She couldn't see past Kirill, but she watched him turn to the sound. His body only stiffened more and it was as if she could fell his tension inside herself. The sudden wave of stress made her sick to her stomach and she felt as if she might retch.

"My King, it's an honor," the same voice said.

Ulyssa took a small step to the side. The man who bowed to Kirill was shorter in stature with long graying black hair. If Kirill was ninety-eight, she could just imagine how old this man was.

Cool, green eyes turned to her. She met the man's stare boldly. Ulyssa wondered at it. She took a step closer to better hear. Before she realized what she was doing, she stood next to Kirill's side. He didn't move to acknowledge her. The old Var eyed her curiously, as did his son.

Under their stares, she did the only thing she could think of. She smiled, held out her hand, and said, "Hello, I'm Ulyssa Payne."

The men merely looked at her strangely.

"And you would be?" she prompted, a little too sternly at their rude silence.

"Lord Myrddin, I know you haven't had the honor of meeting my mistress, Lyssa." Kirill's hand waved dismissingly toward her and he didn't turn to look at her. "Lyssa, this is Lord Myrddin and his son, Master Andras."

Andras was a taller man than his father, with a head full of brown waves. Though, he did have the same cool, green eyes as Myrddin. Neither man moved to acknowledge the small bow of her head as they turned back to look at Kirill.

"Were you to Prince Reid's?" Myrddin asked.

"Ah, just for a walk about the forest," Kirill lied.

"We were most aggrieved to hear of your father," Myrddin said, angling his head so he spoke down his nose at Kirill. "He was a good King. Such men as him will never be replaced."

It seemed like an odd thing to say to the present King. Ulyssa waited in sweet anticipation for Kirill to seize the man's throat and demand respect. To her surprise, he only nodded at the statement and said nothing. Ulyssa snorted lightly before she could stop herself and all eyes turned to her.

"Lyssa, was it?" Myrddin stated. There was no question in his hard tone. She had a feeling he knew about her before their meeting. She also had the distinct impression their meeting here wasn't completely a coincidence. His eyes gauged her as he asked, "Did you have the honor of knowing our King Attor?"

"Yes, briefly," she answered, matching his rude tone with her own. Ulyssa decided she didn't care for the man's attitude. She couldn't help but wonder why Kirill let him talk down to him. A desperate need to wipe the smarmy grin off the man's face overcame her. In a voice so sweet it dripped with honeyed sarcasm, she added, "I believe it was the same day he died. Though, it's hard to say since he kidnapped me and knocked me unconscious."

"I see," Myrddin snarled. His mouth snapped, as he ordered, "Andras, come, we are late."

"My lord." Andras bowed his head to Kirill and moved to follow his father's lead. His face gave away nothing of the exchange.

Myrddin nodded to the King, murmuring, "My lord."

"Lord Myrddin, Master Andras," Kirill answered politely. The men passed. Kirill didn't wait for them to get out of sight before he started walking again toward the palace.

"Who were they?" Ulyssa asked when they were alone.

"Lord Myrddin is a wise, respected man of the Var. He's leader of the old houses and his family maintains most of the shadowed marshes." Kirill still didn't look at her and Ulyssa realized he was livid. Gritting through his teeth, he said, "He and his men were very loyal to my father."

Kirill walked faster, stalking through the trees. Ulyssa jogged to keep up with him. "He didn't seem very noble and wise to me."

"Sacred Cats, Lyssa! Can you never just obey me?" Kirill stopped. His dark eyes narrowed in on her in anger. "I told you to follow behind me and yet still you stand beside me as an equal! Most of the time it doesn't matter, but his ways are of the old and we must respect that. Are you actually trying to cause us more trouble? If I didn't know better I would think you were trying to be my wife! Only a Queen would dare speak the way you just did."

"Hey, buddy, I don't want to be your anything!" she hissed, matching his muffled tone. He wasn't yelling, but he might as well have been for all the anger in his face and voice. "You're the one who asked me to stay. I wanted to leave. Just let me out of our bargain and I'll leave now-- right now! I'll walk into that forest and you'll never see me again."

Kirill slashed his hand through the air to silence her. "I ask you to behave and yet you open your mouth! Can you just never stay quiet?"

"You're a King. You don't have to answer to the likes of him. How could you let him speak to you like that?"

"I have to answer to everyone in this kingdom," Kirill growled. "You gave me your word you would behave for three months until your ride came. If you would have me honor my word to let you go, I will demand you honor yours."

"You still shouldn't let him talk down to you like that. If you won't defend yourself--"

"You dare insult me further by saying I need you to defend me?"

"Argh! You are so ... so *argh!* Who cares if he liked your father better, Kirill? I've got a news flash for you. You're his new King and what's more your father was a jerk. I'm sorry you lost him and I'm sorry he's dead, but that doesn't change the facts. Look at your childhood, your brother's childhood--"

"You're human. There's no way you can understand our ways," he broke in, storming closer to better glare at her. His body was tense and he refused to touch her. "I'm well aware you have no love for my father, Lyssa, but these people do. And more than that, Attor has their respect even in death. You can't undo centuries of loyalty in a week. I know it matters naught to you, for you plan on leaving, but it matters to me! I am stuck here for centuries!"

"Stuck?" Ulyssa gasped in shock. She trembled violently at his nearness, as if she could feel his anger inside herself-- but there was more, a slight edging of fear he'd never admit to and probably didn't know he had. His words echoed in her head as if he yelled inside her rather than whispered angrily before her. She heard roaring echo in her brain and it wasn't her frustration she felt. It was his. She took a frightened step back, her eyes wide. Every nerve inside her tried to push him from her body, not liking the invasion.

Unhampered by her new plight, Kirill stood regally before her. The roaring stopped as he looked her over. Quietly, and without passion, he said, "I must insist you stop your slander against King Attor. If you speak of it again, our deal is off and I will have you punished."

"You said you were stuck here," Ulyssa said instead of answering his threat.

"I used the wrong human word," he dismissed, but she somehow knew he was lying, could feel that he was. "Your language is easy to switch around."

Suddenly, she felt nothing. The silence in her head left her numb. He turned his emotions off, blocked them, swallowed them down until they were ignored. It was as if he invaded her and then left, taking part of her with him. She couldn't explain it, didn't even want to try.

"As for your insolence before Lord Myrddin, I shall sentence you to two weeks of repentance. You may not leave my home until that time is served."

Ulyssa gasped. She watched in silence as he stalked away. Then, glancing around the shadowed forest, she hurried after him.

Chapter Eight

Kirill took Ulyssa home without another word and, to her amazement, left her there alone. It was just as well. She suddenly felt like she had a lot to figure out. A small, yet overwhelming part of her screamed to push everything aside--her pride, her stubbornness--and just hold him whether he allowed it or not. That same part told her to submit completely, to give in so that she could have what she wanted. She ignored that small part, for it wasn't her logic that spoke, but her treacherous heart. Ulyssa refused to become enamored with a barbaric King.

The first week of her repentance passed in anger. She ignored Kirill. He ignored her. She ate alone, bathed alone, sat alone, stared at the wall alone. It was only when she started to have conversations alone that she shook herself from her stupor and began looking for things to do. And, though she found little to occupy her, her thoughts stayed busy.

The second week seemed even longer. Kirill's anger seemed to abate and he began dining with her in the evenings. At first conversation was stilted and short, but it gradually grew to inane topics about Qurilixen weather and food. He tried to ask her personal questions, which she artfully avoided. The only stories she had involved the Agency and that little detail wasn't something she wanted him to know.

By the end of her repentance, an uneasy tension settled in the home. Their eyes would lock and hold for long periods before either of them thought to look away. Kirill would walk across the living room without a shirt, lounging against the doorframe as he spoke, knowing all the time she watched. Ulyssa would allow her body to brush against his when passing by. Or she'd allow ample amounts of cleavage to show in his direction. It was a game and they both knew it--a battle of the wills to see who would cave first. So far, neither was giving in.

The two weeks were complete torture, sleeping on the couch, knowing she had but to crawl onto his bed and offer herself to him. Stubborn pride kept her from going. Stubborn pride was becoming a hard comfort in the late hours of the night when she'd wake up from an erotically charged dream of Kirill and of the magic his tongue could work on her skin.

Once, she'd tried to relieve the sexual tension from of her body by herself. Kirill had stumbled sleepily from the bedroom, sniffing the air, as he passed by to the bathroom. It was as if he'd known what she was doing. She closed her eyes and pretended to sleep. She'd not tried such a thing again.

Another notion filtered in and out of her thoughts when she was alone. Kirill had been honest with her from the beginning. He could feel nothing for her or any woman. He wanted only one thing from her--her body. She respected him for that honesty, but suddenly it became a hard reality to swallow and she didn't know why. Why should it matter if Kirill could care for her or not? Did she really want him to? Did she want more from him than a passionate, adventurous, incredibly wonderful affair of the flesh? Did she want his barbaric heart?

Ulyssa stopped pacing the length of his home. Her world spun as her mind edged closer to the thought. She turned in circles, looking for something solid to hold onto. The couch, the bright fireplace, the living room, it all blurred and streaked within her vision.

"I think I ... *love him*?" she whispered with a confused grimace, right before she fainted dead away onto the floor.

* * * *

Kirill looked out over the balcony adjoining the royal office. He couldn't go back home, not yet. He needed to get away from the frustrating woman who already occupied too many of his thoughts as of late. She was rash, outspoken, reckless--everything Attor had warned his sons against in a woman.

The valley below spread out with trees, the tops of which blended together in a gently rolling plain. Their leaves shimmered in such a way it looked like field of emerald. He loved this land--his land. And he loved the people who lived in it.

Kirill sighed, feeling the weight of his burden tenfold. Only with Ulyssa did he feel it lessen, unless he counted that time when she'd opened her mouth too wide in front of Lord Myrddin and his son. The noble was a well-respected elder and her words had enticed him to anger. Already rumors spread of his distrust of the new King.

It had been Lord Myrddin's nephew that helped to kidnap the Draig Princess Olena. Because of the foolishness of the plan, Brouse and his two cohorts were dead--slaughtered by the Draig Princes in the shadowed marshes. Lord Myrddin had been one of Attor's closest advisors and was also one of the few people Kirill had to worry about. The fact that he hadn't come to the coronation also said he wasn't wholeheartedly giving his support of the new King's reign.

Kirill knew many of the elders wanted him to attack the Draig, to kill off the royal family and avenge his father's death and, on a smaller level, the death of Brouse. Part of him wanted the same thing. It was his father, after all, who'd fallen to the sword. But, Kirill was King now and had to look above his own needs, his own desires. He had to do what was right for his people.

Kirill had never believed in Attor's wars. He believed there could be peace between the Var and the Draig. He'd not ruin that slim chance of peace to avenge a man who'd provoked the battle to begin with. He'd not risk his reign on a temperamental woman who'd be leaving him in a few short months--no matter how sexy he found her, not matter how much his body wanted her these last weeks, no matter how many thoughts she occupied in his brain.

Going into the royal office, he began to pace. "Siren, where's Lyssa?"

"Lyssa is in your home, my lord," the computer's sultry voice answered, as it did every time he asked her.

He asked the computer several times during the morning and afternoon and always it was the same. *She is in your home, my lord.* To Kirill's surprise, she'd honored his decree and had not left his home for the full two weeks. He knew it had to be killing her, being locked indoors.

"What is she doing?" Kirill asked, swallowing almost nervously.

"She's not moving, my lord. Performing scan." There was a short pause, before Siren answered, "Health status fine. She appears to be asleep, my lord."

Kirill sighed heavily, leaving the office. As he came through the door, he ordered, "Siren, lock up."

"Yes, my lord," the computer said. The door latched behind him.

Kirill started to walk home, only to hesitate and stop. A sense of grim determination came over him. He needed to work Ulyssa out of his system. If he had to keep denying himself as he waited for her to come around, he'd surely cave.

Turning around, he stalked down the hallway toward the harem. A few of the women were still there. Surely one of them wouldn't be so averse to pleasuring the new King. Golden blonde-red hair and dark blue eyes instantly appeared in his mind. He was able to remember in full detail the feel of her skin, the taste of her lips. Swallowing over the lump in his throat, he knew it might just take more than one.

* * * *

Ulyssa lifted the sword and swung it around her head. She didn't know how to properly wield it, but that didn't matter to her. She needed to exercise. She needed to vent. She needed Kirill to come back home so she could prove to herself that she merely wanted to sleep with him, not love him. It was two weeks of sexual stress that put the thought in her head. She was sure of it!

After pulling her body off the floor, she'd spent the night on the couch. Not that it seemed to matter. For all she knew, Kirill had not come home. She wondered if he spent the night in the harem--had often wondered if he spent time in the harem. It was insane to believe that a man with such carnal appetites would deny himself, especially without the sexual innuendoes she let fall to tempt him into madness.

Ulyssa grunted, swinging harder so the blade sung through the air. She refused to be jealous. Her feet shuffled on the floor as she moved.

Vaguely, she recalled her train of thought right before she passed out. The next morning, when logic once more reigned over her mind, she knew that she'd probably just drank some of that nef stuff Kirill mentioned. That's why she'd felt all ... *tenderhearted.*

Ulyssa shivered in disgust, swinging the deadly blade again and again. Unbidden, the image of Linzi and Kirill locked in an embrace came to her and she yelled with her frustration. Only when she panted and gasped for breath, did she stop. Her arms fell limp to her sides.

Lifting the sword, she moved to place it back in the weapon's cabinet where she found it. As she let go, the door opened and she turned. Her heart leapt in her throat as she looked for Kirill.

"Falke?" she asked in surprise.

"My lady," Falke nodded. His eyes moved to look over the open cabinet. "You know how to use those?"

It took a moment for Ulyssa to get over the fact Falke spoke more than a few syllables to her, before she answered, "Ah, no, not really. I've done a little with knife combat, but nothing with swords."

Ulyssa's breath caught as she realized what she revealed. Falke gave nothing away.

As if it was no big deal, she said, "Ah, it was self-defense training that all the orphans had to take."

"Orphan?" he inquired. "I am not familiar with that word."

"Those without parents." Ulyssa was beyond feeling bad over her circumstances. She'd been raised in a girl's home for eleven years before she moved to the Agency to begin her training. "My parents died in a shuttle crash when I was a month old. I was raised in a home that takes in children who have no home or family."

"Hum," he mused.

"Are you looking for your brother?"

"No. He sent me to--"

"To check on me," she finished.

"Yes, and to see if you needed anything. Your two weeks are over."

"Need anything? You mean besides out of this house?" Ulyssa laughed.

Falke didn't move from his position in front of the open door. He nodded in approval of her. "You didn't try to escape, so are free to walk about the palace. Was there someplace particular you'd like me to lead you?"

"Just out," Ulyssa said with a grin. She felt almost giddy. It'd been two weeks since Kirill told her she had to atone. If she was caught in public, she'd break her agreement about behaving and he'd be forced to throw her in the prisons. Two weeks confinement was definitely better than being a prisoner. As far as she could tell, gilded bars at the palace were much easier to escape from than iron--if the time ever came when she needed to.

"Out," Falke repeated. He slowly nodded. "Very well. Out. Grab the sword and come. We will go out."

* * * *

'Out' consisted of an empty practice field in the center courtyard of the palace. Four walls surrounded the grassy yard, blocking it in on all sides with a covered walkway of intricate patterns and detailed mosaics. Falke had stopped first to get his own weapon, before leading her to where he'd instruct her.

Ulyssa was very much impressed with Falke's abilities. He was a patient teacher, a capable leader, and a hard commander. She admired all three qualities.

Striking a pose, he thrust the blade before him and drew it back only to pause as he waited for her to copy the move. She did and he repeated the same move several times for her to follow. They worked in silence until she did it to his satisfaction.

After about an hour, Falke turned to her and lifted his blade. "Now, do what I just showed you as I attack."

Ulyssa grinned, excited to try her new skill. With a clang of their sword, Falke stepped slowly through the motions, speeding his attack slightly by each pass until she got use to the weight of his blows.

* * * *

"Siren, find Lyssa," Kirill stated, looking up from desk to the ceiling with a weary sigh, as he stretched his neck muscles. He waited for the standard answer. *She is in your home, my lord.*

Kirill was tired. He'd gone to the harem, hoping to drain the tension from his body, but none of the women would touch him without his mistress's permission first. Taura, Falke's mother, had commanded the women away from him, reminding him of that little hierarchy fact.

It was just as well. It hadn't take him long to realize he didn't want anyone but Ulyssa. The realization was hard to admit, even to himself.

Kirill turned his head back down, ready to continue reading through his father's old decrees, as soon as Siren gave him the answer he desired. He frowned, realizing it was taking the computer a long time to answer.

"She is battling with Prince Falke in the courtyard," the computer's sultry tone said.

"Thank yo--*what?*" Kirill frowned. "Repeat Siren."

"Lyssa is battling in the courtyard with Prince Falke. My sensors detect swords, my lord."

Kirill felt his stomach lurch into his throat. He took a deep breath. Had she tried to escape him again? Did his brother find it necessary to subdue her into staying? Did his threat to punish her cause her to want leave him? And why now after two weeks?

Kirill ran from the royal office. Falke was a great warrior. Ulyssa would be no match for his strength and skill.

Earlier, he'd sent Falke to check on her, not wanting to go home and face her himself. It had either been Falke or Reid and he didn't like the way she'd flirted with Reid when they dined at the tree home.

Kirill ran faster. He didn't like the idea of her leaving him. Over the last couple of weeks, it had given him some small measure of comfort to know she was in his home, waiting for him. Well, maybe not waiting for him, but within his reach all the same. Their evening dinners were a welcome relief to a hard day adjusting to his role as Var ruler.

Rounding the corner to the covered walkways that surrounded the courtyard, he slowed and affected an easy stride. His breath was a little heavy, not from having run half the length of the castle, but from fear that Falke would do something to Ulyssa out of duty. When it came to the law, Falke did not deviate from his responsibility, no matter what.

"Falke!" Kirill roared to see his brother attacking Ulyssa with a sword. It was a vicious blow and for a moment Kirill froze, waiting for her head to roll. To his surprise, she countered the shot, blocking it with ease.

Ulyssa blinked and stumbled back. Falke made sure she was done with her counter-attack before letting down his guard and turning to bow to his brother.

"What goes on here?" Kirill demanded, his words harsher than he intended. He couldn't bring himself to look at Ulyssa. His eyes glowered with golden rage. The anger was easier than the fear and he welcomed it.

"My order was to entertain." Turning to Ulyssa, Falke asked in his serious tone, "Are you not entertained?"

"Yes," she answered in a soft whisper. Kirill felt her eyes on him and couldn't resist the urge to look her over. A light sheen of sweat covered her body, making her glisten in the sunlight. Trails of her hair were plastered to her face and neck, falling from her neat bun. She was beautiful. His heart sped in his chest.

"Leave us," Kirill ordered, glancing back to his brother. A flood of desire invaded him as he watched her and he felt his body lurching to respond. Two weeks was too long a time to hold back from her.

Falke bowed toward them both and turned to go.

"Hey, Falke," Ulyssa called after him. The Commander turned. "Thanks."

He bowed again, letting a smile twitch the corner of his mouth, and left.

When they were alone, Ulyssa turned her wide eyes on Kirill. Her expression fell as she studied him. "Let me guess, my holding a sword is not allowed by your laws and I'm embarrassing you again. How many weeks do I get this time? Three?"

Kirill didn't speak as she moved over to him. Her eyes met boldly with his. He liked the way she looked at him, straightforward, honest. Now that he knew she was safe, he relaxed. Her hand lifted and his breath caught. Instead of touching him, she held the sword out for him to take. His fingers brushed against hers as he took the hilt.

"So am I in trouble?" Her wide blue eyes fell down toward the ground.

She's worried? Kirill was struck with the realization.

"No," he said.

"Then..." Ulyssa was obviously confused. She pulled away and he lifted a hand to her face to stop her.

"Come with me, Lyssa."

"Where are we going?" Ulyssa eyed Kirill, wondering what he was up to. He smiled slightly at her question and her heart skipped. It was clear by his stiff moments that he had been mad about Falke teaching her the sword.

"For a walk," he answered, his hand slid down over her cheek to her neck. His fingers settled against her racing pulse.

"You're taking me to the dungeon, aren't you?"

Kirill chuckled. His eyes fell to her lips and he drew the blade to the side.

"Are you going to lop off my head?"

A slow, predatory grin slid across the corner of his mouth. His fingers tightened on her throat. Ulyssa tensed, wondering at the glint in his dangerous gaze. She shivered, too frightened to move. His nearness wreaked havoc on her senses. She wanted him desperately. She forgot where she was, who they were. Nothing mattered in that moment as she gazed deeply into his dark eyes.

"Come back with me to my home," he whispered, leaning closer. The words sounded like a command.

Her lashes fluttered over her eyes. "Ask me."

His lips brushed against hers, but he didn't kiss her. His fingers glanced down her arm and he took her hand in his. He walked backwards, pulling her with him. Then, reaching the side of the courtyard, he turned and led her into the long halls of the palace. She followed in silence, entranced by him. Her eyes moved over his frame, straying too long at where the laces crossed the tight flesh of his hips. Her finger itched to touch him there, to run beneath the tight material to find his awaiting erection.

When they came to his home, he let her go and moved to hang the sword in its place. She watched him almost in a daze. He moved with stealthy purpose and fluid grace. Suddenly, she shook her head, trying to bring herself back to reality.

"I'm going to take a shower." Ulyssa edged across the living room. His dark eyes turned sharply to her, hot with desire. His arousal was large, pressing unmistakably against his pants. He wanted her. "Alone."

His gaze narrowed and his dark eyes stayed with her, tortured with his passion. Their arousal was so thick that it blanketed the air between them. "Tell me to come with you."

"Beg me to let you," she answered, meeting the challenge in him. If he didn't crumble in that moment, he never would. His jaw lifted with pride and she knew that instant, no matter how badly his body burned, he wouldn't relent. He'd never bow to her. His limbs shook and, with a force of control she'd never seen in a man, he turned and walked slowly to the bedroom.

Ulyssa had to run to the shower to get away from him before she caved to her desires and begged him to sleep with her.

"Shower on," she stated. Instantly, the water sprayed. She hurried into the shower, washing quickly in the warm water. Then, pausing, she slapped her fist hard against the tile wall. Memories of being pressed against the stall invaded her skin. She was hot for him. And, damn her pride, she wanted to give in to him. But, she also remembered his callous words.

See, it's not so bad to be controlled by a man. You didn't mind my dominance over you.

She imagined him in his room, releasing his body's tension without her and the image drove her mad. Playing dominance was one thing, but she wouldn't let him mistake her for property, a slave. She had too much pride for that. So what to do now?

"Argh!" she screeched, slamming her hand against the shower over and over as she fought her own treacherous body. Falling limp, she whispered, "Shower off."

The water stopped. She stepped out, grabbed a towel, and, walking out the door, jerked it over her wet skin. Coming to the bedroom door, she paused. He wasn't there. She stepped in and moved to the closet. Through the rectangular window, she saw him leaning on the stone and iron railings of the balcony, looking off over the distance.

She didn't think as she moved to join him. A narrow door on the side was cracked open and she ducked down to pass through. A rush came over her, not unlike that first morning waking in Kirill's home. There was something quite magical about the view, something that stirred her soul.

The cool air hit her skin, causing her to shiver. The balcony was high off the ground, jutting from the side of the palace. The dusky green-blue sky spread out before them, glistening beautifully over the distance. A majestic display of forest and mountains stretched along to the horizon, cradling a clear lake. Its glassy surface reflected the three suns. Trees lined earth like a pile of discarded emeralds. Their leaves crashed in a gentle symphony of nature.

Her eyes came around to Kirill's back. His body leaned over, supported on the rail. His long dark hair blew to the side, rolling in the wind. His perfect form called to her. He was more handsome to her than the surrounding landscape and she couldn't look away.

Ulyssa stepped forward, her bare feet solid on the stone floor. Her fingers whispered forward to touch his back, startling him to standing up. Hair blew over his strong features as he turned.

Brushing the silky locks off his cheek, she said, "Just ... let's call a truce."

He visibly stiffened and nodded once.

"Tell me you desire me." Ulyssa left her hand on his face, letting her fingers tangle in the silken strands of his hair.

"That much is more than obvious." His voice was low and the rich tone washed over her, making her hot for him despite the chill in the wind. Her nipples stained and hardened beneath the towel. The wind caught the edge of the material, lifting it aside to expose her thighs.

"Tell me what you want," she insisted.

"I want," Kirill hesitated. She was so lovely. He did want her. He wanted her more than he should and there was nothing he could do about it. Denial only made his longing worse. *I want you, Lyssa.* "I want to make love to you."

Ulyssa dropped the towel instead of answering. The wind caught it and carried it away like a bird. She darted forward and pressed her lips to his. A soft moan left them as she explored his mouth with her probing tongue.

Kirill's hands were everywhere at once, gliding over her flesh, cupping the soft globes of her backside, pulling her lower back to him so that he could rub the indention of his arousal into her heating body. It had been too long a wait. Every touch sent a shiver of molten desire through them.

Her fingers trailed over the hard muscles of his chest, running down to his belt. She pulled his waistband free.

The belt fell to the stone floor before sliding off in the wind to join the towel and neither of them noticed or cared that it was lost.

Ulyssa shoved her hand down his pants to grab his hard erection. She moaned into his mouth, pulling back to gasp for breath. Kirill's gasp of pleasure joined hers as she stroked his heavy length in her palm. Then, shoving his pants off his hips, she smiled as they pooled around his ankles.

Ulyssa had wanted to taste all of him since the first moment she'd laid eyes on him. Trailing kisses along his jaw, she nibbled and licked her way to his earlobe. With a gentle shove to his crotch, she backed him to the railing. She lifted her hand and boldly licked her palm as she met his dark gaze. Then, reaching down, she took hold of his arousal, letting it glide in her moist palm.

"Tell me you want this," she demanded of him. She stroked harder, longer. His hips jerked and his breathing deepened. She squeezed, causing him to cry out. "Tell me."

"I want this," he whispered, almost as if the admission caused him pain.

"*Mmmm*, see that wasn't so bad, was it my lord?" she murmured, darting her tongue to lick the seam of his parted lips. For a brief moment, he sucked her between his lips, moaning in delight.

Her hand left his arousal for his chest. She pulled his shirt, sliding the black material up to expose the hard planes of his body. She kissed one nipple and than another, sucking them both hard. Kirill groaned in instant appreciation.

Ulyssa moved along his skin, rubbing her flat palms around his back and across his sides, as she kissed a hot, wet trail down the center of his stomach to his navel. The shirt dropped as she did, hiding him from view once more. Her hands found the taut flesh of his firm backside as she slid onto her knees before him. Coming to his naked hips, she lightly bit at the skin beneath his navel.

"Lyssa," he gasped. His hands were in her wet hair, pushing and pulling as if he couldn't decide what he wanted from her.

Ulyssa drew her cheek along the pulsating length of his hard shaft, moving up from the base to his smooth rounded tip. Her fingers squeezed his backside as her tongue flicked over the head of him. A roar left his mouth. The muscles in his stomach tightened and flexed as he took hold of her head and thrust himself forward between the barrier of her teeth.

Kirill howled in delight as she sucked him into her mouth. The wet strands of her drying hair, whipped from about her shoulders, wrapping around his thighs. The back rail held him up as she worked her mouth along him. Looking down, he knew that seeing her mouth on his arousal was the most erotically charged scene he'd ever witnessed. Her hands grasped him as she controlled the movements of his hips. Seeing was too much, and Kirill tried to jerk her back before the orgasm hit him.

Ulyssa felt his body tightening with release the moment before his hands tried to pull her off. Her fingers gripped his flesh. She sucked harder, shoving him over the edge of his climactic release. His hands gave up their struggle as he came into her mouth, letting her have his hot essence. Only when the last of his trembles subsided did she pull off. Swallowing, she looked up at him through her lashes and moved to stand proudly before him.

"I am sorry," he said, breathing heavy. "I didn't mean to ... I didn't drink the nef since before we ... since before that first time and I--"

"Will not be drinking that wretched stuff again," Ulyssa said, suddenly realizing where all the Var got their rigid control. Whoever invented that drink should've been shot upon its conception.

"We drink it for you," he said, almost lost. "For women. So we don't ... aren't too untamed for them."

Ulyssa pressed her body to his and began to rub. Huskily, she murmured, "You're half animal, Kirill. Untamed is part of you nature. You shouldn't fight your nature, at least not in this, not with us."

Ulyssa found she meant the words. He had to hide so much of himself, suppress his longings, his dreams, his desires, for those of his people. How could she ask him to do the same for her?

His eyes flashed with heated promise as he looked down at her. She felt the almost instant rising of his body against her flesh. To her amazement, he was ready to go again.

"More," he growled, demandingly. It was as if a dam of control broke inside of him. "I want more."

"Good, cause I'm ready to give you more, my lord. Lots more." Ulyssa pulled back, liking the predatory glint to his dark gaze. His jaw lowered and a low crackle began in the back of his throat, as if he would pounce. Slowly, she moved to the rail and placed her elbows down on it, leaning over.

Kirill kicked his pants from his ankles and reached to touch the soft flesh of her offered backside. Almost in a trance, he came behind her. His fingers reached to touch her and he found she had not lied. Her body was wet, ready to take him in. The knowledge was more than he could take.

Kirill guided his shaft forward, teasing her opening with the tip as he parted her to accept him. Then, grabbing both hips, he delved forward. Another roar left him as he slid deep inside her tight body, seating himself to the hilt within her.

Ulyssa cried out in surprise. Kirill didn't stop. He moved his hips, pumping and rocking mindlessly against her. Their primal grunts of passion called out over the distance. The beautiful scene danced before her eyes. Distance spanned from her head to the ground as he pushed her over the side of the balcony rail. The danger of her position only made her heart beat faster in her chest.

"Oh, Kirill, baby, yes." Ulyssa felt tears stinging her cheeks and was glad the wind would dry them away before he saw. Never had she felt so desired, so wanted, as she did beneath the groping, untamed movements of his body. At her words, his hips thrust faster, deeper, harder into her core until he touched her deeper than any man ever had. The tension built like a rocket getting ready to blast into deep space. "Oh, there, there, oooh right there. Oh my ... *Kirill!*"

Ulyssa screamed as the most intense orgasm she'd ever felt racked her from head to toe. Her hot passage clamped down on him and he answered her call with one of his own. He came in long, hot waves inside her body. He stayed deep, letting his essence wash into her, marking her as his, laying claim. If not for Kirill's hold on her hips, she would have fallen off the edge and not cared.

Ulyssa slowly stood up, weakly falling back until she came flush to his chest. She panted for breath, frail and trembling. Kirill kissed her earlobe, sucking it between his teeth.

"More," he whispered. The word was marred by a growl.

Ulyssa's eyes shot round in surprise. "Kirill, I ... give me a second."

"More," he growled louder. Before she knew what was happening, she was swept up into his sturdy arms. His lips pressed into hers--passionate, strong, demanding--with a kiss that stole her very reason. When her lungs nearly exploded for want of air, he let up. She lay weak in his arms. Kirill grinned down at her, and repeated, softer, "More. I want more."

Ulyssa moaned lightly. Without breaking stride, Kirill swept her forward to the door, and into the bedroom. He placed her down on the bed, stood only long enough to undress completely, and then moved to crawl over her with stealthy grace. She giggled, loving the play of his muscles beneath tanned flesh as he came above her legs from the end of the bed.

"Kirill, maybe we--"

His roar cut her off. His hands pushed her legs open. And, before his lips met her center to wet it once more to him, he growled, "More."

* * * *

Ulyssa couldn't move from the bed. Her body was sore. Kirill's more turned out to be a lot, lot more. By the seventh time, she was almost ready to go and find some nef for him just to get him to give her a rest. By the eighth time, she was ready to force the nef down his throat. Luckily, nine seemed to be his limit and he finally let her rest.

His stamina was one thing, but her own surprised her. Just when she thought she couldn't go anymore, that her body would've surely been raw, he'd heat her back up to the point she was squirming and begging for him to finish it. And finish it he did, until she came so hard she thought the whole barbaric planet was falling apart.

Feeling a hand on her thigh, she looked over. Kirill had awakened in a playful mood. He grinned with meaning, as his hands skimmed higher beneath the covers. His fingers found a breast and he tweaked her nipple, rolling it lightly. It hadn't taken him long to discover how sensitive her breasts were and he used the knowledge to his full advantage.

"Mmmm," she moaned in weak protest. "No more, Kirill, no more."

"Are you sore?" he asked, concerned.

"Yes," she moaned. However, the way he played with her nipple was causing her to forget herself again.

With lightening speed, he tossed up the covers and slid over her. The covers settled back over his hips as he rubbed his erection to her swollen opening. "Then let me soothe you."

"I can see why your kind takes so many women," she murmured, jokingly. She reached up to brush aside his tangled hair so she could see his face.

Kirill tensed. A strange look passed over him. "You now wish for me to take another woman?"

"Do you want another woman?" she asked, carefully. Her heart stopped beating and she was sure she almost died in that moment.

"Right now, I want you," he whispered after a length, sweeping to kiss her lips. His body thrust forward and he made love to her slowly, savoring their shared passions. When they both met their release, he rose from the bed to retrieve a box from the closet. Setting in on the bed without comment, he left to take a shower.

Ulyssa sat up. She stared at the box for a long time before throwing aside the lid. Inside were a pair of cross lace pants and a shirt, similar in style to Kirill's but made to fit her. There was also a pair of boots. Her fingers shook as she looked at the gift and her heart skipped in little strange beats. Then, her eyes rolling in her head, she fell back-- fainting again.

Chapter Nine

Life at the Var palace mellowed into a steady routine for Ulyssa. In the mornings, she'd either exercise with Falke or take a stroll about the palace grounds, trying to learn her way around. Kirill taught her a few simple tricks to getting about and, if she ever got lost, all she had to do was ask Siren how to get home. She soon learned the computer could track her at any time, anywhere. So, if Kirill wanted her, all he had to do was ask. Unfortunately, it wasn't the same for her. Despite feeling like she was a prisoner he could keep tabs on, things were pretty good between them.

Sometimes Quinn would walk with her, if he happened upon her in the halls. She had a feeling Kirill sent him to keep her company, or more likely to keep an eye on her and probe her for personal information she'd never give. Quinn never let on and they enjoyed an easy friendship. She found the youngest brother to be good-natured, though he did have the same stubborn streak known to the Var men in his family. It was clear he, like his brothers, put no stock in love or finding a lifemate.

Mostly, she and Quinn would discuss the Var people and their great history--a history the Princes had lived through. She still couldn't get over that Kirill was old enough to be her grandparent. Even with their advanced medical knowledge, humans rarely lived past one hundred. But, when she was with Kirill, she didn't see his age and it didn't bother her as much as she thought it would.

From Quinn, she learned much about King Attor's rule. She couldn't be sure, but it was almost as if he wanted her to understand Kirill by teaching her of their past. Long ago, several hundred years before Kirill's birth, before Attor became King, things had been different for the Var people. It was a wild time, a time when the Var let emotions rule their head and their hearts. They acted rashly, on instinct.

For reasons completely unknown to Quinn, Attor changed the ways of the Var. He was a good King, one who worked hard for his people. He encouraged emotional detachment so that if one half-mate died, there could be others to take her place. It was Attor who encouraged men to have control, to drink nef, to prove their worth and dependability with emotionless detachment. He taught by example that to prove prowess in the bedroom showed prowess in the field of battle, until strength in one meant strength in the other. Many of the elders followed the old King's example and took many half-mates, though none so many as the King. Lifemates were a privilege of the lower classes--tradesmen, farmers, even hunters and lower ranked soldiers, all men who could ill afford to keep many mates on a planet so barren of women to begin with.

Attor's father had suffered the folly of mating with one woman--Kirill's grandmother. She died when Attor was born and his father never recovered enough to have more sons. Although he took women to his bed, he left Attor without any brothers to help lead the Var nation. So, when Attor took over the throne, he became reliant on a few noble houses--like Lord Myrddin's.

Ulyssa slowly reasoned that, even after he had his sons, Attor must have relied heavily upon the old house nobles and it was more than likely Lord Myrddin wasn't happy being out of power. With Kirill as the new King, the old house nobles were no longer needed, for Kirill had his brothers. It was a new era for the Var, and, in politics, the old rarely adjusted well to the new.

Ulyssa suspected there was more to Attor's story than Quinn knew, but she doubted she'd ever get a chance to find out for herself. The King's past had been buried with him and it was just as well. No matter how Quinn sung his father's praises as a King, the fact remained he made a lousy father, and as a man he was little better.

Ulyssa looked up from her place on the balcony, where she watched the subtle color shifting in the dusk-tinted sky as it marked the late evening hour. She doubted she'd ever get used to the brightness of the planet, but at least Kirill learned she liked the curtains drawn at night. It was a small thing, but one he never forgot to do, even without being asked.

Ulyssa sighed, moving back inside Kirill's home. She'd been on the planet for a little over a month and for the last couple of weeks things had been almost like a dream. She was getting too comfortable with him and knew it would be best if she could start to put some distance between them.

Though their bodies came together often, they didn't speak of anything intimate beyond the physical. An invisible wall was between them, keeping emotion from entering into their agreement. He didn't bend to her, didn't beg, but neither did she. They kept their truce and made no demands.

Kirill would leave during the day to be King. When he came home they had a silent understanding that outside concerns didn't come between them. All it took was one look, one touch of his hand, and she'd melt into his arms. Without the aid of nef, he was insatiable. It didn't matter, because so was she.

They spoke of nothing important and made love constantly--in the shower, on the couch, before the fireplace, the closet, the kitchen, the dining table. He'd even managed to get her back into the bathtub with him. Ulyssa smiled at the memory of her body riding over his soapy one, being caressed by water and his hands at the same time.

Their playfulness even overflowed to other parts of the castle, though always in private. When they were alone, he was affectionate, almost sweet. He smiled more. He laughed and joked. He kissed her freely, without thought or hesitation.

However, the few times they were seen in public, he'd ignore her as if she were but a servant waiting to do his bidding. His gaze would harden and he'd become detached, hardly looking at her. When they were again alone, those eyes would soften ever so slightly and he would pretend that nothing happened. Ulyssa hated to admit it, but the change in him hurt her deeply. It was almost as if he were ashamed of her.

A few times, when she first awoke in the mornings, she would catch Kirill watching her. There would be a strange look in his eyes, a look that had little to do with physical desire. In those moments, there was something more between them, something neither one of them cared to explore.

Ulyssa sighed. She didn't want to think about it now either. It was late and Kirill had yet to come home.

Deciding she didn't want to wait around for him, she grabbed a long coat from the closet and went to find what he was up to.

* * * *

"Kirill? Kirill, are you listening?"

"I'm sorry," Kirill answered, sitting up in his chair where he stared absently into the fireplace of the old council hall. He turned to look at his brothers. Reid had been speaking to him, but now a frown marred his face. Slowly, Kirill nodded his head for him to go on.

"I said," Reid continued, "that there have been signs of movement on the Northern borders. The men have found tracks."

"Draig?" Quinn asked from his place on the red carpet floor.

"Boots. It's too hard to be sure if they are ours or theirs, but I have not ordered anyone through the marshes." Reid's frown deepened. His narrowed eyes looked to Kirill, who was again drifting from the conversation.

Kirill sighed. He was tired of discussing the Draig. It's all they'd talked about since Attor's death. Right now, he wanted to just go home to Ulyssa.

"Lord Myrddin's men could have gone through with a hunting party," Falke allowed.

Kirill nodded. All Reid had said so far was merely speculation and hardly worth sending out the troops to investigate. Still, Reid knew the Outland better than anyone and if his gut said something was wrong, there could very well be something wrong.

"Ah, hell!" Reid growled. His eyes glinted with yellow as he glared at Kirill. Kirill blinked in surprise. "I'm your brother so I'm just going to say it. You need to get your head off that woman! She's affecting your duty to your kingdom. She's distracting you just as our father warned a woman would if you let them come too close."

"You speak out of turn, Reid," Kirill warned in low tones.

Reid stood to tower over the King. "Pulling your rank to silence me doesn't make it any less true. Lady Ulyssa occupies too much of your mind."

Kirill stiffened, before gracefully moving to his feet. He'd gone out of his way to make sure his affections for Ulyssa were not shown in public, even if there were times he wanted nothing more than to touch her, kiss her, pull her onto his lap.

Reid glared hotly at him. Falke rose, but his expression gave nothing away. Quinn sat up on the floor, but did not look directly at any of them. Aside from the crackling of fire, the old council hall was silent.

Very carefully, Kirill answered, "Ulyssa is a good lover, but nothing else to me. If my thoughts are occupied, they aren't with her. I thank you for your concern, brother, but it's not needed. I know my duty and I will do it."

Before Reid could speak, Kirill turned and stalked from the room. The King's expression was blank, but his body was stiff and jerked with his anger.

"Well done, Reid," Quinn muttered from the floor. "Very diplomatic of you."

"We are on the verge of war and you wish for diplomacy?" Reid asked.

"There is still time for peace," Quinn said. "If there will be war, let it come and I'll fight it. But do no wish for war and the death of the people you'd think to love. And don't condemn our brother for trying to find some sort of peace or happiness for us. Haven't enough lives been lost under our father?"

"We will not, cannot be considered weak," Falke stated.

"The Draig must wonder why we haven't attacked." Reid placed his hands on his hips.

"Let them wonder," Quinn put forth with a shrug.

"It could be perceived as weakness," Falke reasoned.

"Yes, and it could be perceived as strength." Quinn countered. "When the time for action comes, Kirill will act. I have faith in that."

"As do I," Reid admitted, reluctant. "But, already the rumors grow. He spends too much time with her. He already has her body, what more does he want?"

"You sound as if you are jealous," Quinn put forth softly.

"No, little brother, not jealous." Reid chuckled. "Never jealous of such things. I pity him."

"She is a mystery, that's true, but she's not ... lacking," Falke said. Quinn and Reid turned to him in surprise. Their mouths practically fell open at his words. Falke shrugged a big shoulder and again sat in the chair. "As you said, when the time comes for Kirill to act, he will act. There is no reason to dwell in the meantime."

* * * *

"Siren," Ulyssa said quietly. "Can you open the royal office?"

"Yes, my lady," the computer answered.

Ulyssa waited. The door stayed shut. Rolling her eyes, she stated, "Siren, open the royal office."

The door unlocked and she stepped in. The room was dark. She wandered in toward the desk.

"Siren, light the fire," Ulyssa said. The fire blazed to life. She looked around, expecting Kirill to be sleeping at his desk. She'd caught him there once before. "Siren, where's the King?"

"I'm sorry. That information is not available to level eight security," Siren answered.

Level eight? Ulyssa frowned. "Siren, what is level eight security?"

"Level eight is confinement to the castle, my lady, and limited privileges."

"Who is on level eight security in the palace?" Ulyssa slowly walked up to the desk, not really looking at it in her concentration to hear the computer's answer.

"I'm sorry, my lady, you're not authorized to access that information."

Ulyssa gritted her teeth together. She'd just have to ask in another way. "Is the harem women level eight security?"

"No, my lady," Siren answered.

Ulyssa relaxed. At least she was above the harem security level. That said something at least.

"Most of the harem is level six security, my lady."

Her smile fell. "Level six? Clarify please."

"Freedom to leave the palace, my lady, with limited castle privileges."

Ulyssa's fingers skimmed over the top of Kirill's desk, stopping to tap irately on a pile of folders. Under her breath, she whispered, "I'm on tighter security than Attor kept his women?"

"Yes, my lady," the computer answered, causing Ulyssa to grimace.

"What happens if I leave the palace, Siren? If I just walk out?"

"The guards will be alerted and you will be taken to the prison level and confined," Siren answered. "There you will await trial."

"Estimate how long until the guards find me, Siren, if I were to escape."

"Past record indicates the guards could track a human woman within ten minutes to two hours. Anything beyond two hours is highly unlikely."

Suddenly, Ulyssa frowned. Reaching down, she placed her finger on a piece of paper inside one of the folders and slowly dragged it out on the desk. The emblem in the corner caught her eye first. It was the symbol of the MAPH, *Medical Alliance for Planetary Health.* If not for that, she wouldn't have been able to tell it apart from the other documents.

"What--?" she whispered, before stopping to glance around. She kept her mouth shut, not wanting to trigger a silent alarm in Siren by saying a wrong word.

The MAPH was a cover for the Medical Mafia--a good cover the Agency had been trying to destroy for years. It was the whole reason she'd been sent to Qurilixen. It was her mission and she suddenly realized that it wasn't over. Doc Aleksander might be dead, but this was a document proving his dealings with the Var people.

Ulyssa gulped, looking around the empty chamber again, wondering if she was being recorded. She didn't pick the paper up from the desk as she again pretended to slap the flat stone top with her hand in a great show of frustration. Slowly, she rubbed the back of her neck, peeking down to see the paper.

She had learned enough of the Var language over the last month to make out that it was a trade agreement of some sort between the Var and the MAPH. She couldn't be one hundred percent sure what was going on, but she knew some of the medical ingredients listed on the document were illegal to transport off their native planets. If employed by the wrong person, it would be mass genocide. Ulyssa could only guess what race King Attor had wanted to erase from the history books with his little order of biological weaponry.

The paper was on Kirill's desk, so it was clear he knew about it. Did this mean he planned on going through with his father's plan? It would explain why he hadn't made a move against the Draig when everyone around him pushed for war. He could be biding his time until the Medical Mafia's shipment came. Without an antidote, the Draig wouldn't stand a chance. Depending on the form of the weapon, it would only take one drop into the water supply or one really strong gust of wind.

Ulyssa had seen picture of the devastation caused by biological warfare. The memory alone was enough to turn her stomach. Even if they Draig discovered what caused the plague, the antidote would never reach the planet on time.

"Lyssa?"

Ulyssa tensed to hear Kirill's voice. She swallowed nervously, before pasting an indifferent expression on her face. When she looked at him, his dark features, his piercing eyes, her heart fluttered. She didn't want to believe he was capable of such a monstrous act. But, in truth, she didn't really know him.

"Oh, hey," she answered, doing her best to act cool. Inside she shook terribly. She hugged the long coat to her naked body. She had meant to surprise him in his office, but suddenly didn't feel like playing.

"What are you doing here?" he asked.

"I ... I was looking for you," Ulyssa answered softly. She had to get that paper. Leaning back, she let the bottom of the coat fall open to reveal her boots. Instantly, his eyes turned down before sweeping back up to hers. To her surprise, he hardened against her. A wave of panic washed over her. Had Siren seen what she was doing? Had the accursed computer told him about it? Was that why he was suddenly there?

"Why do you have me on level eight?" she demanded with a frown, hoping to cover her tracks.

"It was before I knew you," he answered with a shrug. "I couldn't allow you to leave the palace."

"Oh," Ulyssa answered, biting her lip.

"Why were you looking for me? Did you need something?" His tone matched the hard look in his eyes.

Ulyssa decided her best course of action was to distract him in the only way she could think of. But, even as she feared him, her body became excited by the game. Besides, he didn't know who she really was--whom she worked for.

With a little hop, she sat on the desk and moved to lean back on her arms. The coat fell open revealing her naked body as she crossed her legs. High boots covered her calves and knees, working their way up to her thighs. Her hand hit the stack of folders and they went spiraling to the ground. "Oh, oops!"

Kirill watched Ulyssa wiggle seductively on his desk. The coat slipped off her shoulders, baring her more. Soft orange firelight alighted on her skin, caressing her in ways he longed to, and glinted off the shiny surface of the boots. His body lurched. Sacred Cats! She was beautiful and bold. Only Ulyssa would dare to enter the King's royal office wearing such vixen attire.

He hadn't been expecting to see her. In fact, he was coming back to the royal office to think about what Reid had said. He was preoccupied with her, but did it mean anything?

Then, he found her in his office, looking at his desk. He couldn't help the suspicions that leapt inside him at the discovery. Always, when she spoke, he had the feeling she hid many things from him. He had yet to discover what that might be. A person merely shipwrecked, waiting for a ride, wouldn't have the need to keep so many secrets. Where was the rest of the crew she was with? It was unlikely she'd be manning her own craft in deep space. What was she doing near Qurilixen space? It's not like they were in a high trafficked area. They were on the outer edge of the Y quadrant--disregarded as a primitive race. It's how the Var and Draig preferred it. It was one of the few things they had agreed upon in the past.

Kirill tilted his head to the side, wondering if she'd mind dropping the coat completely so he could have a better look. Passion filled his loins, making him ache with need. He wanted her, always wanted her. Reid was right, she occupied too many of his hours. He thought of possessing her, possessing more than just her temptress body. He wanted to possess her mind, her soul, perhaps even her heart. He wanted to know who she was. He wanted to know what she was really doing on his planet, in the Var palace, in his bed. He wanted to know if he meant anything to her, beyond a means to find sexual release.

Ulyssa watched a subtle shift of emotions cross his dark features--anger, confusion, passion. The wave of his feeling tried to invade her body but she blocked him from her. Long black hair picked up firelight as it glided handsomely over his shoulders to blend with the black of his tunic shirt. His body was rigid with power. His gaze flickered with gold.

He was dangerous and suddenly she feared him. Graphic images of death and destruction that the Agency had shown her flickered in her mind. She didn't want to believe that Kirill could be a madman about to wipe out an entire race of people without discrimination. She didn't want to believe he'd be so cruel, so heartless. But, the fact was, she knew what sort of man Attor had been. It was likely he'd raised his son to be the same way--ruthless, hateful, vengeful, deadly, and most of all deceitful.

The first lesson of Ulyssa's training had been to trust no one but yourself when out on an assignment. Hate it as she did, Kirill was her new assignment. She didn't need to talk to headquarters to confirm it. She knew her duty. If Kirill was somehow in league with the Medical Mafia, she needed to know about it. If he were involved, she'd have to take him down--regardless of how she felt about him. It would seem her little vacation was over.

Letting an impish smile cross her features, Ulyssa felt something inside her change. Her heart hardened, severing all feelings until she was but a shell. She forced herself to see him as a mission, not a man. It was the only way she could go through with her job.

Kirill took a step forward and hesitated. His shifting eyes studied her. "There's something different about you."

"Mm," she moaned lightly, ignoring his words. Her hands lifted to the bun in her hair. Pulling the red-blonde locks loose, she shook them out, letting the curls pour around her shoulders. Giving him a feminine pout, she murmured, "I made a mess. Let me just get that, my lord."

Ulyssa hopped down from the desk. Not bothering to close the front of the coat, she took a step for him before abruptly turning around. She thrust her leg to the side, showing a boot as she leaned over to pick up a file. Stopping in mid-bend, her backside thrust up in the air, she ran her fingers down over the vinyl-like material. With a flip of her hair, she looked at him through half-lidded eyes and licked her mouth.

Kirill swallowed visibly. His hands clenched into fists at his sides. Grabbing a file, she set it on his desk. Then, cocking her hip to the other side, she repeated the same procedure again, this time stopping to suck her finger into her mouth as she looked at him. He answered the look with a low growl sounding the back of his throat. Still he didn't move as she put the second folder on the desk. Reaching for the last of her mess, she spread her legs wide and bent straight over. Hidden within the folds of the thin coat, she grabbed the trade agreement and shoved it into the sleeve.

She tensed slightly as Kirill stepped up behind her. He threw the coat off to the side to expose her backside and grasped her hips firmly, jerking her back against his arousal. A groan left him as he rubbed his naked shaft along the cleft of her butt. That first shock of flesh against hot flesh reverberated through them, joining them in a way their bodies never could. She felt him inside her, in her mind, trying to connect. Ulyssa hid her thoughts, concentrating on the way he made her feel.

She was caught off balance by the position, but his strong hold kept her steady. His arousal was hot, instantly sparking flashes of desire from where it touched her. Moisture pooled between her thighs, making her dizzy. Slowly, she stood back up, letting her body flex, caressing and sliding against his shaft. She tossed her hair over their shoulders and nestled back into his chest. His face instantly turned, burying in the soft locks to take a deep breath.

"I enjoy your smell," he murmured. "Berries and cream."

The folder slid from her fingers and crashed onto the floor, scattering papers everywhere. Kirill chuckled.

"Pick them up," he demanded hoarsely.

Ulyssa bent over grabbed the nearest paper, not bothering with the rest of them. It crumpled in her hand as she balled it into a fist. Her eyes rolled pleasurably in her head as heat built inside her, spreading like wildfire from his touch. Kirill rubbed himself along her body, groaning in masculine pleasure.

"Ahh," he panted. "On the desk."

Ulyssa stood and reached to put the paper on top of the pile. Everything but the feel of him, the sound of his voice, fell from her mind. Before she could let go, Kirill spun her around to face him.

"No, you," he growled, gasping for breath. "I want you on the desk."

He didn't give her a chance to comply, as he lifted her up and set her on the hard, flat surface. He'd taken his pants off, but still wore the shirt. With a growl, he shrugged it off and threw it aside.

Kirill's eyes glowed with yellow promise. A slow, seductive grin curled onto his features. "Siren, record us. Private file, King only access."

"Yes, my lord," the computer answered.

Ulyssa gasped and moved to cover herself with the coat. She heard movement in the ceiling as four small camera lens came down and turned to the desk. She couldn't let the computer record her!

"Relax," he whispered. His eyes were heated with golden-green promise. "I want us to watch later."

Ulyssa swallowed, as she felt something she didn't recognize at first. It was nervousness. The idea thrilled her more than she thought it would and, against her better judgment, she let the coat go. It fell open once more.

Kirill took himself in hand as he looked her over, stroking his long fingers over his hard length. Then going right for her, he pulled her to the edge, and plunged his ready shaft into her moist heat. His body glided in her juices as he thrust to the hilt. Ulyssa gasped at the sudden onslaught as he filled her. Each time they came together, it was like a feeling of shock overcame her and she was amazed her body still needed to stretch to fit him.

Kirill held still for a brief moment letting her adjust. Her legs dangled off the side of the desk. She braced herself with her hands as he moved. He withdrew only to thrust hard in long even jabs, pushing into her hot center.

His hand slid forward over her flesh to roll a nipple, pinching it into a hard bud. Ulyssa fell back, running her fingers to her own breasts to help him. Sensations exploded from the touch as her fingers mingled with his. Kirill grunted in primitive approval.

His hand moved back to control her, as he pumped in gracefully hard thrusts of his hips. Her body clenched around his, her passage tightening around him as he rode her to the edge of her desires. Their pants and moan mingled in the royal office, growing louder with each torturous plunge of his shaft inside her.

Suddenly, Ulyssa screamed. Her body tensed on the desk, arching beautifully before him as the tremors of release took over her. Kirill grunted in masculine approval and domination. Her passage tightened almost painfully around him, forcing the seed from his body as his orgasm took him in several hard jerks. A cry ripped from his throat.

In the aftermath, Ulyssa mumbled incoherently.

Kirill froze, leaning forward to better hear her.

"What?" he demanded, a little harsh, torn by his duty and his feelings.

Ulyssa blinked as he withdrew from her. Breathless, she answered, "What? I didn't say anything."

"Mmm." Softening a little, he let his hand lift to briefly touch her cheek, before he turned to grab his shirt. "Siren, stop recording."

Ulyssa pulled the coat up over her arms, feeling inside the sleeve for the paper. A sense of guilt overwhelmed her at what she was doing. When Kirill touched her, she forgot everything but him. She knew her duty, what she must do, but for the first time she was conflicted over her obvious choice.

Lacing his pants along his hips, Kirill turned to her. He sighed, looking very tired. "Come, Lyssa, let's go home."

Chapter Ten

"Here."

Ulyssa looked up from the fireplace, where she'd been staring at for hours. She was in such deep thought that she didn't hear Kirill come home. Looking at him, she became lost in his dark eyes. She blinked, not really hearing what he had said. A spark ignited in her, torturing her even more. For a moment, she wished she wasn't an agent and he wasn't a King she suspected of horrific intent. What would happen if he was just an ordinary space pilot and she a ... a whatever it was normal women did? What would happen if duty wasn't between them?

Something changed between them that night they walked back from the office. Neither of them spoke. They didn't fight, didn't say anything important as they made their way back to Kirill's home. It was just as if a wall was built between them, cementing them apart. After finding the document, she'd purposefully distanced herself from him, but she had a strange feeling he was doing the same with her. They'd not come together since.

As he didn't move, she finally looked down to his offered hand. In it was her communicator. Her heart fluttered lightly. She was almost afraid to touch it, as if holding it would connect back to her world, tearing her further away from him. The urge to confess became strong. She opened her mouth, but no words would come from her.

"When we made this deal," Kirill said softly, "I promised to find it. It was broken or you'd have gotten it back sooner. It seems some of the guards scavenged it for parts to fix their music relayer."

Ulyssa stiffly nodded and reached to snatch it from his fingers before she lost her nerve. "Uh, thanks."

"They said you had a gun, too." Kirill looked at her expectantly and she knew he wanted her to explain.

"Oh, yeah," she shrugged, forcing indifference. She'd really like to have the weapon back, but didn't dare push the issue. "My ... uncle gave it to me. I don't really like using it."

Kirill nodded. When she didn't move to turn the communicator on, he frowned. "Don't you think you should call your ride and let them know you're all right?"

"I ... yeah, sure." Ulyssa swallowed nervously. She switched the unit on, hoping it would malfunction like it did in the forest. To her dismay, it lit right up. She looked at Kirill. He eyed her curiously and made no move to leave. She tried to smile and stood from the couch. Walking around the living room, she pressed the button and paced.

"Hello?" a sweet elderly voice asked from the communicator.

"Hey, grandma," Ulyssa hesitated. She glanced at Kirill. He hadn't moved. His arms crossed over his chest and his rigid features gave nothing away. "Can I speak to Uncle Frank?"

"What?" the elderly voice called, nearly screeching. "I can't hear you, speak up!"

"Grandma, get Uncle Frank!" Ulyssa stated, raising her voice. "It's your granddaughter, Ulyssa!"

"Oh, hold on, I'll get Frank. I can't hear you," said the elderly voice, before it yelled, "Franklin!"

Ulyssa knew it was a computer generated cover voice and that an Agency operator really spoke. Careful to keep her finger on the button so the operator could hear her answer his code, she again glanced at Kirill. Ulyssa bit her lip, more for having to lie to him than for her little play she was about to perform, and explained softly, "She's a little senile and deaf and sometimes forgets who I am. My uncle Frank takes care of her in his apartment. I don't know why he lets her answer the phone."

Kirill nodded once in understanding, but didn't move. She turned her back on him and stood, staring at the kitchen doorway. Her foot tapped lightly.

"Uh, ye-hello," Franklin's authoritative voice drawled. "Frank here, who's this?"

"Uncle Frank? Hey, it's me. Ulyssa."

"Ulyssa?" Franklin repeated, sounding warm and affectionate and not quite himself. "Is everything all right? We've been trying to contact you. We've been worried sick!"

Franklin and the Agency had some new information for her.

"My communicator was broken, but I'm fine. Listen, about that ride you're sending. There has been a small change in coordinates. I'm still shipwrecked but found a place to stay. I'm typing them in now." As Ulyssa let Franklin know she was on the same planet, she looked at Kirill expectantly. He softly gave her the coordinates and she typed them into the communicator, adding the word *active* so he would know she was undercover and on to something. "You got it?"

"Yeah," Franklin answered, concerned. "Where is this?"

"It's a palace. The King was nice enough to let me stay while I await rescue," Ulyssa said. Kirill's mouth twitched and she could just imagine what he was thinking. She blushed and turned her back to him once more. There was no way she was telling Franklin about *that* part of the arrangement! He didn't have to know everything. Wanting to get the farce over with, she hugged an arm over her waist and asked, "How is everyone? I miss you guys."

What you got for me?

"Your Aunt Milly's planting roses. She went to that supplier you recommended but they were all out of the thorny breeds--what did you call them again?"

"The Alexis?" she asked very carefully.

"That's the one!" Franklin confirmed. "Milly was sorely disappointed. She wants you to try and find them before you come back. We hate to ask, but she has that dissertation coming up."

Doc Aleksander, Ulyssa thought. Her mission wasn't over.

Ulyssa bit her lip. Franklin wanted to know what she was on to and it sounded like he had something for her. Thorns. That could only mean that the poisonous darts hadn't been recovered by the other team. Doc must have brought the poison with him when he came down to Qurilixen. But why would he need the revenge darts? What purpose would Attor have in a dart that made a woman allergic to her husband's or lover's touch? But, if the darts were on the planet like Franklin obviously suspected, then....

Oh, God, no!

With a sudden clamp of fear squeezing her heart, Ulyssa wondered if the biological weapons were already on the planet, too. She swallowed nervously and began to sweat. She needed to focus, to concentrate. If Nadja Aleksander, Doc's daughter, ran away from him and joined Galaxy Brides, it was quite possible he came to the planet simply to retrieve her. It was a long shot, but it made sense. Nadja marrying a Draig Prince had seemed a little strange, but she'd been too preoccupied with the woman's father to think anything about it.

The Agency couldn't figure out why Doc had bothered to come so far into the Y quadrant, but assumed it was for the ore in the Qurilixen mine. The ore was a great power source for long-voyaging starships and intelligence deduced he was about to plan something big that required long distance travel. That's why she was sent to stop him-- before they lost track of him over the galaxies. But, what if they were wrong? What if Doc only came to retrieve his runaway daughter and meeting Attor was just a happy little side job for him?

The Agency had no clue about the deal going on down here. She had hoped against hope that their intelligence would be aware of the shipment, especially since Franklin would've had Doc's old ship stopped and inspected by undercover agents posing as spaceport authorities. Any ships coming her way would have been scanned and the biological material picked up on the Agency's sensors. But what if they hadn't found anything because the drop off had already been made? And how could she relay such a message to him?

"I'll try my best," Ulyssa said in response to looking for the darts. A few missing revenge darts were the least of their problems. She'd carried the hope that it wasn't as bad as she thought. But, speaking to Franklin, knowing he'd have done his job, she wasn't so sure. Now it was up to her.

What if the biological plague couldn't be contained? What if the Draig panicked and an infected pilot took off for deep space to look for a cure or just to escape the planet's fate? He could go anywhere. The plague could spread beyond Qurilixen to other spaceports.

She was no scientist. All she knew was that she'd been forced to memorize their names in case she ever ran across them. Her department didn't handle this sort of thing. She wasn't trained for this, not really. She had no way of knowing what the ingredients on the list could do or what they even looked like. She could be looking for a small vile or a huge crate. Short of naming them out loud over the communicator, she had no real way of telling Franklin what she was up against.

"Uncle Frank, hold on a second." Ulyssa turned. She glanced at Kirill. He hadn't moved. His face was strangely passionless. "Kirill, do you mind if I have a moment alone?"

She turned, thinking he'd allow her at least that. He didn't move. Instead, he asked, "Why? Do you have something to hide?"

Ulyssa glanced at him. She swallowed nervously. "I ... I just want some privacy, that's all. You know, family stuff."

"What are you trying to keep from me?" Kirill looked suspicious. She swallowed. She saw his nostrils flare slightly. His eyes filtered gold in their dark depths. Did he suspect her? Did he notice the paper she'd taken was gone? She forced her mind to be blank of conscious thought, afraid he might actually try to probe into her thoughts. She'd felt him in her before and suspected the Var might be mildly telepathic under the right circumstances.

A heavy sigh came from Franklin. The communicator crackled. If she didn't hurry up, she'd lose contact.

"Franklin, are you there?" Ulyssa asked, keeping her eye on Kirill.

"Ulyssa? You'd better hurry. We've got a pretty bad flux coming." Franklin paused and she knew he was worried. "I'm about to lose contact."

Kirill hadn't moved. He was waiting for an answer.

Ulyssa took a deep breath. "Uncle Frank. I'm engaged."

Kirill's face paled. A wave of pain crossed his features. The look stabbed at her heart, but also gave her a dim sense of hope.

"What?!" Franklin's voice lost all softness.

"It's a contracted marriage," Ulyssa rushed, turning her back. She couldn't bear to see Kirill's hurt expression. Her throat worked violently. It didn't matter. She had to let Franklin know what was going on and a bombshell like that was just the only way to do it--the only way she could think of. "I haven't met him, but he's a scientist--a biologist--on Ranoz."

There. All the clues should be in that statement. There was a slight pause and Ulyssa knew Franklin was putting it all together. Contract, unknown location, biological, Ranoz. It didn't take him long.

"You ... you're sure?" Franklin asked. "I mean, it's what you want?"

"Yep, contracts as good as signed." Ulyssa paused. She glanced at Kirill. His face was red with anger. "All that's left is the final ... transporting of the bride."

Okay, she thought, *so that last statement was weak. But, Kirill doesn't seem to be paying attention.*

"All right, kid," Franklin mumbled. She could tell by his tone he was distracted with what she'd told him. Saying, for the sake of eavesdroppers, he added, "If that's what you really want, I'm happy for you. I'll relay this new pick up information to the ship. Last I heard they were ahead of schedule. They should be there in about three weeks if not sooner."

"Thanks Frank. Can't wait to be home."

"Yeah, can't wait to have you back safe and sound." There was a pause, and then Franklin added, "Oh, and Ulyssa?"

"Yeah?"

"Happy birthday."

A small, soundless laugh left her. Franklin was the only one who ever remembered.

"Bye, Frank."

"Bye, kid."

Ulyssa turned off the communicator. She waited, unmoving, too afraid to look at Kirill.

Kirill scowled at Ulyssa's back, barely hearing the last of her words as she ended her communication. He felt like she'd kicked him in the gut. She was engaged! No matter that the man was a stranger to her. Why hadn't she told him? Was that the big secret she'd been keeping from him?

Something strange nagged at his brain about the conversation. It was something in her tone, a vibration he picked up on with his sensitive hearing. He sniffed the air, smelling her, pushing past the unique perfume of her body to dig deeper into what was happening. The jealousy left him and he smiled grimly. She was lying.

He didn't know what she was up to, but she definitely wasn't getting married. The grip over his heart released a fraction and he could again breathe. Keeping his voice stern, he ordered, "Come here."

"What?" Ulyssa's wide blue eyes turned to stare at him. Her lips trembled and she sucked it between her teeth to stop it.

"Come," he beckoned. "I want you to come to me."

"But," she frowned. "Didn't you hear what I just said? Aren't you?"

"What? Angry that you are engaged?" he questioned. He forced a light tone to his words as he shrugged. His dark gaze was steady as he looked directly at her. "Why should I be? I don't know the man. You obviously feel no loyalty to him for you have been with me."

"But--you're not...?" Her features fell. Her eyes moved to the floor, but not before roaming down his graceful body. She turned her back on him so he couldn't see the sudden tears in her eyes, the pain crushing her from the inside. He wasn't jealous at all. He didn't care. He didn't care. Nothing between them mattered to him. She was just a diversion. She was ... Ulyssa's heart stopped. She was a King's whore.

"Lyssa," he began. "I would remind you that you promised to stay three months in my home. Just because your ride comes early, doesn't mean you can get out of our bargain."

Ulyssa's stomach lurched. She didn't hear him over the strange buzzing in her ears. Her hand flew to her mouth and she ran for the bathroom. Seeing the toilet, she fell to her knees and threw up into the stone bowl.

Kirill rushed in behind her, helpless as he watched. Worry strained his brow. His hand reached to touch her but he held back, unsure how to give her comfort, unsure if it would be welcome. He knew she lied, but he didn't know why. It might just have been a way to let him know she wasn't interested. Had too many of his feelings shown the last time they were together in the office? He'd been trying hard to fight it. He'd been trying to let her go. Was the lie her way of telling him she didn't want him? Slowly, he took a step back. But he couldn't bring himself to leave--not until he knew she was all right.

"Lyssa?" he asked, the word a mere whisper.

"Don't," she mumbled, gasping for breath as the sickness subsided. Her heart couldn't take being near him at the moment. She choked back tears under the guise of panting. Her words a trembling whisper, she said, "Don't watch this. Just ... go away. I'll be fine. Humans get this stomach flu sometimes. It'll pass, but it's contagious. Just go away, my lord. I don't want you to get sick. I don't know how your body will react to this sickness. I know what I need and I can take care of myself."

"Are you sure? I can send a medic," he offered. His voice was tight, strained with worry but she didn't notice. She was too miserable.

"Yeah, I'm sure," she answered, reaching to pull the cord to flush so she didn't have to look at the vomit.

"How ... where does it come from?" Kirill was still loath to leave her.

"It just does. I haven't been eating right. I've been ... preoccupied. My body just needs to reboot." Ulyssa felt a wave of nausea coming to her again. Hearing his voice was pure hell. She needed him to go. Waving weakly behind her, she ordered, "Go. Get out! I don't want you watching me."

"Siren," Kirill said, so Ulyssa could hear him.

"Yes, my lord," the computer answered.

"If Lyssa has need of me, she has permission to summon me to her or to come find me."

"Yes, my lord," Siren said.

"I won't need you," Ulyssa mumbled bitterly. She pushed to her feet. Kirill watched her stumble across his home. She didn't even look at him. "All I need is sleep. You'd better get out of here. This can get pretty ugly."

Ulyssa knew she was lying. She wasn't sick with the flu, but she desperately wanted to lie down and wallow in self-pity. She wanted to curl into a little ball and sleep, to forget her assignment, to forget the biological weapons and the Medical Mafia, but most of all she wanted to forget King Kirill.

* * * *

"Siren, monitor Lyssa's life functions. Alert me if there is danger to her." Kirill said once he was out of the house. It was almost time to dine and he decided to make an appearance in the banquet hall. He'd been spending his evening meals with Ulyssa and he knew that was one source of the rumors about his over-attentiveness to his mistress. He was about due for a public appearance and now would be as good a time as any. It wasn't like he could go back home.

The banquet hall was filled and Kirill stopped to make small talk with the soldiers as he worked his way to the head table. Reid, Quinn, and Falke were already seated when he arrived and they nodded to him in greeting. Before he even made it to his seat, servants brought out a plate of food and a goblet of wine for him.

Kirill took his seat amongst his brothers. As he picked up his goblet, a hush fell over the hall. Kirill looked up. Taura was waving for silence. Linzi stood next to her. Slowly, the two women came forward.

"My King," Taura said, with a very dignified curtsey. She was a tall, stately woman with long willowy limbs--very characteristic of her Roane heritage. Her gown of gold shimmered as she walked. Her long, golden brown hair shone in waves down her back, mimicked by the hazel-gold of her almond shaped eyes. She was a beautiful woman and all could instantly see why Attor had chosen her as his first half-mate.

"Lady Taura, you grace us with your presence," Kirill answered, honoring her. They all teased Falke about his mother, but the truth was growing up she had been a mother to them all--especially when their own birth mothers had died.

"My King, Linzi has served her month in exile. I bring her before you now seeking absolution from her misconduct." Taura motioned to the dark temptress at her side. Linzi's gaze shyly met the Kings before turning to the floor.

"Granted," Kirill answered. He knew that her exile wasn't her fault. Neither one of them had any way of knowing that Ulyssa proclaimed herself his woman. He stood and motioned to his side. "Please, join the table so all can see that you are absolved."

"Thank you, my King," Linzi curtseyed. Taura led her around the table. Servants came forward to move the Princes' plates over to make room. Taura sat between Kirill and Falke. Linzi took her place at Kirill's other side next to Quinn. She shot the King a small smile and said nothing as a plate of food was set before her. She ate in silence.

Kirill studied Linzi from the corner of his eye. She was a beautiful woman, but he found he wasn't interested. Turning back, he ate, ignoring the women as he thought of Ulyssa in his home, alone and sick. More than anything, he wanted to go back to comfort her.

* * * *

Ulyssa cried herself to sleep, not the wretched sobs she felt inside, but the silent unmoving tears of someone who locked their feelings within. When she awoke, the nausea of a broken heart was gone, but a passionless sense of duty replaced it leaving her numb.

She had no future with Kirill. She'd known it from the beginning. It was her fault for allowing herself to get so comfortable in his home. His family--something she'd never had--had drawn her in. Sure, they were only brothers, but they had taken to her--Falke by training her, Quinn by their walks and conversations, and Reid by his warm home and shared memories of the Var Princes' childhood.

Her memories were of school and the orphanage. Her childhood was a cot in the middle of a long hall, surrounded by the cots of other orphaned children. Her first happy memory was that proud day she finally got her own room at the Agency and didn't have to share it with a hundred other children, or when she got to take a particle bath and change in privacy. Her childhood didn't allow for modesty, for a sense of belonging. She had been a number-- child 71577.

At the Agency, she'd been given a sense of purpose. It was a job in which her self-reliance came in handy. She was a survivor. That's what her folder said. Ulyssa Payne, survivor. She still wasn't sure what that meant, except that she was tough and could get through anything. With the Agency she got to travel. She got to make a difference. She didn't have to share anything. The only drawback was she was still a number--Agent 596.

"I can get through anything," Ulyssa said to herself, pushing from the bed with renewed purpose. "And I can get through this. I *will* get through this. It's just another assignment. Another day, another space credit in my bank account."

She stalked to the closet to change. Sliding on her pants and shirt, she went to the bathroom to clean her teeth with the handheld mouth sanitizer. Next, she pulled her hair back into a bun to get it out of her face. Satisfied that she looked ready to work, she said, "Siren, tell me where to find King Kirill."

* * * *

Ulyssa followed Siren's directions through the maze halls until she heard the loud murmur of a crowd. It only took a second for her to realize the hall was gathered together to dine. The clink of utensils on plates was unmistakable. Ulyssa slowed as she neared the opened hall doors. She'd never been to this part of the castle. Slowly, she came to the narrow slit that edged along the side, between the door and wall, where she could see into the hall without being seen.

Looking in over the banquet hall of soldiers, she craned her neck searching for Kirill. It didn't take her long to find him at the seat of honor at the head table. She froze, her breath sticking in her throat. Unable to move, she saw Kirill next to the dark woman, Linzi. His rich laughter rang over the hall at something she said, pouring down over Ulyssa like a rain cloud to further dampen her soul.

Ulyssa's lips trembled. She imagined there'd be invitation in Kirill's dark eyes when he gazed at the woman--the way he looked when he wanted her. Kirill had never taken her to this hall. He'd never even asked if she'd like to go and here he was sitting and laughing with another woman for all to see. It was too much. Breathing heavily, she covered her mouth and forced down a wave of nausea. In public he always acted ashamed of her, like she was a humiliation.

Ulyssa looked down at her body and for the first time she felt the oppression of feminine doubt. Was she so misshapen? Was she ... ugly? Fat? Frowning, she poked at the slight roundness her stomach. She had been lax in her training, but she hadn't necessarily been eating more. There wasn't so big a change as to make a difference in her overall appearance. Maybe it was her hair. Kirill often started at it. Perhaps it was an odd color for their kind. Maybe he thought it was ugly.

Hearing footsteps, she backtracked and slipped into a little inlet to hide. Two guards walked by, but she was too preoccupied to hear what they said. Then, as she watched, one turned to the wall and pressed his fingers to the circular pattern. Automatically, her eyes memorized the sequence. The wall opened and the guard pressed his hand to the screen that showed, not stopping in his conversation.

Vaguely, she heard Siren's voice say, "Trillon, off duty."

The guards kept talking as they walked away, one mentioning he was going home. The wall closed. Looking around, Ulyssa snuck forward and pressed the same sequence. The wall shifted and opened. She glanced around before reaching in to the computer. She was familiar with the system. It was an older mainframe, but one she could easily hack if she had the right codes. Typing with a fury, she skirted around the computer's basic security protocols, using the programmer's back door. Then, finding her name on a security list, she simply deleted it. Removing her hand as she heard more footsteps, she ran back to her inlet. The computer wall didn't close.

She held her breath and watched as a guard walked by, heading in the same direction as the others. He stopped and glanced around when he saw the open wall. Then, cursing his fellow Var for their laziness, he reached in and pressed a button. The wall slid shut and he moved on.

Ulyssa relaxed. She clung to the numbness she awoke with. Telling herself it was a good thing she'd seen Kirill and Linzi together, she burned the image in her mind. It would keep her strong. Taking a deep breath, and hoping the reprogramming worked, she jogged down the hall in the same direction as the guards. After a minute of searching, she got lucky and found the front entrance to the palace.

Being as Siren has sensors within the palace, there were no guards at the front entrance. Taking a deep breath, she walked through the gate. No alarm sounded. She was free.

The Var city outside the palace was a bustling maze of earthen streets and large rectangular home, whose walls and foundation were constructed of fired bricks held together by mortar. Many of the homes were two stories high with flat roofs. The grand design indicated that most of the Var population prospered.

Ulyssa saw a few people walking along the top of their houses. For the most part, they didn't even glance in her direction as she passed. There weren't many windows that she could see, but that served to her advantage as she slipped further away from the palace.

A few of the homes had a courtyard where she could hear the sound of young boys playing. Clay pots set outside doorsteps, some with flowers and other native plants. The streets were clean and orderly. Beautiful woven rugs hung outside in the sun, drying on lines. There was less intricate tile work than inside the palace, but the city was lovely nonetheless.

Thinking of the Var palace, Ulyssa glanced back over her shoulder and gasped. It stood tall against the blue-green sky. Square turrets reached high into the heavens, commanding the heavens over the city. It was magnificent. Her gaze automatically roamed, trying to detect which part would have been Kirill's home. Realizing what she was doing, she stiffened, turned her back, and didn't look at it again.

No one stopped her as she made her journey north, though she did get a few curious glances. She knew the Draig were to the north of the Var. If she were going to have any chance of finding the biological weapons, it would be with Princess Nadja's help. With a plan forming in her brain, Ulyssa reached the forest, amazed that she actually escaped so easily.

Chapter Eleven

Kirill looked at Falke, his dark eyes weary, before turning to go to the balcony wall. They were alone in the royal office. Pushing a button, the wall slid to the side to show the surrounding countryside. He took a deep breath, as his gaze automatically slid over the distance searching for his runaway mistress.

"I take it there is no news of her?" Kirill asked solemnly. He knew the answer. He'd read it in Falke's hard face. Ulyssa was definitely gone. She'd left him without a word. If not for Linzi explaining what the human flu was to him, he'd have thought something horrific happened to her--like she turned to dust. Though thoroughly unpleasant, the flu didn't sound as tragic as Ulyssa made it out to be.

"Yes, my lord," Falke responded.

"Her information's been wiped from the computer security. I've reloaded her DNA, but she's not in the palace." Kirill turned. His red-rimmed eyes dipped and for a moment Falke saw the rawness of his pain. He'd not slept the night before, hadn't stopped pacing and searching since the moment he realized she had left him.

He'd stayed in the banquet hall a long time, making a great show of laughing and talking to Linzi and Taura. Musicians had been called to play. Wine had been poured in abundance while they celebrated nothing in particular. Kirill enjoyed his home and his people, but when he'd looked to his side, he didn't enjoy the fact that Ulyssa wasn't by him enjoying it as well.

He'd gone back home late in the evening to discover her missing. At first he thought she played a game. Then, when he didn't find her hiding from him, he'd asked Siren to locate her. A dull ache had settled in his chest, making him feel weak and helpless. It had yet to leave him. By the time they discovered the computer had been tampered with, several hours had passed since her possible escape.

"Did ... she say anything to you?" Kirill asked his brother. He knew she'd grown fond of Falke--though he was sure he didn't know what caused such an odd friendship. Falke was hardly a man people took lightly.

Falke's expression softened, revealing he knew how hard it was for the proud King to ask such a question. Ever one to take charge, he said, "Let us gather our intelligence. What happened yesterday?"

"I gave her communicator back to her. She called her Uncle Frank." Kirill answered. He quickly relayed the entire conversation, knowing Falke could be trusted. He left out his own reactions to her words, except to say, "I could sense she was lying about the engagement."

"It's code," Falke stated flatly. His lips pulled into a hard line.

"Code?" Kirill asked. "How can you be sure?"

"Lady Ulyssa has no uncle or grandmother." Falke frowned. "Has she told you nothing of herself? Have you not spoken?"

Kirill's dark face paled slightly. She'd never share anything with him, no matter how gently he asked her. It was like she didn't want anything personal between them. To hear that Falke knew more about her personal life than he did stung bitterly.

"I apologize," Falke stated, lifting his chin. "It is not my place to question it. Lady Ulyssa is an orphan."

Kirill frowned, not understanding the term.

"It is an Earth word for a person without family. Her parents died in a space shuttle accident."

"How do you know this is true?" Kirill inquired, doing his best to hold his emotion back. But the truth was he was worried--terrified. She'd been ill when he last saw her--so pale and fragile. She'd been shaking terribly and he could just imagine the harm that would befall her in the forest.

"It's the truth. I would've detected the lie." Falke paused, waiting for Kirill's nod to continue. "You say she spoke falsely about the engagement right after asking you for privacy. It's easy to assume engagement code for something else. I doubt there was even a shipwreck. If someone knew that there was a possible war brewing between the Var and Draig, they'd know we'd never ask the Draig Princes about a shipwreck on their land. We wouldn't trust them enough to believe them either way."

Kirill nodded. "I always thought it strange that she could understand the Var tongue but not speak it."

"And she's been trained in weaponry, though not extensively to the sword or knife. Her reactions are honed." Falke nodded in silent approval of her skill.

"And she is intelligent," Kirill responded. Just thinking about her made his gut ache. He wanted her back. He wanted her in his home, waiting for him, safe, sound, so he didn't have to worry about her. And he wanted her there now! Keeping his voice even, he continued, "Her mind is sharp. I only have to tell or show her something one time before she understands it. But, the question remains, who is she? Why is she here?"

"A spy?" Falke offered. "An assassin?"

"If she's an assassin, she'd have acted before now," Kirill dismissed.

"What if..." Falke paused, looking slightly uncomfortable. "What?"

"What if the Draig sent her? What if she was meant to kill you and failed?" Falke cleared her throat. "What if she couldn't go through with it?"

"I might not know her past, brother, but I didn't feel murder in her. She's not an assassin." Kirill turned his back on Falke and leaned his head to the window. His eyes searched the distance.

"Spy?" Falke asked.

Kirill knew Falke didn't want to give up his suspicions that the Draig were behind her presence, but for some reason he couldn't lay voice to, he just couldn't see it. Suddenly, an idea struck him. "Attor."

Falke frowned.

"Our father kidnapped her in the forest, or at least he could have. Lyssa mentioned something about blond warriors. It could have been Attor's personal guard. In the last several years he never went anywhere without them. Find the mountain lions and ask them if and where they found her."

For the first time since finding her gone, Kirill felt like he had a plan of action--at least the beginnings of one. If he could find her old campsite, then maybe he could find her. If he found her, he'd drag her back by the roots of her hair and throw her into the prison. Even if he had to chain her up, he'd make certain she never left him again. No matter how much she protested, he would make her stay. He had no choice. He simply couldn't live without her.

* * * *

Ulyssa was tired. Her skin and clothes were covered in dried sweat and mud. Not knowing whether or not Kirill would try to come after her, she knew it was best to mask her scent with the smell of forest. If he did come, more than likely it would be out of pride and not because he missed her. She thought of Linzi and grimaced.

Several days had past since she walked out of the palace. She'd been traveling by foot during that time, avoiding passersby as she tried to find her campsite. Only allowing herself an hour's sleep at a time, she'd jogged toward the northern borders until her legs felt like jelly and she could see the tall red mountain of the Draig palace in the distance. Then, turning east, she slowly backtracked to the campground near where the Galaxy Brides ship landed. From there she was able to navigate toward her old campsite.

When Ulyssa found her campsite, the cloaking device was turned off. It looked as if a wild animal had chewed through the wires in the back. Luckily, her backpack was still inside the collapsed tent and she was able to salvage a pack of freeze dried mineral compound. They tasted gross, but after living on a handful of berries since leaving the palace, she was more than happy to swallow down the dark brown wafers.

Pulling out her backup communicator, she programmed it to call the Agency. It didn't take long for the old woman voice to answer, "Hello?"

"Agent 596."

"Report," came the operator.

"Ulyssa 596, codename Gena, Qurilixen," she answered quickly, glancing around uneasily into the shadowed light of the surrounding forest.

"We've been anticipating your call, patching through secure line to the director."

Ulyssa waited as a series of clicks sounded on the communicator. She searched through her bag with one hand, not willing to be caught without a weapon again.

"Ulyssa?"

Ulyssa let loose a long sigh, "Frank, I'm here. I can't talk long, but right now we're secure. I want to get moving again, but I had to let you know what's going on."

"Is it true? Doc Aleksander stored biological weapons on that planet?" Franklin's voice was tense.

"I think so. I found a trade agreement with the old King of the Var at the Var Palace where I was..." she paused before stating diplomatically, "...undercover. I don't know how much or where it's at or if it's even here for sure."

"Damn it! That's not a lot to go on, agent! We need to know what we are up against." Franklin paused and she could tell he was worried about her. "Listen, why don't you come back? You're not trained for this. There's nothing more you can do."

"I can't leave. I have a plan. Nadja Aleksander is married to a Draig Prince, the Vars' rival. I'm going to make contact with her, see what she knows. I'm hoping she'll help us." Ulyssa frowned, glancing around the forest. The hairs on her neck stood on end. Very carefully, and quietly, she said, "To be safe, I'd send a containment crew in case this gets out. No one should get off this planet alive."

"Agent ... damn it. Ulyssa, listen to me. If this thing blows a doctor won't ... we can't bring you back."

"I know, Frank, I know. If it blows, leave me here to die with the rest." Ulyssa swallowed, nervous about the prospect of dying on Qurilixen. If the weapon was released, she wouldn't have an antidote either.

"I have a team of specialists on their way. They should be there in less than a week. I want you to concentrate on finding transport off that planet. There is nothing more you can do."

"No, Frank, you're wrong. I can at least try. And what if the weapon's released before they get here?"

"You don't have to do this."

"I'm staying. I can't let these people die," Ulyssa stated. She steeled her nerves and repeated, "I'm staying and I'll find that weapon. You're wrong. Saving innocent lives is exactly what I'm trained for."

"But--"

"No, if it goes off make sure you blow up any ship trying to leave ... including one I may be on. The risk is too great to the rest of the galaxy. I ... I don't know what we're up against. Besides, no one should leave, including me. I might already be contaminated."

"Damn it!" Franklin swore only to follow the curse with a long string of other ones. Ulyssa smiled at that, drawing a strange feeling of comfort knowing he felt as helpless as she did. "Fine, proceed with your plan. And you be careful--that's an order."

A twinge rolled over Ulyssa's spine and she knew she wasn't alone. Reaching into her bag, she felt for a weapon. Keeping her tone light, she said absently, "Gotta go, Frank. Out."

"Agent--"

Franklin's voice was cut out as she pressed the button, ending the transmission. Without turning around, she called, "I know you're there. Make yourself known."

A light chuckle was her answer.

Turning around, she saw Falke. He nodded his head in friendly approval, though his features were guarded. "I wondered how long it was going to take you to feel me."

Despite the pleasantness of his voice, Ulyssa whipped her hand from the bag and shot a tranquilizer at him. The bullet pierced the tunic over his chest, sinking beneath the skin. Falke looked down in shock at what she'd done, obviously not expecting her to react to him in such a way. He blinked as his eyes turned a milky white. Ulyssa sprung forward, looking for others as she reached forward to catch Falke before he fell.

Sensing he'd come alone, she relaxed slightly and eased him against the trunk of a tree. With a heave, she hauled his massive weight and adjusted him the best she could. He didn't move and she knew that his arms and legs would be like dead weights. His mouth fell slack and his head rolled to the side. The only thing that moved was his glazed eyes. They glared angrily at her in disbelief.

"You shouldn't have tracked me Falke," Ulyssa said quietly, trying to adjust his arms in what looked to be a comfortable position. His chest lifted in shallow breaths.

Going to her bag, she grabbed a handheld travel decontaminator and began running it over her body. Turning her back to him, she tore off her Var styled shirt and began bathing by running the laser quickly over her skin. As discreetly as she could manage, she did her legs and feet before quickly dressing in a fresh change of clothes. They were a little musty from being stored outdoors, but they were much more comfortable. Then, taking a ring out of her bag, she slipped it on her finger.

Fresh and clean, she tucked the communicator and a gun onto her waist before grabbing a small bottle. She crossed over to Falke. He hadn't moved, but his eyes watched her approach. Ulyssa licked her lips before kneeling.

"Falke, I'm sorry about this. But you must understand I have no choice. I know that it sucks not being able to move. I've been shot with this damned thing four times and it does wear off. You'll stay like this for a few hours." Taking a small pill out of the bottle, she rolled it into his tunic sleeve. "Take this as soon as you come around. If you don't, you'll have a terrible headache that will last for days. I probably shouldn't give it to you, but I'm hoping you'll heed me and just leave me alone."

Falke didn't move, except for the shallow rise and fall of his chest.

Taking a *pulser* from her pack, she shoved it into the ground and turned it on. The domed machine blinked. "This will keep the animals away until you recover."

Falke managed to blink but that was it.

"I'm real sorry Falke--about everything. Tell Kirill you couldn't find me." Shaking slightly, she stood. "Tell him I disappeared."

Not knowing why exactly, she let him watch her. She stood tall before him and turned the ring on her finger. Maybe if he saw her morph he'd listen to her and stay out of her business. She grunted uncomfortably as she shifted and stretch. Her limbs weakened and she trembled. No matter how many times she morphed, she'd never get use to it.

Her red blonde hair grew longer and filled in with a dark auburn tone, erasing all traces of gold and red. Her nose lengthened slightly. The blue of her eyes filled in with green. Her lips bowed and thinned, drawing her features into a permanent pout. The skin around her cheekbones plumped, filling in her features with a roundness she didn't normally possess, and a subtle weight was added to her stomach and legs, softening her sculpted form. Taking a deep breath as the last of the tingling sensations left her limbs, she stood tall.

"Damn I hate that." When she spoke, her voice was no longer her own. It was higher and sounded almost like a whine. Just to hear it again made Ulyssa cringe. She had to listen to it for a month on the Galaxy Brides ship and still hadn't gotten use to the sound of 'Gena'. If she weren't so preoccupied, she'd have cursed Franklin once again for picking the hideous disguise out.

Falke's glazed eyes rounded slightly and he looked at her in a mix of horror and amazement.

"Awful isn't it?" she chuckled without much humor. Then, her new face turning serious, she brushed back a piece of his hair. "I'm truly sorry about this Falke. I did value your friendship while I had it."

With that, Ulyssa left him slouched against the tree. Taking off at a sprint, she jogged toward the Draig palace. Her large breasts bounced uncomfortably, feeling like lead weights on her lungs. She held them up to keep them still. Within minutes she was in sight of the large mountain.

The Draig palace was a magnificent thing built inside the mountain. From the ground, because of the angle, she couldn't see any windows or balconies. It just looked like a large mountain dominating the surrounding valley. The night Nadja killed her father in self-defense, Ulyssa had overhead some of the Draig warriors talking about the palace. If not for that, she wouldn't have known it was there. It was truly an impenetrable fortress.

Taking the long way around through the forest paths, Ulyssa hoped to avoid coming into contact with any of the locals. It was harder to defend herself in her morphed body, and she really didn't want to scare a primitive race by changing back in front of them. She knew they were aware of technology, but she doubted they came into contact with such sophisticated equipment as her morphing ring. Morphing was different than a natural shift. To anyone who didn't know better, it would look like her face was melting from her head. She'd sent primitive races into a panic before with that neat little trick.

Taking a path that led up a small hill to a raised courtyard before the palace entrance, Ulyssa glanced over to the little village in the valley below. It was much different than the

Var city in looks. The villager's homes were of rock and wood, so that even the poorest of families looked to be prosperous. The red earth streets were carved to perfection and the town looked very tidy and planned, instead of the maze-like streets of the Var.

Going into the soft haze of the triple suns, Ulyssa took a calming breath, trying to still her racing heart. She could see some of the villagers down below. They wore light linen tunics and all had long hair, their style very reminiscent of Medieval Earth. Seeing them and their town, she didn't think they looked all the different from the Var. She again wondered what the problem was between the two races.

Walking straight toward the wrought iron gates that were lifted high over the side of the mountain, marking the entrance to the castle, Ulyssa smiled at the blond guard. He was dressed like the rest of his kind, in a tunic. A crystal hung about his thick neck on a leather band, signifying that he was single. He had the handsome, proud features of his kind. Simpering as only Gena's voice could, she purred, "Hello there handsome."

The guard looked momentarily uncomfortable by her open look and cleared his throat. He scanned over the distance to see if she was alone. Then, assessing her and finally deciding she couldn't possibly mean him any harm, he nodded back. "What business do you have in the palace?"

"Actually, this is a little strange." Ulyssa sidled up to the guard and slowly drew her finger along his sleeve. "I'm a friend of Princess Nadja and I wished to seek an audience with her, if I may."

"Uh, I'm sorry, but no one is allowed into the palace without royal escort or permission." The guard glanced down to his arm where her fingers trailed over his bicep in lazy circles. He cleared his throat. To his obvious disappointment, she drew her hand away.

Giggling in her high pitched voice, she let her chest bounce to draw his attention. Ulyssa wanted to laugh for real as he eyes drew down to the monstrous protrusions. Men were so predicable, no matter where she went. Well, all except for Kirill. She hadn't been able to predict him at all. Instantly, her mind sobered and she focused on her work. She wouldn't let him kill all these people.

"But, how can I get a royal escort if I can't first get a royal audience. See my problem, sweetie?" Ulyssa giggled and batted her lashes over her green eyes. "So, do you think you could at least tell Princess Nadja that her friend Gena is here?"

The guard considered her a moment longer. Stepping out of the entryway, he looked up the side of the mountain and gave a low growl. Ulyssa gasped as a man hopped down the side of the mountain with ease to land next to her.

"I have to escort her," the guard said to the newcomer. Ulyssa gulped as he stood possessively close to her. "Watch the entrance."

The new guard eyed her before shooting a jealous glare at his friend. Stiffly, he nodded and took his new post.

At the blond guard's motion, Ulyssa followed him into the Draig Palace. The mountain castle was as picturesque as she would have expected the castle to be. Wide domes allowed light inside the tunneled path of red rock. Entering a front door of thick oak, they came to a series of passageways. The halls were clean and decorated with tasteful paintings and sculptures. Tapestries hung on the walls, alongside banners with the emblem of the royal dragon.

They walked in silence for some time until Ulyssa was sure they were deep into the mountain. Stopping by two large doors, the Draig guard pushed them open and stepped aside.

"You may wait here," he said quietly. His lips twitched and his eyes roamed over her body in a way that was pure dominance. Letting his eyes linger on her breasts, he licked his lips.

"Thank you," Ulyssa purred. The man was handsome and ordinarily she'd have considered taking him up on the offer in his eyes, but as she looked at him she felt cold, dead. The image of Kirill flashed into her mind. No matter how she tried to deny it, she missed him terribly. It didn't matter that he was a tyrant. Her body missed him, as did her heart. And she hated herself for feeling that way.

The guard had taken her to the main common hall of the palace. It had steep, arched ceilings with the center dome for light. The red stone floor was swept clean and her feet echoed off it as she walked into the large room. Lines of empty tables reached across the floor for dining. Banners of the Draig family crest lined the walls with the silver symbol of a dragon boldly wove into it. Compared to the decorative tile of the Var, the Draig palace was very plain--beautiful, but plain.

After a short time, she heard the door open behind her. She turned to see Nadja enter. Her boots clacked lightly as she came across the floor. Nadja was a pretty woman, reserved and quiet in nature. Ulyssa knew the character of Gena had put her off more than once with her brassiness on the Galaxy Brides ship, but the woman had been too kind to say anything about it. At first, Ulyssa hadn't realized who she was, until she saw the woman strapped to the chair by her psychotic father. Doc had threatened to kill her and the baby she carried if she didn't harm Princess Olena, who he'd also kidnapped. Nadja refused and had killed her own father instead.

Yeah, Ulyssa thought. *Nadja Aleksander was a true lady-- despite what her father had been and despite the fact she'd killed him.*

Nadja's long brown hair was swept back into a bun and she wore a pair of flowing gray cotton pants and a fitted blue shirt. Her features were reserved and she had the perfect coloring of white porcelain. The light blue of her eyes was confident, yet refined. At her side was a man, who Ulyssa guessed was her Prince husband.

The Prince's greater height complimented Nadja's slender frame. His green gaze looked her over suspiciously and he stepped protectively closer to his bride. His hand lifted to rest on her shoulder, as they came to stand before the stranger in their midst. The possessive act took Ulyssa by surprise. If she wasn't mistaken, Nadja Aleksander had found love in her marriage.

"Gena?" Nadja asked, taken aback. She glanced at her husband in confusion. "What are you doing here? Didn't you go back on the Galaxy Brides ship?"

"Not quite," Ulyssa answered. She swallowed nervously. "Ah, would it be possible for us to talk alone?"

The Prince's grip on his wife tightened slightly.

"Olek, it's all right," Nadja murmured. "I have a feeling I know what this is about."

Olek slowly nodded. His eyes softened and he said quietly. "I'll be right outside the door if you need me."

Nadja smiled at him, her look a little too dreamy, as he leaned over to place a tender kiss on her lips. Ulyssa glanced away in discomfort. Jealousy surged in her heart to see the couple so affectionate in public. Kirill had never looked at her so openly. He never kissed her so tenderly, so publicly. No, in public he'd treated her like a slave.

"I'll be fine," Nadja answered, pulling away. She motioned to a nearby table for Ulyssa to sit.

Ulyssa sunk onto the bench, not realizing how tired she was until that moment. She hadn't eaten a decent meal in days and all the running around was starting to take its toll.

"Are you all right Gena?" Nadja asked with concern. "Has something happened to you?"

Ulyssa shook her head and took a deep breath. The dizziness lessened and she forced herself to concentrate. "I don't know how to say this, so I'll just say it."

"You want me to try and find you a Draig husband?" Nadja offered. "Where have you been hiding all this time? The Galaxy Brides ship's been gone a long time."

"What?" Ulyssa shot in confusion, before remembering what a pervert 'Gena' had been on the ship. She shook her head in mild annoyance. "No, believe me, a husband really is the last thing I want."

Nadja frowned in obvious disbelief. Ulyssa couldn't blame her.

"Listen to me very carefully, Nadja, please. I'm here to help you. You and your new family are in danger."

Nadja listened in silence as Ulyssa told her about being in the Var palace and finding the document. After she'd finished, the woman sat back and sighed heavily. Quietly, the Princess said, "I thank you, Gena, for bringing this to my attention. I will speak of it with my husband and we'll take care of it."

Nadja stood from the table.

"No, wait," Ulyssa exclaimed. "You ... you don't believe me?"

"If the Var are our enemy, I have no doubt they dream of killing us," Nadja answered. "In fact, they have already tried and failed. I promise to look into what you say."

"No, those things were something else entirely ... what they tried before was nothing compared to what I'm talking about," Ulyssa insisted. "They've got biological weapons!"

Nadja chuckled. "I've thoroughly searched this planet's vegetation. How exactly would they have gotten the type of biological weapons you describe--?"

"Doc," Ulyssa stated. She hadn't wanted to be so blunt about the woman's dead father, knowing the memory would still be fresh in her mind. "Your father brought it here and sold it to King Attor. I believe he stockpiled it somewhere on this planet, but I don't know what to look for. That's why I need your help. Please, help me! Tell me where ... what to look for."

Nadja paled slightly. Her voice a whisper, she demanded, "What do you know about my father? Who sent you?"

The door flew open and Olek stormed inside. It was as if he could feel his wife's distress as his own. Seeing Nadja's pale face, he marched forward. Nadja lifted her hand to him and motioned that she was all right.

Ulyssa felt another stab of jealousy as she watched the loving couple. A quiver ran over her and she wanted nothing more than to curl into a ball and cry. Kirill's face wouldn't leave her and it became hard to concentrate. Her body felt fragile and she swayed lightly in her seat.

"I know who your father is, Nadja," Ulyssa stated in a rush before Prince Olek had her tossed from the palace as a madwoman who upset his wife. "I'm an undercover agent sent here to stop him, only you did it first. My name is really Ulyssa Payne."

Nadja let loose a weakened gasped and reached for her husband's hand. Her mouth worked but no sound came out.

"I'm not crazy. I know how I acted on the Galaxy Brides ship, but that's not how I really am," Ulyssa cried. "Please, you have to believe me. I have to find the weapon or the entire Draig population will be wiped out and possibly a good percentage of the Var--at least those not given an antidote."

At that declaration, Olek stiffened and pushed his wife behind him. "You threaten us?"

"No, I've come to help!" Ulyssa looked around the Prince to Nadja. The woman was pale, shaken. "Here, watch! I'll prove it."

Taking the ring, Ulyssa twisted it on her finger. Her body tingled, as her features appeared to melt from her face. A stabbing pain washed over her as she morphed, instantly sapping her of her energy. Ulyssa blinked, feeling lightheaded. When the change finished, she looked at the couple. Nadja's mouth was agape and she stared at her in awe.

"Gena?" Nadja whispered, amazed.

"See," Ulyssa said. "I'm not Gena. I'm an agent for the Human Intelligence Agency. Ple ... ease, Nadja. You ... have to ... hel ... *phh*."

Ulyssa swayed on her feet, unable to keep upright. Her world spun, blurring around her, as she fell forward. Right before everything turned black, she saw Prince Olek sweep forward to catch her.

Chapter Twelve

"You know, I like this look for you much better."

Ulyssa blinked, trying to come out of the fog that clouded her brain. Looking over at the bed next to her, she saw Nadja smile at her. There was a row of empty hospital beds along one wall behind Nadja. They led to a long hallway where Ulyssa could see three doors. Suddenly, she realized she was in a medical ward in the Draig palace.

"What?" Ulyssa croaked, feeling weak.

"Your face," Nadja clarified. "I like it better without the morph."

"I like that I can breathe without the weight of two spaceships on my chest. You'll never know how hard it was to keep it on for the whole month on that ship." Ulyssa chuckled. Clearing her throat, she asked weakly, "What happened to me? What am I doing here?"

"You fainted," Nadja answered. "The medic said you were malnourished and most likely exhausted. He said it looked like you'd been kept up for days."

Ulyssa closed her eyes and nodded.

"You said you were kidnapped by King Attor. Were you held prisoner for very long?" Nadja asked. She reached a gentle hand forward to brush back a piece of Ulyssa's hair. "Did they torture you?"

"Prisoner?" Ulyssa croaked. Her face lit in instant denial and she had the strongest urge to defend Kirill's honor. Just as she was about to say he'd never harm or torture anyone, she stopped. She didn't know if that was exactly true or not. So, instead, she said nothing.

"At the Var palace," Nadja clarified in answer to her whispered question.

"I wasn't really a prisoner," Ulyssa answered, choosing her words carefully. Her head was a bit dizzy and she felt sick to her stomach. "It was more like undercover."

Nadja nodded knowingly. "Was getting King Attor also your assignment?"

"No, it ... I only saw King Attor that one time when he found me by my campsite. Before that, I'd never heard of him. He died and King Kirill was put in charge of the harem."

"And this Kirill?" Nadja probed. "What sort of man is he?"

"He's a King," Ulyssa answered evasively. "Until I found that document, I really did think he wanted peace. Now, I honestly don't know about him."

"What does your gut say about him?"

"I..." Ulyssa coughed as she tried to push herself up off the bed, but ended up falling back onto the mattress. She couldn't answer that. In her line of work, she relied on facts, not gut instincts. When she looked at Nadja, she had a suspicion that the woman knew something she wasn't telling her. Desperate to change the subject, she asked, "You're not upset about your father? I mean, about me coming to get him?"

Nadja shook her head, though her eyes turned sad. "No, I made my peace with who my father was. My family is here now."

Nadja glanced up and Ulyssa heard a voice from her other side say, "Here, you must be thirsty."

Twisting around, she saw Princess Morrigan and Princess Olena standing over her, listening to their conversation. Morrigan handed her a glass of water. Ulyssa struggled to sit up and drink it. She wasn't surprised to find Princess Pia at the end of the bed watching her as well. Behind her was a reception desk next to several rows of glass cases with medicine bottles.

"Nadja told us who you are," Pia allowed quietly when she saw she had Ulyssa's attention.

"And what you're doing here," Morrigan added.

Ulyssa nodded and handed the glass back. All the Princesses were pretty women. Morrigan, who Ulyssa soon learned had married the future Draig King, Prince Ualan, had dark hair and eyes. She was a thoughtful person with a sharp intelligence. Olena, married to Prince Yusef, Captain of the Outlands, had flaming red hair wild enough to match her carefree personality. Pia, a quiet blonde with hazel eyes, married Prince Zoran, Captain of the Draig armies.

"So, just how close did you get to the King?" Pia questioned, before deducing logically, "You would've had to be deep undercover to find out the information you have. I imagine deep enough to be his lover."

Ulyssa stiffened and got defensive. A little waspish, she snapped, "I did what I had to. It's lucky for you that I did, too, or else you could all be dead. You could still be dead if I don't find that weapon."

Instead of the return of anger that she expected for the outburst, Ulyssa got soft laughter. She stiffened and tried to stand.

"If you're not going to take this seriously, I'll go take care of it myself." Ulyssa looked around. "Which way is the door?"

The Princesses eyed her in what looked to be pity.

"Was it so bad? Being with the Var King? Did he hurt you?" Nadja asked.

"No, he ... I..." Suddenly, for reasons she couldn't comprehend, Ulyssa cried. There was something about the way the women were looking at her--with kindness, pity, compassion. Instantly, four pairs of arms surrounded her, comforting her.

"Hey, I was like this too at first," Morrigan said.

"We all were," Olena added.

Ulyssa sniffed. "Like what?"

"Emotional," Nadja answered. "I still am sometimes, though I do promise it will get better."

"I'm not emotional, just stressed. It's not like I care for him or anything. I'm not in ... in *love*." Ulyssa spat the word from her mouth with a grimace of distaste. Were her feelings that obvious? Well, she rejected her feelings. Simple as that. She didn't care one bit for King Kirill. How could she love a man who would murder innocent people in a race war? What in the hell did that say about her? All right, so she didn't know he would do that for sure, but is sounded better to her ego than 'I can't love a man who doesn't love me'. "The King and I aren't ... together. How could I be? He's ... he's a...."

"Oh, I'm sorry to hear that." Nadja brushed back a piece of Ulyssa's hair. "It must be rough facing that you're going to be a single mother."

"A single...?" Ulyssa paled and she was sure she was going to pass out again. Instead, she started to hyperventilate.

"She didn't know," Olena gasped.

"It's why you've been feeling so weak and why morphing back was so painful. Your morphed body wasn't designed to be pregnant," Nadja explained. "But, don't worry, the baby's fine. We had it checked out."

"You're ... all ... pregnant," Ulyssa gasped between breaths. The Princesses nodded. "And you ... think that ... I'm...?"

"The baby's blood scan showed it was half Var so naturally we assumed that it belonged to…." Nadja paused, looking helplessly at the others. Again, Ulyssa had the strange feeling they knew something she didn't. "When you were sleeping you said his name over and over so we kind of assumed he was your...."

"Lover," Olena inserted when Nadja didn't finish.

"*Ooooh!*" Ulyssa lurched from the bed and straight for the trash shoot to throw up. Morrigan rushed to wrap a blanket around her upper body. Nadja went to the glass case to get some medicine. Ulyssa flinched as Nadja gave her a shot, but soon the quivers in her stomach stopped and she felt like she could breathe again. Slowly, they helped her back to the bed.

As Ulyssa lay down, she whispered, "He's not my lover. He's nothing to me."

* * * *

"No! I forbid it!" Olek yelled at his wife. "You cannot go! What if this is a trap? We don't know that we can trust her."

Ulyssa watched the royal family from the sidelines. They'd come to the main hall from the medical ward where she was introduced to the rest of the royal family. They were having a quick lunch at the lower tables, though no one really seemed interested in the food. Pushing her plate away untouched, Ulyssa sighed. She chose to sit apart from them while they talked about what they would do with the information she gave them.

Nadja looked at her husband and smiled sadly in understanding. "I have to go. I'm the only one who knows what we're looking for. I know my father's traps. I have to go--for us, for our baby. Besides, I believe her."

"Then I will go as well." Olek frowned. It was clear he didn't like his wife's decision. He turned to look at Ulyssa from across the short distance. He didn't trust her, not completely. She couldn't blame him. He loved his wife very much. It was obvious all the Draig Princes had found love. Ulyssa had to look away first.

"I will go. I know the shadowed marshes better than any here," Zoran stated.

"As will I," Pia asserted. She winked at her husband. It was clear she had a thirst for adventure of any kind. "I have a feeling I might be needed."

Zoran looked grimly at his wife, but it was obvious her mind was made up. He gave her a stiff militant nod. "I don't trust the Var to deal fairly with us. They're leading us to the marshes could be a trap."

"The Var?" Ulyssa gasped, drawing attention to herself. "Who said anything about the Var? They don't know that I'm here. We don't have to tell them anything. They're the ones who brought the weapon here in the first place."

The same strange look crossed Nadja's face that she'd worn in the medical ward, the look of secrets. Ulyssa paled dramatically. What was going on here? What weren't they telling her?

"King Attor was the one who brought the weapon to our planet. King Kirill has come here to the palace with Prince Falke to inform us about its existence and to request Princess Nadja's help in disarming it. He's also come to inquire after you," Prince Ualan stated. "He awaits our decision."

Ulyssa paled and shook her head. "Decision for what?"

The four Princes studied her quietly, taking in her nervous reaction.

"Decision for what?!" Ulyssa demanded, shaking violently.

"On whether or not to return my property to me."

The Princes' eyes turned to the door. Ulyssa froze, refusing to move. Her heart pounded wildly in her chest, trying to escape. Her fingers gripped the wooden bench at her side, grinding into the surface as if she could crumble it beneath her. If she didn't look, he'd just disappear. He'd go away. She swallowed nervously. A chill racked its way up her spine, as she felt all eyes on her, watching what she would do.

A hand lightly clamped down on her shoulder, not squeezing or hurtful, just resting, letting her feel its weight pressing against her. Her mouth went dry. A familiar tremor racked through her at the touch, alighting her nerves with fire. Very slowly, she glanced at the hand, recognizing it.

"Kirill," she whispered, unable to look away from the long fingers. She'd missed him so much, her body longed for him still. Her flesh tingled, remembering what it felt like to be held against him. Her body warmed. Her breasts reacted violently until the nipples stood at erect points, trying to lure his hand down to them.

Ulyssa forced herself to remember him next to Linzi in the hall. She could not, would not be a King's whore, the dirty little secret he had to hide from the world. With an angry jerk, she tore her arm away from him and stood. She met with his dark, foreboding features. His brown-black eyes glittered an angry green within their depths. The firm set of his jaw clamped down. His nostrils flared. He was livid.

"Ualan," Morrigan's voice invaded Ulyssa's trance. "Can't--?

"Shhh," Ualan answered his wife. "We have his word that he won't harm her."

"What are you doing here?" Ulyssa whispered, terrified to see him and well aware that they were watched.

Kirill reached into a hidden pocket of his pants and pulled out a crumpled piece of paper. Ulyssa's eyes stayed focused on his hard gaze before twitching over to look at his hand. It was the trade agreement she'd found in his office. "I came to bring this. I found it in your coat."

Ulyssa swallowed, uneasy. Kirill glanced over to the table before stepping forward to grab her arm. With a firm tug, he dragged her across the hall to where they could be watched but not heard.

"Do you even know what it is?" Kirill demanded hotly, letting her go.

Faintly, Ulyssa nodded. "It's the trade agreement with the Medical Mafia to buy biological weapons. An agreement made between the Mafia and your people."

"No, it's an agreement made between the Medical Mafia and my father. Don't you think I would've liked to see it? Don't you think I could have handled this matter on my own?"

"It was on your desk, your highness. You knew about it," Ulyssa accused.

"No, it was part of a stack I had yet to read through. Do you really think so little of me, Lyssa, to believe I would wipe out an entire race of people? Sacred Cats woman! Do you know what you could've done if I'd not found this? You could've started a war between the Var and the Draig! I don't want another war. I don't want to send my people to their deaths because we are different than the Draig--not better, not worse, just different. I want the hatred to stop. I want the death to stop. I don't want blood on my hands!" Kirill shook the paper at her as he spoke. "Do you think they would have trusted me after this? I would've taken care of it--"

"How can I trust you're telling the truth? You might only be here now because I came and ruined your plans," Ulyssa hissed.

"I came because I found this. I came because this little note in the corner reveals who Princess Nadja is. That it was her father who brought it here and my father who paid for it. I came to stop this." Kirill frowned, lowering his arm to his side. "I want peace. I want the prejudices of my father and the older generation to end. I don't want to conquer more land, land which my people don't really need."

"How was I to know anything? I'm ... *was* just your whore," Ulyssa hissed. "Clearly one of many. Why should there be anything between us, especially trust?"

"What do you mean? One of many?"

"Oh, you know very well. I know you go to the harem," Ulyssa snorted in dismissal. "I don't care. I welcome you to those women. Enjoy yourself, highness, in your little brothel. We are over. Done. Finished. I want nothing to do with you."

Kirill stiffened at her heated words. His eyes hardened, becoming blank voids. "Very well. As you wish it, my lady."

Ulyssa didn't know what he meant by that, but his dead tone scared her more than his heated anger. Somehow she doubted he was just going to let the matter drop completely.

Kirill turned and walked away. He didn't have other women, but after her little tirade he wasn't about to tell her that. He'd been so worried. He wanted to go to her campsite to confront her, to see with his own eyes that she was well, but Falke insisted he go instead so none at the palace would suspect her absence. When Falke told him about overhearing her conversation with the 'mission director' and that afterwards he'd tracked her to the Draig palace, Kirill's worry had been replaced by anger. By not trusting him, she could have brought him to the brink of war. If he had not come forward when he did, the Draig wouldn't have ever believed in his innocence.

It sickened him to think of what his father had been planning. It tore at his soul to know Ulyssa thought he was capable of the same. He'd hoped there was more between them--more than just sex. He'd been wrong and it was slowly killing him. An ache rested on his chest, growing worse with each passing heartbeat, squeezing the life from him, the breath from his lungs. He steeled himself for what he must do. He was a King and he would act like one.

"Falke and I will travel with you to the shadowed marshes. I know the area this paper talks about well. It shouldn't take us long to find it." Kirill paused and looked at Ualan. "As a test of good faith, I leave my brother Quinn here in your care. I ask that you send Yusef to my palace for the same. We have no reason to trust each other--"

"Like hell!" Olena yelled, jumping to her feet. The dark Yusef grabbed her arm and pulled her back down next to him. He stroked back her hair and whispered in her ear.

"I give you my word that I won't harm any here, so long as my own aren't harmed," Kirill stated.

"What good is your word to me?" Olena demanded hotly. "I have seen first hand what your kind is capable of!"

"Princess Olena, I apologize for the rash actions of a few, but I did not order your kidnapping." Kirill was tense. He knew the woman was just scared for her husband.

"It was Attor--" she began. Yusef took her and pulled her to his chest. He again whispered to her and she settled down, nestling in his arms.

Ulyssa stepped forward to his side. Kirill glanced at her. She looked pale, sick, and so very beautiful. His arms ached to hold her, the way the Draig Princes held their wives, but, by the way she'd jerked his hand from her shoulder, he knew his touch would not be welcomed.

"If your husband or any Draig is harmed in this," Ulyssa paused. Her round blue eyes met his. They were hard, devoid of life, and they matched his look perfectly. Very warily, she finished, "Then you run his heir through with a sword."

Kirill felt as if he'd been kicked in the gut. His eyes trailed down in disbelief to where her hand was placed on her stomach. Pleasure tried to assault him at her words, but as the whole of her statement set in, he froze. She would dare to use his unborn son as collateral? Did his baby mean so little to her? Did he? He couldn't breathe, couldn't speak.

"But that would also kill you," Morrigan pointed out.

"If it will get this whining over with, then so be it." Ulyssa gazed at them all, fed up with their bickering. She didn't feel like dying any time soon--especially sitting around waiting for them to get their act together. "If we don't get moving soon, it's quite possible we'll all die anyway."

"She's right," Nadja said. "They wouldn't have planned on keeping it in long time storage. If an animal got to it, or a child...."

"So can we come to a temporary truce or not?" Ulyssa demanded. "There is something more at stake than a few petty differences of one planet. If we don't stop this here and now, it's a very real chance that it could spread to other parts of the quadrants. I will not stand by and watch the innocent die because we all can't get along. Hate me if you wish for saying it, but hate me alive."

"My lord," Falke, who'd quietly watched, stepped forward.

Kirill ripped his eyes from Ulyssa and held up his hand to silence his brother, as he forced himself to concentrate. Slowly, he nodded. He didn't like the position she put him in. But, if they couldn't reach an agreement, many Var would die, too. There wasn't enough of the antidote to cure everyone. He hated to admit it, but in the end, his father had been a madman. "It will be as she says. If any are harmed, run her through."

* * * *

To get to the shadowed marshes, they first had to trudge through miles of swampland. The Draig provided Ulyssa and their two Var companions with *ceffyls,* hideous looking creatures with a center horn protruding from their skull. They had the eyes of a reptile, the face and hooves of a beast of burden, and the body of a small elephant. The animals' wide back shifted low, as they trudged through the swamps, taking their passengers through the mucky waters.

The ceffyls' hisses kept most of the large swamp life at bay. Their thick hide could withstand the bite of the poisonous *givre* that swam freely in this part of the kingdom. When Falke helped Ulyssa to mount, he'd warned her to keep her legs from the water. She obeyed, holding tightly onto the horn, her legs lifted onto the strange creature's back to sit crosswise.

The group traveled in silence for about an hour. A diffused light fell over the dense forest in a soft green haze that blended eerily with the patches of hot, steamy fog from the nearby marshland. From what Ulyssa could tell, there wasn't much difference between the swamps and the marshes, except that the marshes seemed dead of all life.

The air was damp in this part of the woods. Moss hung from treetops, unmoving in their windless isolation. They were in an awful place. The rotting smell of molding plant life and animal carcasses masked even the barest traces of scent. Even the insects seemed to have deserted the area.

Kirill didn't look at her once during their trip, but kept his gaze stoically forward. Ulyssa had never dreamt of being a mother and the pregnancy didn't seem real to her. She knew the Agency would never allow her to keep and raise the child. Nevertheless, it hurt that Kirill so readily agreed to run her through. She'd said it to shock him, to hurt him for not denying he'd been with other women since her. She never thought he'd agree to it.

It hurt that he showed her no more notice or consideration than if she'd announced she'd grown a new freckle. Prince Olek and even the stoic Prince Zoran hovered protectively around their pregnant wives, rubbing at their lower backs, guiding their arms, kiss their temples with quiet whispers of concern. Ulyssa grimaced as she looked forward to where Kirill rode near the front of the group, far away from her.

The constant bumping of the animal beneath her made her queasy. She was ready to stop and rest, but would never be so weak as to complain. Gritting her teeth, she stared forward, concentrating on sitting up right.

"You knew you carried his first heir and yet you left anyway?"

Ulyssa jolted and turned to stare at Falke. She'd not heard him ride up next to her. Her eyes had drifted absently to Kirill's back, trying to remember to hate him. Glancing around, she saw no one heard his words.

"I just found out today," she answered quietly, letting her mount fall slightly behind so they wouldn't be overheard.

"Had you known, would you have left him?"

Ulyssa turned to look at him. His eyes weren't judging. If anything, he looked sad. She saw he held no hard feelings about being left paralyzed next to the tree. He didn't mention it, so neither did she. Without flinching, she said, "Yes. You out of anyone should understand that I must do my duty."

"Yes, I out of any understand that," Falke answered. He gave a meaningful glance to Kirill. "But he will not. All he will understand is your betrayal."

"It doesn't matter, Falke. As soon as this mission is complete, I'm gone. If I fail, I die with the rest of you. If I succeed, the Agency will pick me up. I'll disappear and not even the King of the Var would be able to track me down."

"You would take his child from him?" This time when he looked at her she saw a mix of disbelief and horror.

"Yes. This child should've never been conceived. It's against Agency policy for me to have it. They choose me because I have no ties, no commitments beyond duty. My shot must have expired or been defective. When I get back, I'll be lucky to have a choice in the matter. Most likely they'll rid me of it without even asking. Or, if they allow it to be born, they'll take it and find placement for it." Ulyssa gulped, wondering at the intense sadness that flowed over her at the words.

She suddenly felt very empty and hollow. A pain shot over her abdomen, blanketing her chest and heart in agony. She wanted to cry out, but the air was trapped in her lungs.

Kirill abruptly turned around to stare at her. His dark features frowned in question. Ulyssa felt as if he stabbed her with his eyes. Another pain shot through her and she turned to look at Falke. Her face pale, she whispered, "Help."

* * * *

Kirill paced outside the tent where Ulyssa slept. He cursed softly. As they journeyed, he'd been doing his best not to look at the woman who tormented his every waking thought. But then, as a sense of pain and sadness so intense washed over him, he was drawn to give her comfort. It was strange, but he felt her inside him. Her agonizing scream echoed in his head, drilling a hole in the side of his skull.

When he looked back at her, her face had paled and, turning to Falke, she slid off her ceffyl into the stagnant water of the marsh. Falke managed to grab her arm so she didn't go under. Kirill leaped from his mount only to fly through the air to land noisily at her side.

"We camp here," was all he said to the amazed onlookers.

Their Draig traveling companions didn't protest. They watched Kirill carry an unconscious Ulyssa in his arms to drier land, before moving to follow so they could set up camp.

Now, stopping next to the tent, he turned to glare at his brother and demanded, "What did you say to her?"

Falke held still but didn't answer, not flinching at the dark tone. Nadja came from the tent. Kirill stiffened and looked down at the slender woman. She shook slightly before him, but he was too worried to notice.

"She'll be fine," Nadja said. "Just let her rest."

Nadja tried to step away. Kirill reached out and grabbed her arm. Out of the corner of his eye, he saw Olek stand. He instantly let the woman go.

"What is wrong with her?" he asked, his words harder than he intended. He refused to show compassion. As

Nadja's eyes searched his face, she smiled slightly, as if seeing through his façade.

"These little fainting episodes are caused, more or less, by low blood sugar and tremendous amounts of stress. I even suspect that the HIA had her on a heavy birth control that hasn't expired. According to the readings in her blood levels, she shouldn't even be pregnant." Nadja lowered her voice. "I don't know much about the form of birth suppression the HIA uses on their agents, but I can tell you it will be a hard pregnancy for her. She'll be sick and weak for much of the time. She should be resting and watching her diet, not traipsing about the forest. Whatever it is causing her stress, if it doesn't stop, she may eventually lose that child. I didn't say anything to her about this because she already has enough to deal with."

"HIA?" Kirill asked.

"You don't know?" Nadja was taken aback. She paled and tried to step away.

"No, wait, please, tell me." Kirill let the full torment inside him pass over his face. Princess Nadja seemed to be the only one willing to tell him anything. In a hoarse whisper, he couldn't stop the words from escaping him. "Please, I beg you. I have to know."

"H.I.A. Human Intelligence Agency." Nadja paused. "My lord, Ulyssa is an undercover government agent sent here to stop my father from selling these types of weapons. She's in deeper than most men are in the Federation Military. I don't know much, but I do know that most HIA agents never leave the Agency. I honestly don't think they can."

"How do you know all this?" Kirill asked.

"You don't grow up a Mafia boss's daughter and not pick up a few things about the government." Nadja patted his arm lightly. Sighing, she strode across the campground to her husband.

A slight commotion to the side caught Kirill's attention. Pia whispered angrily at Zoran before pointing at Kirill. The Var King stiffened. Zoran growled at his wife, who merely smiled and batted her lashes. Storming over to the Var King, he stated, "Lady Ulyssa is under our protection. Harm her...."

Kirill snarled. Zoran nodded as they came to a silent understanding. For a moment, they held each other's eyes before Zoran stormed back to his wife. Her squeal resounded over the campsite followed by her husband's laughter. Sweeping her up over his shoulder, Zoran carried her into their tent.

Jealousy hit Kirill in a hard wave. He'd never seen or felt such happiness between a man and a woman as he saw in the Draig Princes and their wives. His eyes turned to his own tent, to where Ulyssa slept. It was likely he'd never feel such happiness as long as he lived. Perhaps the Var weren't made to love. Attor had seemed to think so.

"Come, brother, let her rest," Falke said coming from the trees. Kirill hadn't even noticed he left when he spoke to Nadja. Falke stretched his arms wide and noisily yawned. "Come. Join me by the fire."

* * * *

Ulyssa groaned, opening her eyes. The sound of laughter drifted all around her. Sitting up, she saw the reflection of orange fire on the wall of the tent. Beneath her was a padded sleeping mat. For a moment, she blinked, trying to get her bearings.

The laughter again sounded, louder than before followed by quiet murmuring of conversation. Crawling to the front flap, she pushed it aside and looked out. To her amazement, everyone was gathered around a campfire. Very cautiously, she stood, taking a wary step forward.

"We're dead, aren't we? I'm stuck in hell." Ulyssa watched all eyes turn to her. The laughter died somewhat at her words. Nadja and Pia were nestled in their husband's arms. Falke and Kirill were opposite the fire. Kirill stood as he saw her. "You're all getting along, so either we're dead or I've been asleep a really long time."

"Yo--" Zoran began, his word hard.

"Shhh," Pia hushed him. She smiled, and drew his face to her. As if it explained away Ulyssa's lack of manners, she whispered, "She's pregnant. Leave her alone."

Ulyssa grimaced. Kirill stiffened. His eyes dipped to where his child grew in her stomach.

"How do you feel?" Nadja asked, politely ignoring Ulyssa's rude outburst. She rested her head on her husband's shoulder and smiled knowingly. "You had us worried."

THE SAVAGE KING   173

Ulyssa didn't answer, as Kirill's gaze captured her. There was no malice in his penetrating look. He almost seemed like his old self, before their duty got between them. Her heart fluttered in her chest. She swallowed, nervous. His mouth curled up slightly, very handsome the way it pulled up at the edge. She knew that look well. He wanted her.

"You should try to eat, Ulyssa," Pia asserted into their trance. "It'll make you feel better."

Ulyssa blinked, her eyelids still feeling heavy as she looked around her. Everyone stared back, their gazes full of questions, pity, understanding. She nodded in agreement, still feeling like she walked in a dream. The motion was only half finished when she gradually turned and moved to the forest, not saying another word.

Chapter Thirteen

Kirill exchanged looks around the campfire as Ulyssa walked away from them. He didn't know how it happened, but somehow having a joined purpose had helped relations between the Var and Draig. He even suspected being out of the palace and on neutral ground also made it easier for them to set their differences aside. Even Falke and Zoran, longtime enemies, made civil comments to each other. It wasn't a signed peace treaty, but it was a beginning--a good beginning.

Falke frowned and motioned his hand that Kirill should follow Ulyssa.

"Excuse me," Kirill said, standing to move after her. He wasn't sure what he'd say to her when they were alone. He was still angry at her for leaving him in the first place, for not trusting him to be a better man, for questioning his honor, for thinking that he could massacre innocent people--whether they were Draig or not.

Sniffing the air, it didn't take him long to detect her scent. Jogging forward, he saw the outline of her body in the dusky light of evening. She leaned against the trunk of a tree, staring absently at the ground. Her face was sad and it tore at his heart to see it.

"Lyssa?"

Ulyssa turned. Her wide eyes looked at him. Slowly, she pushed away from the trunk. Swallowing, she answered, "This doesn't change anything."

Before Kirill could respond, Ulyssa's hands were on his face, pulling his mouth to hers. The first touch in what felt like ages exploded through them, tearing over their flesh like lightening. Ulyssa's loud moan joined his, the sound agonizing. Her hands dug beneath his clothing, pulling desperately to free him of it.

When he would pull back and speak, she kissed him harder, thrusting her tongue into his mouth almost desperately as she drank of his taste. Her teeth nipped his lips as she devoured him in the kiss. He didn't resist, returning her passion full force, letting her take whatever she wanted from him.

"Just kiss me, Kirill," she said into his mouth. "I want to feel anything but this fear and uncertainty. I don't want to die here."

"We're not going to die," he answered hotly. He pulled back to look at her face. She was vulnerable, fragile as she looked up at him. "If it goes wrong, there is an antidote. I will make sure you are amongst those who get it. I promise."

"No, you don't understand. If it goes wrong my bosses won't let anyone off this planet alive--antidote or not. They can't afford to stop and ask questions. They'll kill us all. If we fail, we're dead." Ulyssa moved to kiss him again. He still held her, but he moved his head back to study her.

"Kirill--?"

"Why did you stay? Falke said you were ordered to leave by your boss." Kirill's eyes searched her. He waited a long moment for her answer.

"I stayed because it's my job. I was sent here to stop Doc and whatever it was he planned. I never quit a mission." Ulyssa shook violently, but her words were calm. "I couldn't leave just to watch innocent people die--not if there was something I could do to stop it."

"Is that the only reason?" he demanded. Even though his head stayed back, his arms held her tight to his body.

"What other reason could there be?" she whispered.

Kirill groaned a low throaty sound as an answer, no longer able to hold back. Tugging her tight pants off her hips, he stripped her of her clothing, as if he wanted desperately to be buried inside her.

Ulyssa kicked the pants off her feet, helping as he undressed her as he pulled at her shirt. Reaching for his waist, she freed the hard length of his arousal, gasping in pleasure as she caressed the smooth shaft.

Kirill grunted, forcing her back against the tree. Eagerly, he lifted her up, parting her wide to accept him. He'd missed her so much. The perfume of her longing filled his head, calling to him like a drug. He was helpless against her and he no longer seemed to care. There was no point in fighting their desire.

Without needing to test her depths, he plunged himself forward. His body slid deeply into hers, conquering her. Ulyssa cried out, urging him on with her soft pants and whimpers of pleasure. Kirill answered her call with one of his own. Animalistic grunts of pleasure escaped them. His hips rocked into her, pumping fast and deep, as he tried to brand her to his touch.

Ulyssa's back rubbed against the bark of the tree, but she didn't care. She'd missed him, as if a piece of herself had been missing. His hands gripped the cheeks of her butt, holding her firm as he filled her completely, sliding in the cream of her body. At their fevered pace, it didn't take long for the trembling of climax to seize them both. Her body clenched his hard, milking the seed from him as he came inside her.

Ulyssa moaned, leaning forward to bite lazily at his shoulder. Kirill's palm cupped her face, urging her back to his mouth. He kissed her gently, still buried deep, still trembling, and held her tight. In this moment of ecstasy, nothing else mattered.

Ulyssa let him kiss her for a long moment before drawing back. A look of pain crossed over her features, as she demanded, "I need you to tell me you had nothing to do with this."

"You should know that answer for yourself. I shouldn't have to tell you. Why did you leave me?" Kirill asked. "Was it because you're pregnant?"

"I left..." Ulyssa took a deep breath, before starting over. "I left because of the biological weapons."

"I don't believe you," Kirill growled. He pulled his body from hers and laced his pants. Ulyssa stepped away from the tree and retrieved her clothing. Her legs wobbled, as she dressed. When they finished, he stated, "I can sense you're lying to me. Please, Lyssa, for once, trust me. For once, tell me the whole truth."

"I left because it was my duty to go. I was never shipwrecked. I was sent by the Human Intelligence Agency to stop Doc Aleksander. I hid on the Galaxy Brides ship with the other Draig brides and when it landed I made camp in the forest. But, before I could get to him, Nadja killed Doc. I thought my mission was over. I called the Agency for a ride and found out I was going to be stranded here for awhile." Ulyssa's tone was hard, matching her expression.

Kirill had figured much of the puzzle out already, but nodded anyway.

"I didn't lie about Attor kidnapping me. That much was true. The night you found me wandering the halls I was trying to escape." Ulyssa pushed wayward strands back from her face and sighed. It felt good to be telling him the truth. "Any idiot could see the Var and the Draig were at each other's throats. I wanted to stay out of it."

"So why then did you agree to stay with me?" he asked.

"What would you have picked? Three months in a forest being eaten alive by bugs, or three months in the lap of luxury?" The answer was honest, but it wasn't the whole truth. It barely even skimmed the surface of the whole truth. Before he could probe further, she said, "I ran across the trade agreement by accident that night in your office. I thought you had something to do with it, so I waited for my opportunity, and left."

"And do you still believe I am capable of such things?" he asked.

"No," she answered, knowing she never really had. She'd been confused, mostly because of how she felt. But, it wasn't the trade agreement that sent her fleeing the palace-- not really. It was seeing Linzi by his side in the hall, before all his people--a position he'd never allowed her to take. It was knowing he could, and probably did, take others to his bed.

"And your Uncle Frank?" he asked unnecessarily to see if she would lie to him.

"My mission director," Ulyssa said. "I have no family. I was raised in a home for children who have no family, called an orphanage."

Kirill's hand lifted as if he would touch her, glad that she was being honest. When she didn't move, he let it fall back to his side. "And what will you do now?"

"My mission," she stated simply.

"And if we survive it?" he inquired.

"Then I'll go on to my next mission," she answered. "And after that the next one. It's what an agent like me does."

"What about my child?" Kirill's expression hardened. "Do you think that I'll just let you leave with my heir inside you? Doesn't the baby deserve a father? A home?"

"Like the father you had?" she questioned. It was a low blow and she knew it, but his questions were only bringing her pain because she didn't want to think about the answers.

Kirill's dark features turned red with anger. His jaw tightened and for a moment, she thought he might actually hit her. She wouldn't blame him. Part of her wished he'd hit her so hard she never woke up.

"Don't worry about the baby, Kirill. The Agency will take care of it," she said. Tears threatened her eyes at the prospect, but she knew she wouldn't be given a choice. The Agency was her whole life. She knew it signing up, knew she was giving a piece of herself over, and hadn't done so blindly. For the first time in her life, she regretted that decision.

"What do you mean?" he demanded hotly, gripping her arm.

"I mean they'll take care of it!" she yelled.

"You would kill my son?" His face drained, leaving his dark features ashen.

Ulyssa couldn't bear to look at him. The raw hurt in his eyes tore into her gut, making her ache. She wouldn't, but the Agency just might.

"It's ... it's not really a baby," she whispered, nearing tears. She couldn't think of it as real. She turned her back on him, trying to hide how she felt. "It's just a cluster of cells right now."

"*He's* my son, Lyssa. Our son."

"I can try to have it ... *the child* sent to you after his birth," she whispered. "But, I can make no promises. The Agency will view it as a liability to my concentration. They will see it as impeding my work."

"And don't you think the child deserves a mother?" he asked, ignoring her statement about the Agency. He didn't give a damned about the Agency. They had no authority on his planet.

"I know the Var ways, Kirill. He would have a mother, it just wouldn't be me." Ulyssa stalked back toward the campsite. His low words stopped her.

"I never went to the harem, Lyssa. I haven't been with anyone since you. I know you don't care, but I wanted you to know that."

* * * *

Ulyssa expected knowing looks when they walked back to the camp, but everyone had retired for the evening, except for Falke. The Commander merely nodded at her in greeting. As she watched, Falke easily shifted into the form of a large white tiger. His bright blue eyes blinked at her before he lifted his clothes into his mouth and took off into the forest to sleep. Since there were only three tents, she guessed he went to lie in the trees.

When Falke was gone, Kirill lifted the front flap. He eyed her warily, as if he expected her to refuse to share his tent. She said nothing as she brushed past him. Coming in behind her, Kirill kicked off his boots and pulled his shirt over his head. Crawling forward with his usual liquid grace, he stayed on all fours as he came over her legs. He looked at her for a long moment. His dark gaze penetrated into hers. Slowly, she rolled onto her back and he crawled forward over her.

Kirill's eyes went to her lips. Bending at the elbows, he brought his mouth to hers in a light, tender kiss. Ulyssa met him willingly, not protesting. They didn't speak as Kirill made love to her slowly, worshiping her body with his hands and mouth. And, when they finally met their earth-shattering release, Ulyssa fell asleep in his arms. She spent the whole night with Kirill by her side.

The next morning, camp broke early. They didn't speak as they quietly dressed. A somber mood came over the group, as they mounted up and rode deeper into the marshes.

Kirill traveled by her side, not speaking. He wasn't sure what he should say to her if he did. Ulyssa was just as quiet.

The further they journeyed, the darker the marshes became until it almost looked like night. The stagnant smell only got worse. Kirill frowned, pulling his ceffyl to a stop. He looked around the marshes, before pointing up toward a rocky incline next to the path they traveled.

Turning to Falke, he nodded. They were on Lord Myrddin's land. Neither Falke nor Kirill had been surprised to discover the old noble had something to do with hiding the biological weaponry.

Swinging down from his mount, Kirill drew the attention of the others. Instantly, they followed suit and did the same. Pulling the paper from his pocket, Kirill looked it over. A slight frown marred his brow as he again pointed up. No one spoke as Kirill shifted to panther form. His clothes fell on the ground, next to the paper. Leaping with his mighty paws, he moved from ledge to ledge, up the stop incline until reaching a small cave. After a short time, he poked his human head over the side and unrolled a rope ladder down over the edge.

Ulyssa grabbed Kirill's clothing and bundled them beneath her shirt to free her arms for the climb. Without waiting to be told, she started up the ladder first. Reaching the top, she felt Kirill's hand on her arm, helping her in. She stood, her eyes searching for him in the dim cave light. Her eyes instantly moved down over his naked body. At her attention, his loins twitched and filled.

She blushed in embarrassment that she could be thinking of such things at this moment. Her gaze flitted up to his. He stared at her protruding stomach where she hid his clothes. His hand lifted as if he would touch her and a look of longing passed over his dark features.

Ulyssa looked down, realizing it looked as if she were pregnant. Swallowing nervously, she pulled the clothes out and handed them to him, meeting his searching hand. For a moment, he stood, arm extended. But, as the ladder wiggled, signaling that the next person came to join them, he quickly slid into his clothing and didn't say a word.

"Kirill, listen," Ulyssa rushed to his turned back. "I have to tell you something."

He pulled the laces on his shirt and moved to look at her.

Ulyssa glanced over her shoulder. A hand poked up from the side. "I never thought you had something to do with this ... not really. It's not the exact reason why I left. I just wanted you to know that in case we don't make it--"

A grunt interrupted her as Zoran heaved his body into the cave. He looked around, stopping briefly to study the couple before turning to motion at the others that it was safe. Ulyssa merely nodded at Kirill, unable to finish as the rest of the traveling party joined them.

"It should be down here," Kirill stated to the group when everyone was up. He turned, leading the way into a narrow tunnel. Ulyssa made a move to follow him. Falke put a hand on her arm and shook his head. He went in next, turning to the side to fit.

"Stay here. Guard the entrance," Zoran said to Pia, handing her a knife. He moved behind Falke. It was a tight fit for the two large commanders and they made slow progress.

"I'll be right behind you," Olek said to his wife. Before Nadja could go in, Ulyssa slipped into the tunnel behind Zoran.

The tunnel led to a large cavern. Crystal formations protruded from the ceiling. They reflected the outside light, causing spots to dance on the walls like little rainbows. Little inlets and tunnels spiraled off from the side walls. Kirill turned and marked their entrance with a scrape of a rock.

"Wow, it's beautiful," Nadja whispered, looking around.

"What exactly are we looking for?" Ulyssa asked her.

Nadja swallowed, almost embarrassed, as she unbuttoned her pants and turned around. Easing them down, she showed them a black swirling tattoo design on her back hip. "It will have this symbol stamped on it. It's the mark of the Medical Alliance. I'd assume a crate or a metal container."

"Spread out. Don't go too deeply into the tunnels. We don't want to lose anyone," Kirill ordered. Ulyssa began to move, but his arm snaked forward to grab her. With a stiff nod of his head, he ordered her to follow him. Not wanting to cause a scene, and slightly discomfited by his nearness, she obeyed.

Spreading out in all directions, they searched the cave. Kirill hopped up on a ledge, before reaching down to pull her up behind him. Ulyssa's hand rested on Kirill's arm, as she found her footing. When she didn't let go, Kirill gave her a reassuring smile and leaned forward to nudge her face with his own in a silent show of affection. Reaching for her hand, he led her forward. Ulyssa was amazed, looking around to see if he realized they were in view of the others. He didn't seem to care.

They'd only been looking for about a half hour before Falke called, "I think I got something."

A dusty brown crate was settled in a dark corner with the imprint of the Medical Alliance burned on the top. For a long moment, they all stared. Ulyssa kneeled to touch it. Kirill grabbed her arm and jerked her back. He looked at Nadja.

"Open it," Nadja whispered. Falke reached forward to open the lid, prying it with his strong hands. Kirill hugged Ulyssa to his chest. She blinked, looking up to his face. His body was tense, but felt so good pressed against her. If she were to die, there was nowhere else she'd rather be.

The crate was packed with grass and leaves. Falke frowned and didn't reach in. He looked back at Nadja.

"There should be a container inside," Nadja said, nodding for him to go ahead.

Falke reached his hand in. No one breathed. Ulyssa gripped tightly to Kirill's waist. Falke pulled out a glass jar. Frowning as he studied the contents, he turned the jar around.

"What is this?" Falke asked, just as an eyeball floated by the side.

Nadja turned pale to see it. She closed her eyes briefly. "It's human remains."

"I don't get it," Ulyssa said, lifting her head from Kirill's chest.

"It's how they get it past the bio scanners. Your computers write it off as biological waste or research materials. Besides, when they do ship checks, who in their right mind would open that thing up? The real weapon's inside." Nadja frowned. "It doesn't look as if it's been compromised, but we should get it out of here just in case."

"The Agency will have a safe lab where it can be analyzed." Ulyssa felt queasy just looking at the jar. "We should keep looking. There could be more."

"No, there won't be," Nadja said. Almost ashamed, she whispered, "There'll be enough in that jar to kill five planets."

Olek tucked his arm around her.

"All right, let's get it out of here." Kirill nodded at Falke who placed the jar back in the crate.

Zoran stepped around to the other side and they managed to slowly carry it to the front entrance. Pia was waiting for them at her post. Seeing the crate, she nodded solemnly. It took some doing, but the men managed to rig a pulley to get the crate down from the steep cave. And, as they left the marshes, no one really spoke.

* * * *

Ulyssa sighed, looking around Kirill's living room. Since his palace was the closest to the cave, and since the Agency would be coming for Ulyssa at that location, they carted the crate there. The Draig sent word to their palace that everything was fine. Not surprisingly, the Draig royal family arrived that same evening. Kirill had guest chambers prepared for them and everyone agreed to meet in the morning.

Ulyssa's hair was still wet from the shower she'd taken. To her disappointment, Kirill didn't join her, allowing her to go first. Turning to the bathroom door, she watched him step out. A towel was wrapped around his waist and his body glistened with remnants of water.

He looked her over. "Did you contact your people?"

Ulyssa held up the communicator. "They're entering the Y quadrant. They should be here tomorrow. I'm supposed to request that you allow our doctors to check everyone who came in contact with that box."

"Fine. We welcome the second opinion." Kirill nodded and turned to walk to the bedroom.

"Kirill?" Ulyssa stood from the couch and hesitated. Loudly, she stated, "Fire."

Kirill was confused as the fireplace lit. Ulyssa pulled a tattered piece of paper off the couch. She held it up. It was the trade agreement. Crossing over to the fire, she tossed the paper into the flames.

"I'm going to do my best to keep you and your people out of this. Without any evidence, they won't be able to press intergalactic charges. I know your planet is out of the treaty zone, but you really don't want that sort of attention. You'll have every space reporter, pirate, curiosity seeking nutcase knocking on your front door." Ulyssa sighed. "My record's impeccable, which will help. I'll have to tell them about King Attor's involvement, but I will try to keep it vague. I'll also tell them of your honor in helping me."

Kirill nodded. "Thank you for protecting my people."

Ulyssa walked around the couch to meet up with him. "I'm not doing it just for them. I'm doing it because I owe you. I'm sorry I almost started a war between you and the Draig. That wasn't my intent."

"In the cave, you said you knew that I didn't have anything to do with the weapons. Why then did you leave?" Kirill didn't touch her. His eyes searched her face, needing to know.

"It doesn't matter now." Ulyssa yawned, tired. "It's over. Tomorrow the Agency will come and take me away with them. It will all be over."

"If there wasn't an Agency, would you want to stay here?" Kirill took a step closer. Her head was forced back on her shoulders to look up at him.

"There's no point in dwelling on such things. There is an Agency and--"

"What if I asked you to stay?" His tone dipped sending chills over her spine. "Would you at least try?"

Ulyssa thought of Linzi. No, she wouldn't stay. She could never share him with other women. Even if she believed that he hadn't taken any since her, she knew that eventually he would. It was the way of his people and he was King. The very idea tore at her heart and made it hard to breathe. If he was asking for her and not just the baby, she could have considered it.

"No," she whispered. "It would never work. You're ashamed of me and I can't live like that."

"Ashamed? What is this human word?" he asked.

"Oh, that's a hard one." Ulyssa shrugged. "It doesn't really matter."

"Tell me anyway," he murmured.

"You act strangely with me in public, as if you are embarrassed to be seen with me," Ulyssa answered.

"You think I act strangely?"

She nodded.

"I do not mean to. You know I cannot be..." He frowned. "In public, a King cannot--"

"Shhh," she hushed. "It doesn't matter. There's no reason to think about it. I'm leaving tomorrow and no discussion will change that."

The light in his eyes faded some at the comment, but he nodded.

"But we still have tonight," she continued, soft and light. Her hand lifted to his neck, ready to memorize every inch of him. She'd hold onto the memory in the life to come. Running her fingers down over the rigid muscles of his chest, she felt him shiver beneath her touch. His skin was warm and smooth. Her fingers stopped above the steady beat of his heart. Slowly, his fingers reached up to cover hers.

"I got something for you," he said. Ulyssa smiled, her eyes traveling down to the obvious protrusion coming from the towel. Kirill chuckled. "You can have that, too."

"Then?"

"Wait here." Kirill turned, disappearing into the kitchen. When he came back, he held a small box. "When you were on the communicator, Frank told you Happy Birthday. I thought ... well, it probably isn't really your birthday, but here. I got this for you."

He shrugged lightly, handing her the package. Ulyssa's fingers shook as she took the lid off. Inside was a delicate necklace of gold and pearls. She gasped. "It's beautiful. I didn't know you had such oceans here as we do on Earth."

"We don't. The necklace is from Earth. My mother brought it with her when she came here. I thought maybe it should belong to another Earth woman." Kirill paused, frowning slightly as her fingers trembled. "Is it all right? Falke thought I should give you a sword, but this seemed better suited to a woma--"

"I love it!" Ulyssa gasped, throwing her arms around his neck and kissing him soundly. Inside she cried, *I love you, Kirill.* "It's perfect."

"Then why do you look ... sad?"

"I've never had a birthday present before. Well, except one year Frank gave me a day off." She sniffed. "Thank you."

Kirill grinned, pleased that she liked it. Though, his expression was still overshadowed by deep thought.

"Now," she murmured, running her hand down to grab his towel. Pulling it free from his hips, she said, "About this other present."

Kirill swept her up into his arms. She clutched the box in her hands as he carried her to the bedroom. Taking the gift from her, he set it on the mantel by his crown. Then, slowly, he undressed her, taking his time as he licked and kissed her entire length. His mouth brought her to a fevered pitch, making her squirm beneath his hold.

Ulyssa pushed him on his back, wanting to take her time to give him the same treatment. Pinning his arms above his head, she held him down, straddling his waist with her legs. The moisture from her body slid between them, as she rubbed along his strong stomach. Her teeth bit his earlobe, before sucking it gently between her lips. Kirill groaned, arching against her. He tried to reach for her hips and she stopped kissing him.

Sitting up, she grabbed the side laces from her shirt. Her gaze steadily on his curious dark ones, she tied his wrists together. Then, securing his arms to the top of the bed, she grinned.

Raking her nails down his arms to his shoulders, she began with the slow torture of her mouth on his chest. Kirill moaned and writhed beneath her. Her hand found his arousal, stroking him lightly in her palm as she rubbed her breasts against his heat. She knew if he wanted to, he could escape, but he didn't. She'd finally taken complete control of him, but the victory was bittersweet and control no longer seemed to matter.

"Please, Lyssa," he begged, thrusting his hips.

She lifted her body up and guided his hard shaft to her opening. Impaling herself on him, she cried out. He filled her deeply, completely. She sat on him, lifting herself up so he could watch her body above his. Slowly at first, she rode him, building the rhythm until they were both thrusting and straining for release.

Primal grunts escaped them as they neared their climax. Ulyssa touched her breasts, squeezing them, pinching the nipples. Kirill's eyes stared at her hands, her body. His groans of approval urged her on. She knew he liked watching her touch herself and, as the tempo of their bodies increased, she ran her fingers down her stomach to her rub the sweet spot of her desire.

Instantly, her hips jerked as she came hard atop him. The tremors racking through her caused him to find his own release. His yell joined hers as her body milked him of his seed.

Ulyssa collapsed on top of his chest. Their hard, gasping breaths mingled as she turned her lips to his. Lazily kissing him, she never wanted the moment to end.

"Promise me," he whispered. Stiffening, he pulled hard, breaking the laces so he could wrap his arms around her.

"What?"

"Promise me you'll try to save our child's life." Kirill swallowed. "Please, Lyssa, say you'll try. Don't let them kill our son."

"I can't promise it will work, but I promise to try."

Chapter Fourteen

There was no time to talk the next morning. Siren awoke them with the dawn to inform them that a ship of Agency scientists had landed. They were covered in airtight, white protective suits complete with plastic hoods. Kirill gladly handed over the Medical Mafia crate to Dr. Elliot, the woman in charge of the group. He was very relieved to see the biological weapon leaving his planet.

Franklin was the first to step off the second Agency ship. He was a lot younger than Krill guessed him to be from his voice. His shortly cropped dark brown hair was trimmed to militant perfection and he walked with rigid purpose, very unlike the liquid grace of the Var.

Automatically, he stepped up to Ulyssa. She made a quick introduction between the two men. Franklin nodded, bowing politely and saying all the right words. Then, turning to Ulyssa, he bid her into a private conference. Kirill offered the use of the royal office, but Franklin refused, choosing instead to take Ulyssa onto his ship. That had been two hours ago and he was still waiting for her to come back off.

"The palace is clear, your highness," the dark haired Dr. Elliot said to Kirill. She stood before him, the airtight suit replaced by a lab coat. With nearly a hundred scientists working, Dr. Elliot's team had swept through the palace fairly quickly. She held a computerized clipboard and motioned slightly to a group loading equipment. "My scientists have done a final sweep of the grounds and are loading the equipment back onto our ship."

"Thank you, doctor," Kirill answered. He nodded down at her from the main hall table. The hall had been set up as a temporary headquarters for the HIA and Kirill was actually sorry to see them leaving. For, when they left, it meant Ulyssa would be leaving too. Falke approached. The Commander took a seat at the head table where Kirill sat with Quinn and Reid.

Dr. Elliot looked at the brothers before taking a step forward. She lowered her voice. "Your highness, I request permission to stay on your land. I'd like to explore the caves where the crate was found and run some tests."

"Has there been a leak?" Kirill asked alarmed.

Dr. Elliot shook her head in denial. "No, but it never hurts to be careful."

"Dr. Elliot found a piece of mud caked to the crate and analyzed it. She believes there is something strange about our marshes. She wishes to run some tests," Quinn put forth.

The woman's face tightened and she shot Quinn a hard look. For a moment, she looked as if she wanted to deck the Ambassador Prince. This fact aroused Kirill's interest far more than her request. When he glanced at Quinn, his brother gave nothing away.

"All that, naturally, would be in my report, your highness. The HIA will also do a planetary scan. It's just as a precaution and only with your permission, of course. I'll set up camp with a team of three. You won't be bothered by us. We're scientists and won't cause any trouble. We wish to analyze the cave to make sure we've gotten all biological weaponry off the planet that might be missed with a scan. Surely you can see the wisdom in that. At the same time, I'd like to do a concise analysis of the land. If anything, my findings might actually benefit you and your people, making for more viable farmland."

"What does your Agency say?" Kirill asked.

"I don't work for the Agency. I was contracted for this one job. Their people couldn't make it here in time." Dr. Elliot paused then shrugged. "However, if you would rather have government hacks traipsing about your kingdom...."

"Write you proposal, doctor," Kirill answered, suppressing a grin at her boldness. He was secretly glad someone would be checking out the cave to make sure all the Mafia's stuff was gone. If she wanted to play in marsh mud while she was at it, what did he care? As an afterthought, he mischievously added, "Give it to my brother, Prince Quinn. He'll give it his approval and oversee the project."

"But, your highness!" the doctor began, swallowing. She glanced nervously around the table. Slowly, she nodded, "Thank you."

When they were alone, Kirill said to Quinn, "Approve her plan if you can. We need to have those caves checked out and she's the only expert I know of on this planet. Besides, she has an honest face. I think we can trust her."

Quinn nodded. A strange look crossed his features.

Kirill sighed, dejected as he watched the scientist continue packing. Ulyssa still hadn't come back from her meeting.

As if sensing his pain, Reid asked Kirill, "Have you asked her to stay?"

Kirill blinked in surprise, turning to study his brother.

"Ulyssa," Reid prompted. "Did you ask her to stay?"

Kirill's voice was hard, as he said, "I offered. She refused."

"Did you beg her to stay?" Quinn insisted.

Kirill swallowed. "What would Attor say to such a question? A King can never bow to a woman. You know that. I asked. She said no. It's the end of it."

"After all you have learned, you're still listening to our father's nonsense?" Falke shook his head in disbelief. "Are you really so foolish? Stop her. Forbid her from leaving. Do what you must."

"What would our people say? What of my reputation?" Kirill asked. He didn't really care about his reputation for personal vanity, but knew he had to care for the sake of his rule.

"They love her," Falke answered with a shrug.

At that, Kirill blinked in surprise.

"It somehow was leaked how she selfishly put her life on the line to save the Var and the Draig." Falke grinned into his drink. "Her staying would be good for peace. I'm sure the Draig will soon know of her selflessness as well."

"Monogamy isn't for me, nor was it for our father. But, for you...?" Reid shrugged.

"We won't tell you bowed this one time." Quinn grinned.

Kirill looked at Reid. "Wasn't it you who said I was going to be looked at as weak?"

"This is not our father's rule. It is yours. You must make your own destiny." Reid grinned. "Besides, my prowess will more than make up for your lack of."

"Having her at your side would not be so bad," Falke interjected. "She is good with a sword. She learns fast. Her sense of duty is strong."

"She has a fine look to her features." Reid motioned his hand through the air, as if to outline a woman's body. Squeezing once he reached the invisible butt, he added, "And a really nice, firm--"

Kirill glared in warning. The brothers chuckled.

"She is steadfast," Quinn said. "And beyond that, you love her."

"But she does not love me," Kirill answered with a heavy sigh. The admission caused him great pain.

"How can you be sure?" Falke asked.

"Because the woman willfully speaks her mind and she has never once said that she does." Kirill stood. "I have my duty and she has hers. Even if she wished it, her honor would take her away. Now leave me be on it. It's better not to dwell on the choices we can't make."

* * * *

"What about Nadja?" Franklin asked.

"She's no threat. She helped in the recovery." Ulyssa looked around the metal cabin of the spaceship, as Franklin finished debriefing her. She'd told him everything he needed to know. Watching him sign the computer screen then push a button to file his report, she knew that her mission was finally 'officially' over.

Franklin sighed.

"Are we done here?" she asked softly.

"Almost," he answered. He crossed his hands behind his head and leaned back in his chair. His dark green eyes studied her for a moment. "The doctors gave me a copy of your lab reports."

"Oh?" Ulyssa whispered. She looked at her hands.

"Care to tell me who the father is?" he asked.

"King Kirill," she answered without hesitation.

"I thought as much. He seemed pretty possessive of you," Franklin allowed.

"No, that's just their Neanderthal ways." Ulyssa forced herself to shrug. "He would like the baby, however. I've got some vacation time coming to me after this. I'd like to file for permission to have the baby and send it to him."

Franklin nodded quietly. "What's this King mean to you?"

Ulyssa opened her mouth to lie, but Franklin saw right through it before she even started to say the words.

"That's what I thought." Franklin sighed and drew forward to lean his arms on the desk. "I'll see what I can do about the child, but I can't promise anything."

"Thank you, Frank." Ulyssa stood and turned to go.

"Is there anything else you'd like to say, Agent?" he asked from behind.

Ulyssa swallowed and shook her head. "No."

"Very well. The ship leaves in an hour. I've been informed the scientists will be done by then."

* * * *

Ulyssa stepped into the mosaic tiled banquet hall, pausing to look at its beauty. She was surprised to see the Draig and Var sitting together at a table, enjoying a late meal. She wore the tight black uniform of the Agency, looking oddly out of place compared to the relaxed comfort of the two royal families. Seeing her, they all stood. She motioned them to be seated as she came to the table.

"I just came to say good-bye," Ulyssa said to the group as a whole. She couldn't meet Kirill's dark gaze so instead looked at everyone else. "My ship's getting ready to take off."

The Princesses came forward to give her hugs, Nadja the most enthusiastic of all. The Draig Princes were more sparing in their send off, but politely smiled and wished her well. Falke shook her hand firmly. Reid grinned and gave her a jaunty bow, kissing the back of her hand. Quinn kissed her lightly on the cheek. Her heart fluttering, she finally turned to look at Kirill.

Kirill cleared his throat, moving to offer him his arm. "Here, let me escort you."

Ulyssa took his arm and let him lead her out of the hall. When they were alone, she said, "It looks like everyone is getting along. Maybe you will find peace between you yet."

"Yes, it does look hopeful. We're drafting a treaty and a betrothal agreement. I have great hopes that it will go well." Kirill nodded solemnly.

"Betrothal agreement?" Ulyssa asked.

"It's more of a formality. If one of them is to have a daughter, which is unlikely, she will marry my oldest son." Kirill's eyes instantly moved down to her stomach. He tensed beneath her hand.

"I spoke to Franklin. I think there's a good chance they'll let me send you the child after he's born. I..." Ulyssa swallowed. They neared where the ship was docked next to the palace wall. She wasn't saying anything she wanted to. Closing her eyes, she bit her lip. Very aware that some of the ship's crew watched them, she held out her hand. "I wish you the best of luck with your reign, King Kirill."

He looked down at her offered hand and took it in his. He didn't shake it, but merely held it. His mouth opened and for a brief instant she thought to see pain in his eyes. Lightly, he bowed his head. "Good luck, Agent Ulyssa Payne."

Ulyssa nodded once, turned on her heels, and walked away. As the small lift took her up into the spaceship, she watched him, unable to move. Then, as the metal side blocked her view, she felt a tear slip down her face. Leaving Kirill was the hardest thing she'd ever done.

* * * *

Kirill couldn't force himself to go back to the banquet hall and he didn't want to go home, which would only remind him of Ulyssa and their time together, so instead he went to the royal office. Sitting on the chair before the fire, he muttered, "Siren, I want Lyssa."

"I'm sorry her DNA is no longer on file. Would you like me to page her?"

"Siren, let me hear Lyssa. Let me see her. Bring her back here." He whispered in agony. His hand trembled. Tears filled his eyes, but he didn't let them fall.

"Yes, my lord," Siren answered in her sultry tone. "Would you like me to sound the all alert to the guards?"

Kirill chuckled darkly, feeling no humor in the situation. "No, don't send out the guards."

"Relax," came a whisper that sounded unmistakably like his own voice. "I want us to watch later."

Kirill shot up from the chair, looking across his office. No one was there. Instead, he saw the holographic projection of the time he recorded them making love on the desk. He watched for several moments.

"Siren, why are you playing this?" Kirill demanded. He tried to turn away, but his eyes were caught by Ulyssa's pleasure filled face as his holographic form brought her to climax.

"You asked to see and hear Ulyssa. This is the only file in the archives. King access only, private file 10065," Siren answered. "Would you like me to search the archives again?"

"No," Kirill whispered. He stepped forward. His hand reached out, falling across her cheek like air. Suddenly, Ulyssa screamed. Her body tensed on the desk, arching beautifully before him as the tremors of release took over her. Kirill ran his hands over her neck, as if he could feel her. He ignored his recorded grunts of masculine approval and domination, as a cry ripped from his holographic throat.

Ulyssa mumbled something, but it was too faint for him to hear. Kirill froze, leaning forward.

"What?" his recorded self demanded.

Did he really sound so harsh when he spoke to her? Kirill frowned.

"What?" she'd answered him. "I didn't say anything."

"Siren, replay last ten seconds and magnify Lyssa's speech." Kirill swallowed, staring at her face, edging closer though he knew the words were recorded and not actually from her holographic throat.

"God help me," Ulyssa whispered. "I'm in love with you."

"Repeat!"

"God help me, I'm in love with you."

"Siren, repeat!" Kirill demanded again, unable to believe his ears.

"God help me, I'm in love with you."

"Siren, all alert! Arrest Lyssa!" Kirill hollered, running from the office. His heart exploded with her whispered confession. Why hadn't she told him sooner? If she truly loved him, then they would find a way to be together.

He ran through the hallways, not caring who saw him. Bumping into a servant, he shook him and screamed, "She loves me!"

The servant yelped in surprise. At the commotion, the royal families came from the banquet hall. They watched the King race by, instantly following him to see what the commotion was all about. Kirill nearly tripped over his feet to get to the side of the palace.

"Let go of me! How dare you!"

Kirill grinned. Two of his guards had Ulyssa in their grip. She struggled to get free, looking damned sexy in her Agency uniform. Her wide blue eyes flew to him.

"Kirill! Tell these goons to get off me! I'm not stealing anything! It's mine!"

"Goons off," he obliged, grinning from ear to ear.

The guards let her go and Ulyssa turned to shove them away. Irritated, she turned to him. "I just came back in to get this and they tried to arrest me!"

Kirill's eyes moved down to her shaking hand. The necklace he gave her was clutched in it. He didn't stop in his progress, as he marched across the side walkway. Catching Ulyssa in his arms, he pulled her to his chest. Ulyssa gasped. Kirill kissed her soundly before she could protest. He didn't care who saw him. This is what he wanted--*she* was what he wanted.

Ulyssa's protest turned into a moan. She weakened as her arms wound around his neck. When he pulled back, her lids had fallen lazily over her eyes.

"Everyone can see," she whispered.

"Let them see." Kirill mouth came to hers once more, kissing her soundly. When he pulled back, he declared, "I love you. Stay with me. Life is a living hell without you. Don't let me be burned alive for the rest of my days."

Ulyssa blinked in surprise. She pushed back. His face fell at her rejection.

"No, I ... I can't." Ulyssa's eyes moisten. "I have my job and you have ... Linzi."

"Linzi?" Kirill questioned.

"It's the reason I left here. I saw you with her in the banquet hall. I can't be one of a hundred, Kirill, I just can't."

"Lyssa," he murmured, trying to draw her back. "You're right. You can never be one of a hundred, because you're one of a kind. I only want one. I only want you."

Ulyssa cried. Tears streamed down her face, but she still shook her head in denial. "I ... can't! Why did you have to make this harder on me? They won't let me go."

"We may not let you go, but I can reassign you."

Ulyssa blinked, turning back to Franklin. He stepped up to her. Lightly, he grazed her jaw with his knuckles. Then, glancing to the stunned royalty that had followed Kirill outside, he said, "I think there is much to be done on Qurilixen."

Kirill frowned.

Franklin merely smiled at him. "If Princess Nadja is willing, the Agency would like more information on the Medical Alliance--how they work, how they transport, suppliers, anything. Her identity will be kept a secret, of course."

Nadja swallowed nervously but, after glancing at her husband, she nodded in agreement. "Whatever I can do to help others."

Ulyssa looked at Kirill, meeting his dark eyes. He saw her tremble.

"And," Franklin continued, his words light and unassuming, "if you agree to let Dr. Elliot and her team stay. I'll need someone to report their findings to me."

Kirill nodded in agreement.

Franklin nodded back and continued, "And, after discovering that a whole planet might have been wiped out by the Medical Alliance, I've determined that it's best if we place someone here permanently--just to keep an eye on the savage Var King. In case he gets it in his head to try and buy black market chemicals like his father."

Ulyssa squealed, throwing her arms around Franklin. The man stiffened in surprise and didn't return the hug. She let him go.

"You mean...?"

"You're deep cover now, agent," he answered. "Only I know how to contact you and you report only to me."

"Frank, I ... thank you."

"Don't thank me. I expect a report in about..." Franklin looked at her stomach. "...seven and a half, eight months. However long these things take."

Ulyssa nodded, again mouthing, "Thank you."

"You take care of yourself, kid, and those nine lives of yours."

"I will." Ulyssa felt her eyes tearing up.

"Come on, let's get out of here!" Franklin yelled at the remaining crew. He waved his arm, as he jogged back to the spaceship.

"I ... ah ... I guess I'm staying," Ulyssa said, turning back to Kirill. Her heart thumped wildly in her chest. "Did you mean what you said?"

Kirill swept down on one knee before her. Loud, so everyone gathered could here him, he announced, "I bow to you, Lyssa, my love. I belong to you. All I ask is that you stay with me always ... as my Queen."

"No harem?" she whispered, shaking.

"No one but you--ever."

Ulyssa nodded, going to her knees to join him on the ground. Wrapping her arms about his neck, she kissed him soundly. She felt the tentative connection that had been trying to build between them since they first met spark to life. Suddenly, she felt him in her body, her head. She heard his thoughts, felt his desire for her and he felt hers for him.

Gasping, she pulled back. "What just happened?"

"We're married. You're my Queen, my property."

"Property?" Ulyssa repeated, hurt.

"What? Is that not the right word?"

"Ah, mmm, Kirill?" Kirill turned to Quinn. Quinn shook his head and whispered, "That was Attor's word and it's not exactly a compliment. I think you mean she's your briallen, your woman."

"Is that not what I said?" Kirill turned to Ulyssa. He looked so innocently confused, she laughed. He grinned, not caring, so long as she was happy.

"All this time when you called me property, you meant woman?" Ulyssa shook her head in amazement. "It doesn't matter what you call me, Kirill--property, woman, *briallen*. I belong to you, my King, my husband. I belong only to you."

"And I you, my most beautiful queen."

THE END

Printed in the United States
58721LVS00003B/151-873